# GIVE OUR REGARDS
# TO THE ATOMSMASHERS!

# Give Our Regards to the ATOM

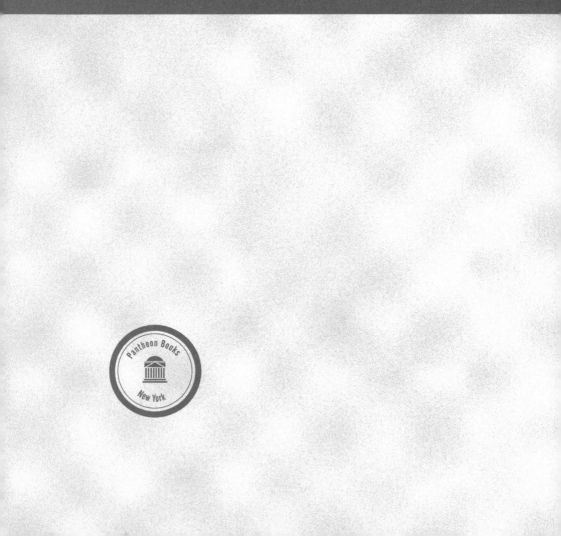

Pantheon Books
New York

# SMASHERS!

## WRITERS ON COMICS

EDITED AND WITH AN INTRODUCTION
BY SEAN HOWE

*Illustration on page 34: The Glorification of Saint Ignatius* (detail) by Andrea Pozzo, 1691–99,
Scala/Art Resource, New York.

*Additional illustration credits:* pages 2, 118, 134, 208: Marvel Comics Group, New York; page 24:
Casterman, Paris, Tournai; page 44: Chester Brown—Drawn and Quarterly Publications, Montreal;
page 52: Marvel Comics Group, New York & DC Comics, New York; page 70: First Comics, Evanston,
Illinois & Howard Chaykin; page 78: *Classics Illustrated,* The Frawley Corporation; pages 96, 166,
188: DC Comics, New York; page 108: Jim Woodring—Fantagraphics Books, Seattle; page 152:
Fantagraphics Books, Seattle; page 178: JC Productions; DC Comics, New York; page 194: (top) Renée
French—Dark Horse Comics, Portland, Oregon; (bottom) Chris Ware—Pantheon Books, New York.

Library of Congress Cataloging-in-Publication Data
Give our regards to the atomsmashers! : writers on comics / edited and with an introduction
by Sean Howe.
p.    cm.
ISBN 0-375-42256-0
1.  Comic books, strips, etc.—United States—History and criticism.    2.  Authors, American—
Books and reading.    I. Howe, Sean.
PN6726.G56 2004
741.5'0973—dc22      2003069349

www.pantheonbooks.com      Book design by Johanna S. Roebas

Printed in the United States of America
First Edition
9 8 7 6 5 4 3 2 1

# CONTENTS

CONTENTS

vi

# INTRODUCTION

Sean Howe

I learned to read from comic books. The first word sequence I ever sounded out, as my eyes moved from left to right, was "red" followed by "tornado"—an outrageously odd pairing that named a member of DC Comics' Justice League of America. Burned immediately into my four-year-old mind was this equation: reading = comic books. For a whole decade, I didn't look back.

I spent nearly every dime that came my way on superhero comic books, memorizing origin stories, first appearances, and creators' names. From comics I learned geography; I learned the names of Norse gods, Greek gods, and Roman gods; I learned to draw; I learned scientific principles (though comic book science would turn out to be pretty unreliable). When I was eight years old, I bought a comic book price guide, and got a crash course in the rules of supply and demand (this was the eighties, after all). But more than anything else, I learned about language. I learned the meanings of dozens of extracurricular words, like "invincible," "incredible," "astonishing," "uncanny," "suspense," "titanium," "talisman," "vigilante," "deviant," "havoc," "quasar," "peregrine," "celestial," and, best of all, "tatterdemalion."

The very use of these words in grade school would have been enough to earn ostracization, so I quickly learned to keep a lid on both my vocabulary and its source. At this late date, though, I can't parse whether it was my deep, dark secret of comics that first made me feel apart, or the feeling of apartness that drew me further into comic books. It's perhaps a cruel irony that comic books simultaneously confer outsider status and offer supplication to the outsider: Walter Mosley recently wrote an article expressing his gratitude for the example of "otherness" that *The X-Men* had provided him. Salman Rushdie has pointed out that "unlikeness, the thing that makes it impossible for a writer to stand in any regimented line, is a quality novelists share with the Caped Crusaders of the comics." In sixth grade, I was no novelist, but I knew better than to talk about comic books with any but a few close friends.

What was it about superheroes that I needed? It was the comfort of continuity in my life that they offered; it was the deathless, ageless characters with whom I was already sharing years of memories. Up to the age of twelve, for better or worse, my strongest memories had to do with comics. This is partially because (unlike a first crush or a family vacation) the memories of reading can be constantly reinforced and relived, easily and vividly. For the legions of aging readers, what else are serial superhero stories but perpetually running narrative machines—an endless supply of nostalgia?

I became a student of comic book history, working backward to the works of Jack Kirby, Steve Ditko, Robert Crumb, Wally Wood, Harvey Kurtzman, Will Eisner, and Carl Barks. My tastes grew to include the slightly more respectable "alternative" comics published by companies like Kitchen Sink Press and Fantagraphics. Still, the weight of social burden remained. For all that was written about the 1986 hat trick of Art Spiegelman's *Maus*, Alan Moore's *Watchmen*, and Frank Miller's *Batman: The Dark Knight Returns*, for all the newspaper headlines about how comics had grown up . . . a comic was a comic was a comic. (This is perhaps best illustrated by those very newspaper headlines, which invariably began with two or three hokey sound effects, pilfered from the *Batman* TV show). The stigma of "funnybooks" left no graphic publication, no "sequential art" collection untouched. It was only a matter of time before I caved in. Publicly, I could pursue interests in "proper" literature, in film, in music. I just didn't have enough *solitary* time to keep up with comics.

In my dreams, it's not unusual to see businessmen reading comics on subways, librarians recommending Joe Sacco and Brian Michael Bendis and Charles Burns, and *Tom Strong* knocking Tom Clancy off the bestseller lists. But we're still battling the shame that's been heavily indoctrinated over the decades, still striving to be taken seriously. Although I've long accepted its permanence, the very nomenclature "comic book" connotes humor even when there's no comedy to be found. The fragility of the stapled pamphlet, hardly designed to withstand travel, is testament to the medium's resignation that *there will be no exposure to the outside world.* And the superhero comic—the genre of men in tights—simultaneously dominates and embarrasses the rest of the medium.

And yet . . . perhaps there's a silver lining to all this. During my college years, it seemed that everyone I knew was devouring the edgier comics: Peter Bagge's *Hate*, Dan Clowes's *Eightball*, Chester Brown's *Yummy Fur*, and Adrian Tomine's *Optic Nerve*. Each the work of a distinct, brilliant vision, they were being proudly read and left around on coffee tables (though, it occurs to me now, I don't remember anyone ever actually talking about them). As a result of their hipness, they at first seemed more like stylish accoutrements than intimate totems—until one day, when I was all alone, I actually took the time to *read* a few of these comics, and realized what I had been missing: the private ritual. It was the accursed stigma, I think, that had forced me into a more intimate relationship with the medium. In a twisted sort of way, my childhood shyness about comics—which had once driven me away—helped me to fully appreciate them. Because although they're considered a pillar of "trash" culture, their enjoyment often, in fact, hinges on dwelling, on meditating.

As a medium that is read, the comic book inherently relinquishes a degree of control to the audience that movies, television, theater, and records do not. The pace and tone are subjective, even pliant. In the everyday melancholia of Adrian Tomine's work, for instance, the reader feels an inclination to slowly and intently take in everything on the page. Even the shortest of passages—elliptical, silent panels to bridge scenes—are limitless in the time they can command. In the filmed adaptation of Dan Clowes's *Ghost World*, a teenager's mutterings and put-downs are punctuated with laughter from the audience, laughter that perfectly fills the allotted pace of comedic timing. In the original comic book, though, her self-consciously sarcastic comments just echo on the page. We feel the discomfort as the words hang in the air; time is frozen as we linger on the panel. Once we've absorbed the mood, and only then, we move on. This is not something we do even when reading a novel: there's no *looking* to give respite from the more linear act of pure *reading*. A comic book's inclusion of visual information is probably the major reason for its intellectual ghettoization, the idea being that words are harder earned information than pictures. Conversely, images can invite the reader to reflect, to slow down, in a way that pure text never will. There is, intrinsically, a greater sensory relation to the characters and setting, an almost guaranteed involvement. Nothing tops comic books for the mysterious one-two punch of active engagement and submissive escape. When you get right down to it, *that's* the common thread of this art form. And that effect—that unique, sublime, hypnotic state—is heightened when you're alone.

One great advantage of movies: they can validate a subculture like no other medium. The shared experience of cinema gives moviegoers instant zeitgeist access, an opportunity for the general public to make a long-secret world their own—to investigate, for example, modern superheroes without having to wear a trenchcoat to a comic shop. Upon the release of the *Spider-Man* adaptation, it suddenly seemed that everyone was a lifelong fan, testifying (in conversation, in the *New York Times*, in the *London Review of Books*) to a long, personal history with Peter Parker's struggles. *Spider-Man* wasn't a sequel—how did they know all this? My God, I remember thinking as the audience cheered every in-joke, there really *are* this many comic book readers. They've just been hiding. Maybe the dream of a comic book–friendly world is becoming reality, after all. Comics are physically changing. Newsprint is no longer the standard; it's being replaced by glossy, more durable paper that does justice, at last, to the artwork. Even the familiar, flimsy pamphlet format is slowly but surely on its way out, as paperback collections gain popularity. This, in turn, is moving the focus away from thirty-two-page stories, and narrative possibilities are widening. High-profile hardcovers like Chris Ware's *Jimmy Corrigan, The Smartest Kid on Earth*, Neil Gaiman's *The Sandman: Endless Nights*, and Ben Katchor's *Julius Knipl, Real Estate Photographer* have greeted cautiously curious hordes of highfalutin intellectuals and eased them into the fold. Comics are regularly reviewed in mainstream magazines and sold in chain bookstores (finally out of the "humor" section and blessed with their own "graphic novels" placard), and they are happily integrating into the literary world that's ignored them for so long.

Writers, fittingly, bear much of the responsibility for bringing comics into literary circles. Their once furtive formative obsessions have slowly been revealed. In Rick Moody's *The Ice Storm*, protagonist Paul Hood uses an old issue of *Fantastic Four* as a metaphor for domestic breakdown. Michael Chabon's *The Amazing Adventures of Kavalier & Clay* lovingly chronicles two comic book creators (fictional amalgamations that fit, Zelig-like, into our own history). And passages of Jonathan Lethem's *Fortress of Solitude* miraculously telegraph the very experience of reading a comic.

Still, these are all filtered through the guise of fiction, each loving testimony ultimately serving the greater purpose of a made-up narrative. There have been numerous scholarly essays on the topic—over the years, esteemed intellectuals from George Orwell to Robert Warshow to Leslie Fiedler have waxed philosophical on the comic book—but there's been a dearth of personal writing about this most personal of art forms. The truth is, comic book fans have been tight-lipped about their forbidden love, and their ruminations about comics have incubated. For some writers these thoughts have evolved, been colored and silently revised by the intervening years, waiting for a release. For others, they've remained frozen as a time capsule of adolescence. What sort of dialogue, then, would be created if all these suppressed musings were to rise to the surface, if everything that had been quietly cherished could suddenly be discussed?

Many of the writers I approached for this book told me (after asking, "How did you know I love comic books?") they'd wanted to write about this for years, wanted to share their long-whispered lingua franca, wanted to come clean with their secret identities. Solitude might make for better reading, but after a while, it's good to share. And so here, making up for lost time, are seventeen of my (soon to be your) favorite writers, better known for their historical fiction, science fiction, music criticism, short stories, coming-of-age stories, memoirs, and thrillers, divulging what reading comic books means to them. Along the way, there are tales of childhood, adulthood, obsession, education, romance, patriotism, drugs, and religion. That's a lot to cover, sure, but they've been waiting for a long time to talk to you about this.

# GIVE OUR REGARDS
# TO THE ATOMSMASHERS!

## THE RETURN OF THE KING, OR, IDENTIFYING WITH YOUR PARENTS

## JONATHAN LETHEM

"I dreamt last night that I'd write this essay in panels of prose, mimicking the style of a comic book, in which meaning lurks in the gaps between, Sue!"

"But Reed, what about the *baby*?!?"                    →

In the mid-seventies I had two friends who were into Marvel Comics: Karl, whose parents were divorced, and Luke, whose parents were among the most stable I knew. My parents were something between: separated, or separating, sometimes living together and sometimes apart, and each of them with lovers.

I would never have been able to name that difference in 1975, however, let alone account for how it felt. The difference I understood was this: Luke had an older brother, Peter, whom both Luke and I idealized in absentia. Peter had left behind a collection of sixties Marvel comic books, in sacrosanct box files. These included a nearly complete run of *Fantastic Four*, the famous 102 issues drawn by Jack Kirby and scripted by Stan Lee, a defining artifact (I now know) of the Silver Age of comics.

Luke was precocious, worldly, full of a satirical brilliance I didn't always understand but pretended to, as I pretended to understand his frequent references to "Aunt Petunia" and "the Negative Zone" and "the Baxter Building." He was disdainful of childish pursuits and disdainful of my early curiosity about sex (I didn't catch the contradiction in this until later).

Luke didn't buy new comics so much as he read and reread old ones. Luke's favorite comic book artist was Jack Kirby.

Karl was precocious, secretive, and rebellious, full of intimations of fireworks and drugs and petty thievery that frightened and thrilled me. He was curious about sex, and unaware of or uninterested in the early history of Marvel superheroes. For him Marvel began with the hip, outsiderish loner heroes of the seventies—Ghost Rider, Luke Cage, Warlock, Iron Fist. His favorite comic book artist was John Byrne.

Karl got in trouble a lot. Luke didn't.

Though all three of us lived in rough parts of Brooklyn, Karl and I went to a terrifying public school together, in an impoverished neighborhood, while Luke went to St. Ann's School, safe in moneyed Brooklyn Heights. It was this, I'm certain, that tipped my allegiance to

Karl in those years. Karl and I, in our schooldays, had been forced to adopt a stance of endurance and shame together, a kabuki of cringing postures in response to a world of systematic bullying. That was a situation I could no more have explained to Luke than to my parents. Karl and I never discussed it either, but we knew it was shared.

In 1976 Marvel announced, with what seemed to Karl and me great fanfare, the return of Jack Kirby, the "King" of comics, as an artist-writer—a full "auteur"—on a series of Marvel titles. The announcement wasn't a question of press conferences, mind you, or advertisements in other media, only sensational reports on the Bullpen Bulletin pages of Marvel comics themselves, the CNN of our little befogged minds at the time. Kirby was the famed creator or cocreator of a vast collection of classic Marvel characters: the Fantastic Four, the Hulk, Thor, Silver Surfer, Doctor Doom, the Inhumans. In a shadowy earlier career (as captives within the Marvel hype machine, Karl and I had bought into a view that nothing really existed before 1962) Kirby was also the creator of Captain America—his career reached into what was for us the prehistory of comics. The notion that he was about to reclaim his territory was rich and disturbing. In fact, what he would turn out to bring to Marvel was a paradoxical combination: clunkily old-fashioned virtues that had been outmoded, if not surpassed, by subsequent Marvel artists (John Byrne foremost among them), together with a baroque and nearly opaque futuristic sensibility that would leave most readers chilled, largely alienated from what he was trying to do. Later, I'd learn, Kirby's return created rifts in the ranks of the younger Marvel writers and artists, who resented the creative autonomy he'd been granted and found the results laughable. At the time all I knew was that Kirby's return created a rift between myself and Karl.

· · ·

5

Kirby hadn't been inactive in the interlude between his classic 1960s work for Marvel and his mid-seventies return. He'd been in exile at DC, Marvel's older, more august and square rival. In the sixties, DC, despite its stewardship of Batman and Superman, had lost much ground to Marvel—due to Kirby and Lee's great creations, of course. Then, after Kirby's relationship with Stan Lee had become aggrieved, DC plucked him away and handed him, for a while, full creative control of an epic series of Kirby-created titles called "The New Gods." In doing so, they'd gotten more, and other, than they'd bargained for— the New Gods comics were massively ambitious, and massively arcane. Though acclaimed by some as masterworks, they never found much traction with the readership. The reason for their commercial failure is pretty specific. The comics were hard to relate to. While Kirby's most "cosmic" creations at Marvel—Galactus, the Silver Surfer, the Inhumans, etc.—were always bound to human-scale stories by their relationships to prosaic earthly characters—i.e., for the most part, the homely and squabbling Fantastic Four themselves—at DC he created a pantheon of gods but didn't bother with the humans. Similarly, at Marvel his all-powerful monster-strongman types—Hulk, Thing, and, in another sense, Thor, all had fragile human identities to protect or mourn. At DC, Kirby seemed to have flown off into his own cosmic realms of superheroes and supervillains without any important human counterparts or identities. The feet of his work never touched the ground. The results were impressive, and quite boring.

What he unveiled on his return to Marvel was more of the very same, in two new venues: *The Eternals,* which introduced another dualistic pantheon of battling gods, and *2001,* ostensibly based on Kubrick's film. Each of these series indulged, from the concepts at their foundation, Kirby's most abstracted work in his most high-flown cosmic register. Each introduced dozens of colorful but remote characters, and each abandoned or distended traditional storytelling to such a degree that the audience—I mean me and Karl—was mostly baffled.

But if           And
This were        a
Drawn by         part
Kirby in         of
The 1970s        me
It would         aches
Be a Massive     to
Gleaming         reveal
Hysterically     to
Hyper-Articulated you
Psychedelic      that
Edifice of       daunting
Mechanistic      inhuman
Prose            spectacle
Adrift           in
In               Jack's
Space!           honor!

Studying Jack Kirby now, I'm bewildered that one man can encompass such contradictory things. By contradictory I don't mean his diversity of accomplishments in so many different eras of comics history—his creation, with Joe Simon, of the patriotic anti-Nazi type of superhero in Captain America; his creation, also with Simon, of the basic mold for the "romance" comic; his dominance in the "movie-monster" style of comics that preceded the explosion of inventions at Marvel; that selfsame explosion, which includes at least a share in the invention of both the star supervillain (Doctor Doom) and the ambivalent antiheroic type (whether craggily pathetic à la the Hulk or handsomely tormented à la Silver Surfer and Black Bolt); the psychedelic majesty (however thwarted) of the New Gods work at DC. Those aren't contradictory, only boggling in the sense that the accomplishments of a Picasso or a Dylan or a Shakespeare are boggling. By contradictory I mean the fact that in that DC work and then especially in

7

the return to Marvel, Jack Kirby, the greatest innovator in the history of comics, gradually turned into a kind of autistic primitivist genius, disdained as incompetent by much of the audience, but revered by a cult of aficionados somewhat in the manner of an "outsider artist." As his work spun off into abstraction, his human bodies more and more machinelike, his machines more and more molecular and atomic (when they didn't resemble vast sculptures of mouse-gnawed cheese), Kirby became great/awful, a kind of disastrous genius uncontainable in the form he himself had innovated. It's as though Picasso had, after 1950, become Adolf Wolfli, or John Ford had ended up as John Cassavetes. Or if Robert Crumb turned into his obsessive mad-genius brother, Charles Crumb. Or if Chuck Berry evolved into Sun Ra.

Speaking of Chuck Berry, there's something about my childhood that I've never been able to explain, but I want to attempt to now. I suffered a kind of nerdish fever for authenticity and origins of all kinds, one which led me into some very strange cultural places. The notion of "influence" compelled me, at irrational depths of my being. Any time I heard mention that, say, David Bowie was only really imitating Anthony Newley, I immediately lost interest in David Bowie and went looking for the source, sometimes with the pitiable results that the example suggests. So I was always moving backward through time, and though I was born in 1964 and came to cultural consciousness some time around 1970 or '71, I particularly adored the culture of the fifties and early sixties: Ernie Kovacs, *The Twilight Zone*, the British Invasion, Lenny Bruce, the beat writers, film noir, etc. I tended to identify with my parents' taste in things, and with the tastes of my parents' friends, more than with the supposed cultural tokens of my own generation. It was with Luke, in fact, that I went to see a Ralph Bakshi film called *Heavy Traffic*, which contains an unforgettable animated sequence that accompanies and illustrates with crude (and rude) drawings the Chuck Berry song "Maybellene." Thanks to the film I fell in love with Chuck

Berry, and while every kid in freshman year of high school was defining their identity according to whether they liked A: Jimi Hendrix and Pink Floyd and the Doors or B: The Clash and the Specials and the Bad Brains or C: Cheap Trick and the Cars and Blondie, I was looking into Z: Chuck Berry and Bo Diddley. It's a commonplace, of course, that we seventies kids were doomed to glance backward, out of our impoverished world of Paul McCartney and Wings, to the era of the Beatles—but I was the only twelve-year-old I've ever known who got into an extended argument with his own mother about whether the Beatles were better before or after *Sgt. Pepper*—my mother on the side of "I Am the Walrus," me on the side of "Drive My Car."

I identified with my parents in other, murkier and more emotional ways, of course. Not that those are separable from the cultural stuff. Put simply, I was in fearful denial of my own childish neediness. I wished to be an adult in order to be forever spared sympathy or condescension, which reminded me too starkly of my helplessness.

At the moment in my childhood I'm describing now, bodies were beginning to change, and the exact degree and nature of their changes provided psychological opportunities, and thwarted others. Karl at thirteen grew tall, handsome, and dangerously effective at cutting an adult profile. Luke and I each stayed, for the moment, small and childlike.

Karl identified, as I've said, with Marvel's existential loners: The Vision, Warlock, Ghost Rider, etc. By becoming tall and rebellious—he'd begun to write graffiti, smoke pot, fail in school, all pursuits I only barely flirted with—he'd eluded childishness by a bodily rejection of it, and by rejecting obedience. The cost was exile from continuity with what was attractive in our parents' worlds, of course. That cost didn't impress Karl, not at that moment anyway.

So here was how, for a time, I tilted back to Luke: he and I were partnered in a more baroque strategy, of rejecting childishness by identifying with our parents, and by sneering at rebellion as childish. As paltry new teenagers we adopted a "you can't fire me, I quit" position.

But Marvel was complicit in my muddled yearning backward—ours, I should say: mine, Luke's, even Karl's. By the time of Kirby's return, the internal discourse around Marvel's greatness was explicitly nostalgic. Any counterargument, based on a typically American myth of progress, that our contemporary comics might be even more wonderful, was everywhere undermined by a pining for the heyday of the sixties. This was accomplished most prominently in Stan Lee's two books: *Origins* and *Son of Origins,* which reproduced and burnished the creation myths of the great sixties characters. The odor of grandeur, not to mention sanctimony, that clung to any discussion of the Silver Age boom was impossible to clear from one's nostrils, after reading the *Origins* books. There wasn't any way to imagine that the first issues of *Iron Fist* or *Deathlok the Demolisher* would ever be collected in equally biblical compendia. Nostalgia was further propagated in Marvel's reprint titles: *Marvel Tales,* which offered rewarmed *Spider-Man,* and the too-aptly-titled *Marvel's Greatest Comics,* which put forward—you guessed it—the Kirby-Lee run of *Fantastic Four.* This was somewhat akin to Paul McCartney and Wings playing Beatles songs on *Wings Over America.* We seventies kids couldn't have been issued a clearer message: we'd missed the party.

Speaking of the Beatles (i.e. famous sixties culture breakups and their seventies legacies), I ought to give at least a moment to the whole question of the Lee/Kirby authorship controversy. In a nutshell, in the *Origins* books, Lee notoriously undersold the contributions of his artist collaborators—that is to say, mostly Kirby, but also Steve Ditko, the penciller of Spider-Man and Doctor Strange. Later, in a dispute over the ownership of Kirby's actual drawn pages, Kirby was given extensive chances to play a grouchy old David against Marvel's corporate Goliath, and the comics world rallied around him. He also made public claim to being the sole author of the great characters that had made the Lee/Kirby partnership famous: the Fantastic Four and all their sublime villains and supporting cast; Hulk; Thor; Silver Surfer; etc. (He even once threw in Spider-Man for good measure.) Lee and Kirby *were* a kind of McCartney-Lennon partnership, in several senses: Kirby, like Lennon, the raw visionary, with Lee, like McCartney, providing sweetness and polish, as well as a sense that the audience's fondness for "hooks"—in the form of soap-operatic situations involving romance and family drama, young human characters with un-God-like flaws, gently humorous asides, etc.—shouldn't be undernourished. And, after the breakup, it was Kirby, like Lennon, who the audience tended to want to credit as the greater genius, and Lee, like McCartney, who took on an aura of the shallow and crafty businessman.

Whoever should be given the lion's share of credit for "inventing" (i.e., designing outfits and powers, creating the origin myths and distinctive personae) the Marvel Silver Age characters, it is unmistakable that in Marvel's greatest comics—I mean, in the *Fantastic Four* issues which were reprinted in *Marvel's Greatest Comics,* the originals of which Luke's brother had assembled and Luke now accessed—Lee and Kirby were full collaborators who, like Lennon and McCartney, really were more than the sum of their parts, and who derived their greatness from the push and pull of incompatible visions. Kirby always wanted to drag the Four into the Negative Zone—deeper into psychedelic science fiction and existential alienation—while Lee, in his scripting, resolutely pulled them back into the morass of human lives, *hormonal* alienation, teenage dating problems and pregnancy and unfulfilled longings to be human and normal and loved and not to have the Baxter Building repossessed by the City of New York. Kirby threw at the Four an endless series of ponderous fallen gods or whole tribes and

11

races of alienated antiheroes with problems no mortal could credibly contemplate: Galactus and the Silver Surfer, the Inhumans, Doom, etc. Lee made certain the Four were always answerable to the female priorities of Sue Storm, the Invisible Girl, Reed Richards's wife and famously "the weakest member of the Fantastic Four." She wanted a home for their boy Franklin, she wanted Reed to stay out of the Negative Zone, and she was willing to quit the Four and quit the marriage to stand up for what she believed.

I seriously doubt whether any seventies Marvel-loving boy ever spared a dram of sexual fantasizing on Sue Storm. We had Valkyrie, Red Sonja, the Cat, Ms. Marvel, Jean Grey, Mantis, and innumerable others available for that. We (I mean, *I*) especially liked the Cat. Sue Storm was, to our conscious minds, truly invisible. She was a parent, a mom calling you home from where you played in the street, telling you it was time to brush your teeth. And the writers and artists who took over *Fantastic Four* after Kirby and, later, Lee departed the series seemed impatient with the squareness of Sue and Reed's domestic situations. Surely these weren't the hippest of the Kirby/Lee creations. Nevertheless, if you (I mean, *I*) accept my (own) premise (and why shouldn't I?) that the mid to late sixties *Fantastic Four*s were the exemplary specimens, the veritable *Revolver* and *Rubber Soul* and *White Album* of comics, and if you further grant that pulling against the tide of all of Kirby's Inhuman Galacticism, that whole army of aliens and gods, was one single character, our squeaky little Sue, then I wonder: Invisible Girl, the most important superhero of the Silver Age of Comics?

I'm breaking down here. The royal *we* and the presumptive *you* aren't going to cut it. This is a closed circuit, me and the comics which I read and which read me, and the reading of which by one another, me and the comics, I am now attempting to read, or reread. The fact is I'm dealing with a realm of masturbation, of personal arcana. Stan Lee's rhetoric of community was a weird vibrant lie: every single *true believer,* every single member of the *Make Mine Marvel* society or whatever the fuck we were meant to be called, received the comics as a private communion with our own obscure and shameful yearnings, and it was miraculous and pornographic to so much as breathe of it to another boy, let alone be initiated by one more knowing. *We* and *you* don't know a thing about what *I* felt back then, anymore than *I* know a thing about what *you* felt.

Specifically, I'd be kidding if I claimed anyone much cherishes the comics of Kirby's "return to Marvel" period—*2001, The Eternals, Machine Man.* Even for souls who take these things all too seriously, those comics have no real place in the history; they define only a clumsy misstep in a dull era at Marvel, before the brief renaissance signaled by the ascent of the Chris Claremont *X-Men.* Here, joining the chorus of the indifferent, is Kirby himself, from an interview with Gary Groth of *Comics Journal,* one which ranged over his whole glorious career:

> Groth: It always seemed like your last stint at Marvel was a little halfhearted.
> Kirby: Yeah.

Anyway I want to withdraw the Lennon/McCartney comparison, because there's something else I've sensed about the Lee/Kirby partnership: it seems to me that Kirby must have been a kind of ambivalent father figure to Lee. Kirby was only five years older, but they were crucial years—crucial in defining two different types of American manhood. Kirby came of age in the thirties, was toughened by his Depression boyhood and perhaps privately, stoically scarred by his frontline experiences in World War II. Lee seems more like the subsequent kind of American male, the coddled fifties striver who lived in the world his parents had fought for and earned. Lee was more a wannabe beatnik—Maynard G. Krebs, let's say. This difference per-

13

haps underlies the extremes of their contribution to *Fantastic Four*: Kirby concerned himself with the clash of dark and light powers, and passionately identified with alien warrior-freaks who, like John Wayne in *The Searchers*, were sworn to protect the vulnerable civilian (or human) societies they were forever incapable of living amid. His vision was darkly paternal. Lee was the voice of the teenage nonconformist, looking for kicks in a boring suburb, diffident at best about the familial structures by which he was nevertheless completely defined.

John Wayne in *The Searchers* is, crucially, a Civil War veteran, made strong and ruined by what he'd glimpsed on the battlefield. Similarly, the first thing to know, and the easiest thing to overlook, about the iconic hard-boiled detective of the Raymond Chandler–Dashiell Hammett–Humphrey Bogart type is that he wears a *trench*coat—i.e., he's a veteran of the First World War. I was once told by a biographer who'd researched Jimmy Stewart's years as an air commander in World War II that the crucial material in Stewart's war record was sealed. (Stewart, unlike others who served less vitally but wore their experiences on their sleeves, tended not to talk about the war.) The biographer wondered if Stewart might actually have led a portion of the raid on Dresden and been protected from infamy by his government. The biographer also wondered if whatever was sealed inside that war record had fueled the deepening and darkening of Stewart's postwar work— the alienation and morbidity and even cynicism that the great and formerly gentle leading man displayed in films like *Vertigo*, *The Naked Spur*, and *Anatomy of a Murder*. Now, when I consider the steady alienation from humankind of Kirby's bands of outsiders—from the Fantastic Four to the Inhumans to the New Gods to the Eternals—I wonder if he might be one of those who could never completely come home again.

·  ·  ·

But he did try to come home in 1976, to Marvel. And Karl and I bought the hype, and bought the comics. And Karl didn't like them, and I did. Or, anyway, I defended them. I pretended to like them. Karl immediately took up a view, one I've now learned, in my research, was typical of a young seventies Marvel fan: he said Kirby sucked because he didn't draw the human body right. Karl was embarrassed by the clunkiness, the raw and ragged dynamism, the lack of fingernails or other fine detail. Artists like Neal Adams and Gil Kane had, since Kirby, set new standards for anatomical and proportional "realism," and those standards had soon been made peculiarly normative by (to me, much less interesting) artists like John Byrne and George Perez: superhero comics weren't supposed to look at all cartoonish anymore. Karl had no tolerance. I, schooled both in my father's expressionist-painter's love of exaggeration and fantasy, and in Luke's scholarly and tendentious devotion to his older brother's comics, decided I saw what Karl couldn't.

Of course, in my defense of Kirby I was conflating comic art and comic writing. I need to quit conflating them here. That is to say, it's possible to debate the moment in the seventies when Kirby's pencilling began to go south. He was good; he got worse. What's undebatable is the execrable, insufferable pomposity of Kirby's dialogue-writing in the Marvel work without Lee. Or the deprivations involved in trying to love his galactically distant and rather depressed story-lines. As a writer, as opposed to an "idea-man," he always stunk.

I did try to love the storylines. It mattered to me. With Luke's help I'd understood that Kirby represented our parents' values; the Chuck Berry values. In Kirby resided the higher morality of the Original Creator. That which I'd sworn to uphold, against the shallow killing-the-father imperatives of youth.

Luke, it should be said, never cared about Kirby's return. Luke was a classicist, and didn't buy new comics. I was on my own, hung out to dry by *The Eternals*.

15

Karl and I were also drawing comics in those days. Well not really comics; we were drawing superheroes—on single pages we'd design a character, detail his costume and powers and affect, then speculate on his adventures. I was profligate in this art, quickly generating a large stack of characters, whose names, apart from "Poison Ivy" and "The Hurler," I can no longer retrieve from the memory hole. Karl drew fewer characters, more carefully, and imparted to them more substantial personalities and histories. One day in Karl's room he and I were arguing about Kirby (we really did this: argue about Kirby) and I formulated a rhetorical question, meant to shock Karl into recognition of Kirby's awesome gifts: Who, I asked Karl, besides Kirby, had ever shown the ability to generate so many characters, so many distinctive costumes, so many different archetypal personas? In reply, Karl turned the tables on me, with a weird trick of undercutting flattery. He said, *you*.

At the time my ego chose to be buoyed by Karl's remark. But really he'd keyed in on an increasing childishness in Kirby. None of Kirby's army of new characters at Marvel were ever going to be real, were ever going to mean much to anyone. They weren't fated to live in meaningful stories. They were only empty costumes, like my own drawings. There was something regressive about Kirby now—he'd become self-referential, the outsider artist decorating the walls of private rooms.

The comics Karl and I actually relished in 1976 and 1977, if we were honest (and Karl was more honest than I), were *The Defenders, Omega the Unknown,* and *Howard the Duck,* all written by a mad genius named Steve Gerber, and *Captain Marvel* and *Warlock,* both written and drawn by another auteur briefly in fashion, named Jim Starlin. As far as the art went, Gerber liked to collaborate with plodding but inoffensive pencillers like Jim Mooney and Sal ("The Lesser") Buscema. Those guys moved the story along well enough. Starlin's figures were drawn in a slickly hip and mildly psychedelic style exaggerated in the direction of adult comix like *Heavy Metal*, but with the "realistic" musculature that the moment (and Karl) demanded, rather than the Franz Kline kneecaps and biceps of Jack Kirby. Gerber's tales were wordy, satirical, and self-questioning, and stuffed full of homely human characters dealing with day-to-day situations—bag ladies, disc jockeys, superheroines' jealous husbands, kids who faced bullying at their local public schools. His attitude to the superhero mythos was explicitly deflationary. Starlin was more into wish-fulfillment fantasies of cosmic power, but he was droll and readable, and the scrupulous way he drew his psychedelia was actually (I see now, paging through the stuff) indebted to Steve Ditko's early version of *Dr. Strange*. Enough: I fear I'm losing you. The point is, Gerber and Starlin were the two creators whose (commercially nonviable) work was pitted in the day-to-day contest against "The Return of the King," and they were winning, hands down, even in my muddled and ideological heart.

Local ironies: the alienated, noble, loner type that Karl responded to most of all—embodied by Warlock and Omega the Unknown, Karl's favorites—was plainly a distillation of pure Kirby characters like Silver Surfer and Black Bolt. But I couldn't lead Karl to appreciate—why should he have?—Kirby's authorship.

And: Steve Gerber, who in his postmodernish anti-sagas seemed to us utterly our "contemporary" (I have to put that in quotes so that you don't think we literally believed Steve Gerber was fourteen years old), was engaged in a *killing-the-father* imperative of his own, one that leapfrogged over the Silver Age, and also right over my and Karl's heads at the time. That's to say, reading Gerber now, I see that three of his best characters were sly parodies of midcentury comics which Gerber must have grown up reading. Omega the Unknown, a handsome blue-costumed and -haired humanoid from a destroyed planet, and

17

with a kinship with a human boy, was Gerber's undermining of both Superman and the original Captain Marvel (known to us only as the pathetic replicant Shazam). *The Defenders'* Nighthawk, a powerless millionaire with a utility belt and a flying cape, was basically a Batman parody. And Howard was a corrupted Disney duck.


The moment I'm describing would come to a precipitous end. Karl and I were in intermediate school in Brooklyn together until the summer of 1977. Though our friendship was strained toward the end of that time, both by Karl's physical maturation and by the increasing distance between his rebellious nonconformity with the adult world and my parent-identifying nonconformity with the teenage world, we certainly continued to sporadically buy and evaluate Marvel comics together until the end of eighth grade.

It was high school which severed our connection, for what would become years. I went off to Music and Art, in Manhattan, a place much populated by dreamy nerds like myself, and perfectly formulated to indulge my yearning to skip past teenagerhood straight to an adult life; many of my best friends in high school were my teachers. Karl was destined for Stuyvesant High, where he drifted into failure and truancy. Later he'd land at one of our local public high schools, John Jay, and there be forced to continue battling a world of bullying I'd left behind.

Luke, meanwhile, was still safe in the preserve of private school, where his negotiation with the call of teenagerhood, and beyond, might be subject to the push and pull of peer pressure, but was better isolated from the starkness of the bankrupt city around us. Our friendship, mine and Luke's, was restored somewhat during those high school years, though I suspect I sometimes eluded him. My public school experiences had made me worldly in ways that Luke's stubborn cognition, and the advantage of his older brother's influence, couldn't quite match. As for physical maturation, I now shot ahead, to catch up with Karl (though he wasn't around for me to make the comparison), while Luke still lagged slightly. Now, I think, I was to Luke as Karl had been to me; I was his Karl. No rebel, I had nonetheless begun to smoke pot, which Luke still distrusted. No whiz with girls, I was at least comfortable with my puppyish interest, while Luke remained, for the time being, gnarled up regarding that subject.

For me and Luke, Jack Kirby was still a tacit god, but only on the strength of his canonical sixties work. Luke and I, righteous in our reverence for origins, didn't between us acknowledge Kirby's continued existence. It would have been unseemly, like dwelling on the fact that Chuck Berry, rock-'n'-roll's progenitor, had had a seventies novelty hit called "My Ding-a-Ling."

Whether Karl continued to buy comics I couldn't know. And what of the place our argument about Kirby had been left, in the end? That was lost, along with much else, in the denial surrounding the state of our friendship, which had attenuated to an occasional "hello" on the streets of the neighborhood.

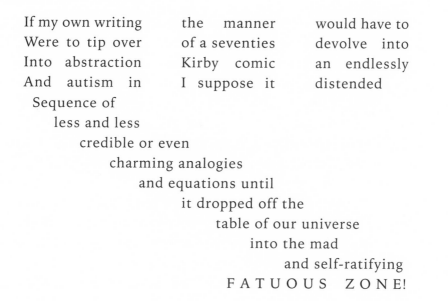

If my own writing the manner would have to
Were to tip over of a seventies devolve into
Into abstraction Kirby comic an endlessly
And autism in I suppose it distended
  Sequence of
   less and less
    credible or even
     charming analogies
      and equations until
       it dropped off the
        table of our universe
         into the mad
          and self-ratifying
          F A T U O U S Z O N E!

And there it would spiral forever, oblivious to contempt:

Kirby

Equals

Chuck Berry

Equals, god help me                          Equals

Sue Storm          I don't know,          John Lennon

Equals                        um,                    Equals

Paul McCartney          Anthony Newley?          Father

Equals                    (or, Jonathan?)          Equals

Stan Lee                                        Luke

Equals                                        Equals

Maynard G. Krebs                    John Wayne

Equals                                  Equals

Pink Floyd              Black Bolt

Equals          Equals

Karl

The last year of high school, before college changed everything, Luke and I still drifted together occasionally. Now it was he and I who drew comics—not innocently wishful superheroes, but what we imagined were stark satires, modeled on R. Crumb and other heroes of the "underground." Luke had by then begun dating girls too, and one of our last collaborative productions was a Kirby parody called "Girlfriends from the Earth's Core." A two-page strip, it reworked the material of a failed double date of a month before, when Luke and I had taken two girls, soon to be our first bitter exes, to a fleabag movie theater at the Fulton Mall. Luke "pencilled" the pages, and I was the "inker"—I specialized in Kirbyesque polka dots of energy, which we showed rising from the volcanic bodies of the two primordial girlfriends.

I know them both, Luke and Karl. Luke's parents are still married, and Luke and his wife live in a New England town. The oldest of their children is named Harpo, which strikes me now as more of the reverence for early-twentieth-century culture that always drew us together. Luke works (as Kirby once did, when his comics career was demoralized by the failed return to Marvel) making animated films. His conversation still features Fantastic Four–derived phrases like "Aunt Petunia" and "Clobberin' Time." Kirby is in Luke's DNA; I see it flashing in his eyes. I know for him it is more real than it ever was for me, as real as an older brother who'd slipped out of the house and left Kirby behind.

Me, I'm a fake, my Kirby-love cobbled from Luke's certainty, Karl's resistance, and Stan Lee's cheerleading. My version of an older brother was Karl, and Karl wasn't reverent about Kirby. Karl was only curious—Kirby was merely on the menu of the possible, alongside Starlin and Gerber, alongside Ghost Rider and Warlock, alongside forgetting about comics and getting into girls or music or drugs instead. Karl never had that kind of crush on his own or other kids' parents—a crush on the books on their shelves, on the records in their collections.

Karl, though, still lives in the Brooklyn neighborhood to which I've returned, and which he never left. He lives down the street, and we're both only a few blocks from the once-treacherous precinct of our shared school. Last week I had him over, and we dug out a box of Marvel comics. These were the same copies we'd cherished together in 1976 and 1977—for, in an act surely loaded with unexamined rage, I'd purchased Karl's comic collection from him in the middle of our high school years, when his interest drifted, when our friendship was at its lowest ebb.

Karl isn't urgent about contemplating our old comics, but he's willing. This day, while we were browsing the Kirbys of the Return Era, he corrected my memory in a few specifics. Most crucially, he raised the possibility that the argument about Kirby, which had seemed to me loaded with the direst intimations of the choices we were about to make, the failures of good faith with our childhood selves we were about to suffer, had mostly been conducted in my own head. It was when I put a stack of Kirby's *2001*s in his hands.

"I really got into some of these issues," he said. I could see his features animate with recollection as he browsed Kirby's panels, something impossible to fake even if you had a reason to do so. "I remember this comic book really blew my mind."

"I thought you never liked Kirby," I said feebly, still stuck on my thesis. I explained what I thought I remembered.

"No, I remember when he first came back I was a little slow to get it," Karl told me, after I'd finished explaining. "But you had me convinced pretty quickly. I remember thinking these were really trippy. I'd like to read them *again,* actually."

"Oh," I said.

"I just never liked the way he drew knees."

# THE CLEAR LINE

## LUC SANTE

In a corner of my office, on top of a bookcase, lies a hunting horn—a sort of bugle, curved in the manner of a French horn. It has occupied a place in my inner sanctum wherever I've lived since childhood. Such horns are not hard to find secondhand in the Ardennes Mountains of southern Belgium, since these days there's not much call for them by hunters of the stag and the boar. The reason I talked my parents into buying me this horn can be found in the fifth panel on page four of the sixth adventure of Tintin, *The Broken Ear*. The panel shows Tintin visiting ➡

an artist's garret, a low skylit room with a bed on the floor amid a panoply of artistic bric-a-brac: a plaster bust, a horseshoe, a sixteenth-century helmet, a skull, a few paintings and sketches, and, directly above the pillow, a hunting horn. Since I wanted to be an artist at an age when most kids want to be firefighters, I knew that I would one day live in a room just like that, and wanted to get started accumulating the props. Possession of such a horn would ensure my future as an artist. The Tintin albums were never wrong about such things. Had I wanted to be a sea captain instead, I would have pestered my mother into knitting me a blue turtleneck sweater with an anchor motif on the chest, the kind worn by Tintin's friend Captain Haddock. The sweater would automatically have conferred upon me the authority to command a vessel.

But if the adventures of Tintin were my guide to life (and worryingly, perhaps, they still are; just a few years ago I bought a floor lamp at a flea market because it looked like the sort of thing Tintin would have in his living room), they were also the reason I wanted to be an artist. I was not alone. Because of Tintin, kids in Belgium, where the series and I both originated, aspire to draw comic strips the way their American counterparts want to start rock bands. I was typical: as soon as I could draw recognizable figures, I started working on a comic strip featuring an adventurous lad and his faithful dog. But even Belgians with no such ambitions have incorporated Tintin and his worldview into the fiber of their beings. The boy reporter made his debut in 1929 in the children's supplement of a Catholic newspaper, crudely drawn at first, but with his personality and that of his white terrier Milou (called "Snowy" in translation) fixed almost from the first panel of *Tintin in the Land of the Soviets,* the first adventure. That he was an ageless kid, of less than medium height and of an uninsistent modesty despite his many accomplishments, answered to the best aspects of the suffering Belgian self-image. Overnight, or almost, he became a national icon.

Tintin is of indeterminate age; he can drive a car and shoot a gun but is said at least once by another character to be "hardly more than a child." He is invariably called "the boy reporter" in the fictional newspaper and radio accounts that are quoted within the panels, but is never seen doing any reporting or writing, nor is any such work ever otherwise alluded to. He has a nice apartment and a substantial library although no apparent income; his constant travel might be paid for by law-enforcement agencies—Interpol, maybe—since the trips always lead to the solving of some crime or other, but he is never seen being assigned, debriefed, supervised, or compensated. He has no parents or any other relatives unless you count the all-male elective family he accumulates over the course of the series: Captain Haddock, the eccentric Professor Tournesol ("Calculus" in translation), and the twin detectives Dupont and Dupond ("Thompson" and "Thomson"). Milou (I can't bear to call him "Snowy") goes with him everywhere, including to the moon, where he has his own four-legged spacesuit. Tintin has a little tuft of blond hair sticking up in front, and unless he is in costume or disguise, he wears the clothes of a jaunty youth of the 1930s, including plus-fours with argyle socks. My father, who was short, blond, and usually wore plus-fours, was called "Tintin" by his friends back before the war, although by the time I knew him his hair had turned black.

I began absorbing Tintin before I learned to read. I know that my father's mother gave me a subscription to the Tintin weekly magazine before she died, which was sometime around my fourth birthday. I'm pretty sure the magazine was then serializing *Tintin in Tibet*, the twentieth of the twenty-three volumes—twenty-four if you count the one left in rough sketch form by the death in 1983 of Georges Rémi, known as Hergé, who wrote and drew the series and refused to consider a successor. Hergé attained his peak of productivity in the forties, right in the middle of the war, when he published his strips in the Brussels daily *Le Soir*. The paper from those years is referred to as *Le Soir volé*—the stolen *Soir*—because it was overseen and censored by the German occupiers. Unlike most collaborators, Hergé got little more than an administrative slap after the war, and hardly any public opprobrium, because it was so clear he was an innocent by nature. His ideology was conservative, but it was molded for all time by the Catholic Boy Scouts. His worldview was that of a serious-minded twelve-year-old.

A serious-minded Belgian twelve-year-old in, say, 1939 would think of the colonial subjects in the Congo as simple, happy people who derived enormous benefits from being colonized. You couldn't expect them to understand complex matters, but at least you could send in the White Fathers to convert them to the Roman religion and stop them from eating each other, or whatever it was they did. *Tintin in the Congo,* book number two, makes for painful reading today, and not only because Tintin is so determined to bag every sort of big game that, unable to shoot a rhinoceros, he blows it up—although he uses too much powder and is left with just the horn. The caricatures of foreign cultures in the Tintin books are hardly virulent, just indicative of a smug ignorance pervasive throughout the Western world then, but the treatment of the Congolese is shocking because its grotesque simplifications had to have been based on self-serving firsthand accounts by the colonizers. To confirm this, all I have to do is look in my family album. My Uncle René, a drunken ne'er-do-well who lived in the Congo in the 1950s, is pictured with a much more mature-looking African gentleman standing a few paces behind him; this man is identified on the back of the photo as his "boy." The English word was used to mean "manservant" for obvious reasons—it wouldn't do to think of the Congolese as adults. Tintin is not an adult, either; he is the champion of youth, fighting the scary and corrupt adults of the world on their behalf. In the Congo these inimical adults are nearly all white, while the natives belong to Tintin's constituency regardless of their ages—it is the only country he visits where everyone recognizes him. When he leaves, the people cry.

Possibly the most striking thing in the Tintin universe is the almost complete absence of women. Of the 117 characters pictured in the portrait gallery on the endpapers of the hardcovers, only seven are female. Women are thin-lipped concierges or very occasionally the silent consorts of male characters; few have more than walk-on parts. The only significant or recurring female character is the overbearing diva Bianca Castafiore, who periodically appears to sing the "Jewel Song" from Gounod's *Faust*, a performance that has the effect of a gale-force wind. This is not so much misogyny as, again, the perspective of a nerdish presexual twelve-year-old. There are no young girls, or attractive women of any age, because the frightened boy is determined not to see them. Tintin has been psychoanalyzed voluminously—the critical literature is vast, and canted upon every sort of postmodern theoretical framework—so that I'm certain that some academic somewhere has already suggested how much Tintin's family, as it were, resembles the Holy Trinity: the boy reporter as Jesus, Captain Haddock as an irascible Old-Testament Jehovah, and Milou—small, snow-white, and ever-present—as the Holy Ghost. You might still expect women to hover on the periphery of consciousness as mothers and whores, although both would distract from the serious business of adventure and crime-fighting, and introduce all kinds of unwanted ambiguity. Hergé, ever the Boy Scout, simply excised them.

Hergé redrew the first several stories (with the exception of the irredeemably crude *Land of the Soviets*) for their postwar publication in album form. Nevertheless, they are set in a period that while undefined necessarily predates May 1940, when the Nazis invaded Belgium. Even the later stories seem to take place in the 1930s, although none of us kid readers of the late fifties and early sixties minded or even noticed, since until the "economic miracle" of 1964, postwar Belgium itself effectively lived in the prewar era, at least with regard to technology. The world of Tintin's adventures is one in which servants wear livery, savants wear long beards, men emerge from fights with their false collars jutting out, and the lower orders are identified by their caps. The world is big enough to include little-documented countries you've never heard of, although no subject is so obscure that

29

there isn't in Brussels some smock-wearing expert who knows all there is to know about it, and possesses the book- and artifact-stuffed apartment to prove it. It is a cozy world in which every detail is correctly labeled and filed away on the appropriate shelf. The world may contain its share of evil, but it is regularly swept and, like Belgian sidewalks, washed every week. There are no areas of grey. Villains—they are most often drug smugglers, sometimes counterfeiters—look and act like villains, and if heroes have their share of human failings (Captain Haddock's alcoholism being the major case in point), there is nevertheless no doubt about the purity of their souls. Sex, of course, would mess up everything.

The clear moral line is beautifully articulated by Hergé's graphic style, which is in fact called "clear line." This method of rendering the world accurately, sensuously, and yet very simply by distilling every sight down to its primary linear constituents derives most obviously from the eighteenth- and nineteenth-century Japanese popular woodblock-print style called *ukiyo-e,* and its masters Hiroshige and Hokusai. Those graphic artists were introduced to European eyes in the late nineteenth century, when their work had a particular impact on the French Impressionists, especially Manet and Degas, who learned from them the value of cropping and of visual shorthand. Hergé absorbed not just those lessons; he swallowed their style whole. He enclosed every particle of the visible, no matter how fluid and shifting, in a thin, black, unhesitating line; made that line carry the burden of mass and weight without modeling; and endowed the line with an accomplice in the form of pure, clear, emphatic but not garish color. The style makes the world wonderfully accessible, in effect serving as an analogue to its hero's mission: Just as Tintin, a mere boy, can travel the world and navigate its dark passages and defeat its oppressors without himself succumbing to corruption, so you, too, whether you are eight or eighty-eight (the advertised age range of the weekly), can confront the overwhelming variousness of the perceptual universe and realize its underlying simplicity without sacrificing your sense of wonder. And that is the core of Hergé's genius: to mitigate his young audience's fears and convert them into sensual delight.

When Tintin, menaced by Chicago gangsters in *Tintin in America*, must exit his hotel room through the window and make his way to the next one by inching his fingernails and shoe soles along the mortar between the bricks, the young reader prone to acrophobia (me, that is) can translate his trepidation into pleasure at the magnificent geometry of those many unyielding rows of windows as depicted very precisely from a dizzying oblique angle. The terror of suddenly coming into an entirely foreign landscape—notably, Shanghai in *The Blue Lotus*—can give way to joy at the immense panels of streets crowded with very individual pedestrians and surmounted by overlapping ranks of colorful banners and signs filled with intriguing if indecipherable Chinese characters. (For this volume Hergé sought the advice of a young Chinese artist then resident in Brussels, Chang Chong-Jen—who became a character in the story—so that the details possess particular authenticity.) The great heights, deep cold, and blinding snows of Tibet; the *horror vacui* inspired by the featureless Sahara; the threat of a tempest at sea as experienced on a raft; even the empty and unknowable surface of the moon (circa 1955)—all of these can be not only managed but appreciated. To say that Hergé domesticated those locations and experiences would be putting the emphasis in the wrong place. What he did was to bring them into the child's compass, not only through the heroic surrogate of the boy reporter, but also visually, by scraping away murk and muddle and purifying it, revealing the world as an awe-inspiring but comprehensible series of planes.

In every way but the visual it is easy to dismiss the simplifications of the series. They are the legacy of the comfortable worldview that rationalized colonialism—that complacently taught African children in French possessions to remember "our ancestors, the Gauls." They are of a piece with the creed of scouting as devised by Baden-Powell, with pen-pal clubs and ham radio and collecting stamps, which Walter Benjamin said were the visiting cards left by governments in children's playrooms. They belong to the same branch of literature as the Rover Boys and Tom Swift and the fantasized travels of Richard Halliburton. They are predicated on nostalgia for a world in which strength rested upon ignorance, and this was so even in the ostensibly simpler times in which Hergé conceived them. Their world is the cosmos of childhood, after all, and childhood past is what all nostalgia refers to, even if wrongheaded adults insist on situating it within historical coordinates. The visual, by today's lights, might be diminished just as easily, you might think, considering by contrast the dark abstract tangles that represent the world in many of today's strips, including some of the better-known superhero adventures, or noting that the heirs of the clear line, most famously Joost Swarte, have applied it to an ironically jolly delirium in which there are not only no moral certainties, but not even any definite up or down or inside or outside. But Batman has one foot in the adult world these days, even if politicians are no closer to growing up. That the adventures of Tintin remain unsullied by maturity or experience allows them to preserve their power as a visual primer. They are an Eden of the graphic eye, in which every object—each shoe, each road, each flame and book and car and door—is in some way the first, the model that instructs the beholder on the nature of the thing and makes it possible to grow up knowing how to cut through fog and perceive essentials. What Hergé did is as serious and as endlessly applicable as geometry. Small-minded, reactionary, immature, he is not the Rembrandt or the Leonardo or the Cézanne of the comic form—he is its Euclid.

# COMICS IN A MAN'S LIFE

## GEOFF DYER

In 1928 D. H. Lawrence wrote a beautiful essay, "Hymns in a Man's Life," in which he reflected on the way that the hymns he heard as a boy "mean to me almost more than the finest poetry, and they have for me a more permanent value, somehow or other." It didn't matter that the words of these hymns were often banal or incomprehensible to him; what mattered was the "sheer delight" they inspired in "the golden haze of a child's half-formed imagination." Even at this late stage of Lawrence's life—he had less than two years to live—the sense of "wonder" engendered by these hymns was "undimmed." I feel the same about the superhero comics in my life. →

I remember with absolute clarity the first Marvel comic I bought. *The Amazing Spider-Man* #46, "The Sinister Shocker." This was the issue of March 1967 and it cost 10d. I was eight, a working-class boy in a small town in the mid-west. The English mid-west, that is: specifically, Cheltenham, in Gloucestershire—the heart of the Cotswolds.

I was entranced, obviously, by the costumed acrobatics and spectacular fights but I also liked the ongoing soap opera of the life of Spidey's alter ego, Peter Parker. This was the phase in Parker's life when, having been spurned as puny and stuck-up, he was at last becoming integrated into the fashionable, semialternative life of college. At the end of issue #46 he moves out of his Aunt May's place and into an apartment with Harry Osborne (whose father, unbeknownst to him, is Spidey's recurrent enemy, the Green Goblin). At one point Peter turns up at a coffee bar with Mary-Jane, one of two gorgeously hip women he's become friendly with.

"What's shakin', Tiger?" says Mary-Jane.

"Nothing much! We were just getting set to spin a few platters!" replies Harry (who, as if having the Green Goblin for a father were not trouble enough, will later, in issues #96–98—notoriously unapproved by the Comics Code Authority—develop serious drug problems). In Spider-Man guise, Peter has injured his arm fighting the Shocker; when he asks M-J if she wants to go for an ice cream, she replies, "Not while the juke is jumpin', dad! Since you can't shake up a storm with your wing in a sling I'll take a rain check till the coins run out." Also on the scene is Flash Thompson, one of Peter's longtime tormentors, and, in one of the ironies milked to death by Stan Lee, Spidey's biggest fan, who is about to be drafted into the army and will go to Vietnam ("Mmm! There's something about a male in uniform! It's wow city!" sighs Mary-Jane).

Lots of this, it goes without saying, went way over my little English head. In future issues I would come across all sorts of references—to Woody Allen, to Dear Abby—that meant absolutely nothing to me but, from issue #46 on, I was caught in Spidey's web. By the age of twelve, I was fairly fluent (albeit with a Gloucestershire accent) in the kind of Marvelese quoted above, that sanitized version of hip American youth-speak. Although Spider-Man remained my favorite, I also got into Thor, Daredevil and the Fantastic Four.

Now, one of the reasons Marvel had an edge over its main rival, DC, was the way that its brand of superheroics did not take place in a fantasy vacuum but in the turbulent here and now of American life. In issue #68 (January 1969) Spidey becomes caught up in the "Crisis on Campus." In issue #78 (November 1969) Hobbie Brown, a young black window-cleaner burdened by domestic problems, is fired by his racist boss and decides to try his luck as a supervillain, the Prowler. Spidey beats him but, instead of turning him over to the cops, tells him to go back home to his girlfriend ("that's where it's really at"). In this racially diverse respect *Spider-Man* lagged behind *Fantastic Four*: Black Panther (who was subsequently granted independence in the form of his own magazine) made his first appearance in issue #52 of July 1966. DC would later follow suit with the famous 1971 "drugs" issues of *Green Lantern/Green Arrow* (with outstanding art by Neal Adams) but, back in the late 1960s, Marvel's knack for siphoning the zeitgeist into the action meant that a version—albeit a heavily distorted one—of contemporary American history was finding its way across the Atlantic to me in England. Take LSD, for example.

Ang Lee's film *The Ice Storm* opens with the adolescent Paul Hood on an ice-bound train, reflecting on the latest issue of *Fantastic Four*. For the previous year—as Rick Moody explains in the novel on which the film is based—the FF have been in trouble: Sue (The Invisible Girl) is living apart from Reed Richards (Mr. Fantastic) who has been too bound up with scientific experiments and world-saving "gizmos" to have fulfilled his role as husband and father. In issue #141 ("The End of the Fantastic Four") this protracted family drama comes to a head in the Negative Zone, "that universe beside our own," as Moody puts it, "where the laws of nature were subtly altered." For Paul—and for the larger ambitions of the book and film—*FF* #141 tells "some

37

true tale about family," thereby providing a mythic, timeless dimension to what is happening at home in the suburban here and now (from our point of view, the suburban there and then).

Reed first entered the Negative Zone on an urgent parental errand in issue #51 (June 1966), and returned ten issues later in April 1967, and again in the *Fantastic Four King-Size Special* #6 of November 1968. It's no accident that these first three trips into the Zone coincided with the period when the liberationist potential of LSD in America was peaking. From the late 1950s, a gradually expanding group of initiates—including, most famously, Aldous Huxley—had been discreetly exploring what lay in the "other world," beyond "the doors of perception" but, by the mid-sixties, a significant portion of Americans were—to borrow the title of Jay Stevens' seminal account—storming heaven. In the chapter conveniently—for our purposes—titled "In the Zone," Stevens records the attempts of Richard Alpert, one of the prime movers of the acid vanguard, "to push the envelope, to pierce the final veil that stood between himself and enlightenment." Curious punters arrived for weekends at Millbrook, the demented mansion where Timothy Leary, echoing the grey-templed tones of Mr. Fantastic, aimed to show how "man's brain, his thirteen-billion-celled computer, is capable of limitless new dimensions of awareness and knowledge." Some guests would be frightened off, fearing, as Leary himself put it, that they had "fallen into the hands of a mad scientist," a Dr. Doom–style supervillain.

Paul Hood reckons the Silver Surfer was "definitely created by a mind on psychedelics"; certainly, Stan Lee and others at Marvel's mission control—"the bullpen"—must have been aware that an increasing proportion of readers wanted stuff they could freak on while coming down or, more mildly, stuff that could serve as a vicarious trip. And that, accordingly, is what these adventures in the Negative Zone are: trips. When Reed first enters the Negative Zone "the universe seems," in language reminiscent of Huxley's *Heaven and Hell*, "to be tearing itself apart." "It's almost more than human eyes can bear!" he declares. "I'm actually witnessing a four-dimensional universe but the effect of seeing it with three-dimensional vision is indescribable." Colors deepen, shapes and patterns swirl around him. "Everything is moving faster now! The universe has become a vast kaleidoscope of light and sound!"

By the time of *King-Size Special* #6, Reed is, like Leary, an old hand at guiding people through "the Gateway to the Beyond." Surrounded by psychedelic forms, he councils Ben Grimm (aka the Thing) and Johnny Storm (the Human Torch) that "we're entering the initial distortion area. Our human vision needs a few minutes to readjust itself, to correctly transmit such images to our brains." By 1973—by the time of *The Ice Storm*—trips to the Negative Zone were a favorite pastime for the FF and their readers. And even when not enacted in the Zone itself, more and more of the FF's adventures—and those of spin-off characters like the Silver Surfer—were being spent in some erupting corner of the cosmos which, in graphic terms, was indistinguishable from it.

The attraction of this for Paul Hood, apprentice stoner, poised to graduate from bongs to blotters, is immediate and obvious. Less obviously and less immediately, I wonder now if my own subsequent interest in psychedelics might not have been initiated by Marvel comics. What is absolutely certain is that after family memories of the Battle of the Somme and the Airfix-generated re-creation of the Second World War, the fantastic version of American life offered by Marvel comics was my most important exposure to extracurricular history. Like the two World Wars, this comic book America was something I learned about—began to find my way around, to make sense of—independently.

Even more important, especially when Spidey battled the Vulture (in issues #48 and #49) in a vertiginous city of spectacular skyscrapers, I began to get a sense of—to feel imaginatively at home in—the architecture of Manhattan. The cityscape in these comics—fifty-story buildings, billboards, water towers, fire escapes, elevated trains—was,

39

of course, unlike anything I had ever seen in real life. When—as children do—I tried to imagine myself in Spidey's place, web-swinging through Cheltenham, it was impossible: the buildings were too spread out, too low, too homey. (Spidey never made it to Gloucestershire but he did come to London in April 1971—issue #95—after Peter Parker accidentally got caught up in a terrorist sky-jacking!) By contrast, from my earliest exposure to it, the Marvel New York was a place where the quotidian was suffused with the mythic (most obviously—and ludicrously—in the case of Thor).

*The Dandy* and *The Beano* were simply comics; Marvel was a universe. The more deeply you got into them, the more encompassing Marvel comics became: characters from one title would guest in another (the Human Torch and Spider-Man were always crashing into each other's pages) so that each magazine offered a different glimpse of—and take on—a world that was imaginatively complete. Events in one corner of this universe (in issue #38 of *Daredevil*, for example) have a knock-on effect in another (in issue #73 of *Fantastic Four,* for example).* Events in the various titles are "cohesive and interconnected." "There is no such thing as the isolated Marvel event"; Marvel "gives all of itself in each of its fragments." These quotations are from Roberto Calasso's book about the Greek myths, *The Marriage of Cadmus and Harmony*: I have simply substituted the word "Marvel" for "myth" or "mythic."

Ken Kesey said that the superhero sagas were the real myths of the United States; the United Kingdom did not have any contemporary

---

*A few days after seeing Ang Lee's film *The Ice Storm*, I saw John Woo's *Face/Off*, in which John Travolta and Nicholas Cage end up inhabiting each other's bodies, thereby reprising the storyline of *Daredevil* #38, "The Living Prison," in which we see (to quote "The Mighty Marvel Checklist") "Daredevil in the body of Dr. Doom, battling against Dr. Doom—in the body of Daredevil." By the time of *FF* #73, Daredevil and Dr. Doom are back in their respective bodies but the FF are unaware of this: cue a "Guest Star Bonanza" in which Reed takes on Daredevil, Thor hammers it out with the Thing, and Spidey and the Human Torch run rings around each other.

version of the mythic (for that you had to go back to the Second World War, to "our finest hour," the Battle of Britain). This was the first glimmer of what in later years would become a position associated with a number of critics, namely that American novelists had the advantage over their British counterparts of automatic, unlimited access to the mythic, the vast. And this, in turn, was why it was American—rather than British—writers who shaped the literary sensibilities of the generation of British readers who are now in their forties.

I have always tended to assume that my life began to stray from the template laid down by class and family when I fell under the influence of my English teacher at grammar school, when I was encouraged to read books like *Sons and Lovers*; that is when I took my first steps on the well-worn path of the scholarship boy. Now, I realize, it started much earlier, when I bought that copy of *Spider-Man #46*.

Superhero comics not only had, to use Lawrence's phrase, "a profound influence on my childish consciousness," they also formed my tastes as a reader and, to a degree, my style as a writer. The very pervasiveness of their influence in this regard makes it difficult to pin down precisely.

In a well-known essay on the composition of *The French Lieutenant's Woman*, John Fowles recounts how he saw his first film when he was six and has, since then, seen at least one a week. "How can so frequently repeated an experience not have indelibly stamped itself on the mode of imagination?" Fowles concludes that this "mode of imagining is far too deep in me to eradicate." For me, that mode of narrative imagining was, initially, *comic*-derived.

Marvel comics—which, for a three-month spell, from September to November 1965, billed themselves as "Marvel Pop Art"—also provided me with the first sense of discrimination in the visual arts. It wasn't just that I liked some artists more than others; some artists were *better* than others. Accordingly, after a hiatus of six or seven years, from O levels to university, instead of unswerving loyalty to Spider-Man or the Fantastic Four, I collected whichever issues of any

41

comic happened to be drawn by particular artists: Neal Adams, Berni Wrightson, Barry Smith, and, especially, Jim Steranko. Artists like these had begun to carve out more and more freedom for their own highly personal visual styles. Typically, they would peak in a few masterly issues and then, unable to keep to the grueling deadlines of monthly production, there would be a marked deterioration or they would move on to another title. Steranko's best work, for example, is scattered among a dozen panel-bursting, genre-advancing issues of *Nick Fury: Agent of S.H.I.E.L.D.*, three sensational issues—#110, 111 and 113—of *Captain America*, and the iconic cover of *The Incredible Hulk King-Size Special* #1. The work of Neal Adams was even more widely dispersed: after several extraordinary issues of *The Avengers* and *The X-Men*, he moved to DC where he revivified *Batman* and *Green Lantern/ Green Arrow.*

The years passed. Through comics I became interested in other artists: first, Roger Dean (who designed those trippy album covers for Yes and Osibisa), then the really big hitters like, um, Dalí. Even when I got a broader sense of art history my preferences and special interests were profoundly influenced by that early exposure to Marvel comics. To put it simply, I liked Michelangelo because the obsessive and extreme torsion of his figures was so obviously derived from that of Jack Kirby (virtuoso creator of the FF and mentor of Steranko).

Then, in the autumn of last year, I experienced what I can only think of calling a moment of intensely *heightened* autobiography. The church of Saint Ignatius in Rome is famous for the trompe l'oeil cupola by Andrea Pozzo. Before you get that far into the church, however, you look up at the vault of the central nave, at the epic fresco, also by Pozzo. Completed in 1699, *The Glorification of Saint Ignatius* shows—to lift a phrase of Moody's—"the dead saints of antiquity" slugging it out in a zone of sheer spectacle. Amid dizzy perspectival foreshortening, the continents of the world are represented by four corbels. On one of these—on one panel, as it were, of the huge graphic myth of the ceiling—a woman with a spear sends two beefcake figures tumbling from her precarious perch (identified by the single word AMERICA) into the emptiness of illusionistic space.

According to Freud, there is no time in the unconscious; at certain intensely charged moments, however, there is no time in consciousness itself. Looking up at the image-crammed ceiling I experienced a sensation that mirrored what was depicted above, a kind of temporal vertigo. The thirty years that separated the man staring at this baroque fresco in Rome from the boy who had bought his first Marvel comic in Cheltenham *fell away,* became compressed into a single instant of undimmable wonder.

# AIMEE BENDER

On the second day of fiction writing grad school, writer and teacher Judith Grossman won my heart for the third time. Several months before, she'd sent out a reading list that included, sandwiched between the works of Dostoyevsky and Henry James, the words "fairy tales." That addition alone radically rearranged my understanding of what writing would be acceptable in graduate school, but on this opening day, at our orientation meeting, she performed, I felt, two more extraordinary feats: first, she spent the better part of the hour telling us where to buy good bread and coffee in the strip-mall conglomerate of Irvine, California, and second, when someone asked what she was reading, she spoke very enthusiastically about Los Bros Hernandez's comic book series, *Love and Rockets*.  ➔

Praise for graphic novels was building at that point, but it still felt like an act of bravery to blur the line between literature and comics so casually. Especially on an introductory day.

Judith was a seminal teacher for me, and the comic books come up here because they, like the fairy tales, set in motion a sense of permission that changed the way I thought about writing. They underlined and rejuvenated my love of symbolic language and imagery. Judith, a wonderfully educated person, had none of the doubts I felt about my own range of reading interests; in fact, when she left the following year, it was Glen David Gold (who I believe is also in this book, as well he should be, as inside his eyeball's pupil lives and breathes a small comic book) who decided wisely that for her going-away gift we should get her an autographed copy of *Love and Rockets*. When she left, cleaning out her office, she put books outside her door for free pickin's, and I took A. M. Homes's *The Safety of Objects,* an annotated edition of *Jane Eyre,* and a delectable-looking series of comic pamphlets called *Yummy Fur,* written by one Chester Brown.

I gobbled up *Yummy Fur,* stories of a guy and his dealings with adolescence and women, drawn with clean direct lines expressing pensive faces and lonely landscapes.

In *Understanding Comics,* Scott McCloud's wonderful book about the history and complexity of the form, he talks about how the plain face, the less realistically drawn face, can be taken in more swiftly by the eye than something more thorough and detailed. Chester Brown, for example, suggests layers of teenage self-consciousness simply through the quick lines that show scruffy hair and the hunched burdened look of his protagonist's shoulders. He is both a real teenager and the symbol of a teenager. This is a tried-and-true method; even Chekhov agrees with McCloud. In a letter to Maxim Gorky in 1899, he states: "You understand it at once when I say, 'the man sat on the grass'; you understand it because it is clear and makes no demands on the attention. On the other hand, it is not easily understood, and it is difficult for the mind, if I write, 'a tall, narrow-chested, middle-sized man, with a red beard, sat on the green grass, already trampled by pedestrians, sat silently, shyly, and timidly looked about him.' That is not immediately grasped by the mind, whereas good writing should be grasped at once—in a second." There's an immediacy to iconic words and pictures, and like Chester Brown's scruffy hair, the plain word allows the reader to digest an image with a different part of the mind; when we read that swiftly, we sidestep the ultra-aware reader, jumping more directly from image to unconscious.

It was, again, Judith who showed me how words can point toward myth, finally clarifying why a word like "bookstore" meant so much more to me than seeing Barnes and Noble—or, better, Powell's—on a page. Much as I love Powell's, the iconic feel and texture of the word changes instantly as soon as it is specified. Girl vs. Jolene. Red riding hood vs. a pullover from the Gap that cost $19.99 in their spring sale.

Words like "robber," or "swamp," or "beast," or "plate," or "bone," evoke landscapes of flat characters, moving through symbolic forests meeting animals who can speak. It is the world of my childhood reading, where the images ran straight into a formative memory bank, and where reading was all about stirring and nourishing the imagination. Comics know this intuitively—Charlie Brown's hair curl evokes his entire personality, and each friend of Chester Brown's is drawn so simply and directly that I can map my own high school friends right onto them.

Comics also seem to be acknowledging, overtly, the visual pleasure in reading that happens with text, too, but doesn't seem to be talked about enough. I love "oo" words—moon, broom, stoop, balloon, crook—but admitting that makes me sound like some kind of flake. But the visual experience is so crucial to reading, and it's why books-on-tape just don't cling to my mind in the same way. For example, when reading, how often does your eye drift to the line below, only to replace a noun with one that occurs in the next sentence? How often, when reading a mystery or encountering suspense, does the eye float to the bottom of the page, take in new information, return to the

47

initial paragraph, and then read forward? Sometimes I have to put my hand on the page to block the end of a scene because I don't trust my eyes on their own. We are always making rubber band pin-art with the page, moving words around, creating a visual scheme. Comics take this reading experience to a more primal level—we graze from a picture, down, to the side, up the diagonal, merging imagery and words effortlessly. Also, the words in comics are active: they will tangibly tremble, sweat, or exclaim; it's a more physical reading activity in that way. Gertrude Stein knew the pleasure of this like the back of her hand: "Miss Furr and Miss Skeene" is not just an aural feat and a cubist party of meaning, it is also a picture, and seeing all those repeating g's and l's is just as much what compels me to her work as the sound and the game she's playing with content:

> To be regularly gay was to do every day the gay thing that they did every day. To be regularly gay was to end every day at the same time after they had been regularly gay. They were regularly gay. They were gay every day. They ended every day in the same way, at the same time, and they had been every day regularly gay.

Also, if, as Chekhov says, the mind takes in simple words or images with ease, then we're freed up to expend brain effort in other ways. There is more room, perhaps, for unlinked scenes and looser transitions.

In issue #26 of *Yummy Fur,* there's an example of that exact advantage. The main storyline is about a character named Chester who will not say "fuck" in school. The bullies relentlessly tease him about this, and try to force him to swear. But on page 13, there's a brief aside about his mother in the car, talking to young Chester about her bra size and how women need to appear to have similar breast sizes, which is why, she explains, she wears a padded bra. The two storylines never nod to each other explicitly; they just share a page. In fiction, this quick aside might be the equivalent of an inserted paragraph, or even just a sentence that takes the reader somewhere new. Here, since the "fuck" storyline and the Mom storyline coexist, each ends up deepening the other. Visually, we read them both almost instantly, and although the rage in each storyline is different, only in reading them together does the page begin to thrum with it.

These days I use comics in my fiction classes as a way to show how time can be manipulated. It's one of the best ways I know to illustrate the difference between "showing" and "telling," that most common (and therefore dangerous) mantra of writing workshops. Show Don't Tell surfaces in classes because a student will often write a "told" line like "she was dismayed" and in class we will discuss if it might be better conveyed with an action or gesture that shows the same feeling. In comics, the "box" at the top of a comic, the narration, introduces the storyteller's voice, whereas the "scene" or "showing" happens below, with dialogue, picture, gesture, action, immediacy. Pow! Showing is about immediacy, and telling is one of the fiction writer's most powerful tools, but if I try to explain both to my class, I trip over my words because there are so many ways to combine the two and any kind of reductive teaching rule makes my stomach sink. In the world of comics, we see both showing and telling, laid out on the page, visually interacting in a range of ways. Time slows in that top box, where the "voiceover" occurs. Enter the storyteller. Some examples: "It was 1972 and I was twelve years old. I was returning home from school . . ." opens up the first sequence in one issue of *Yummy Fur*. In *Ghost World*, Enid tells a flashback of her first sexual experience and uses a lot of narration to cover the internal reflections: "After it was over, we watched *Star Trek IV* on cable without saying a word." The pictures in the panels there need to be silent—faces with closed mouths, arms crossed, eyes blank—but the narration box fills in that blankness. With someone like Lynda Barry, who writes very character- and voice-

49

driven comics and novels, sometimes the narrative box is so exuberant it takes over the panel, and the drawing is just a tiny squished addition at the bottom.

Ideally, all this gives the class a new way to talk about the balancing act of narration and scene, which comes up again and again in their stories. In fact, how a fiction writer moves between a narrative voice and an active scene-building voice is one of the keys to pacing. What the students hopefully learn through the comic exercise is something about how to play with time. There is amazing flexibility here, and seeing how a comic book writer can jump around—speeding up years inside a box, or slowing down to the crucial seconds in a drawing—is a good reminder of the lavish freedoms available in a paragraph. I have my students write a three-panel comic with both "showing" and "telling" to show me they've digested the information. It's often their funniest work all semester long. I feel like I'm getting away with something taboo as a teacher when I'm sitting at home, reading and grading comic strips, the same way I feel like I'm getting away with something illegal as a writer if all I want to do is write about a swamp or a robber. I'm starting to think that this looking-over-the-shoulder, "getting away with something" feeling is maybe a good guide to where the permission is blocked, and where, as a reader and a writer, there is joy to rediscover.

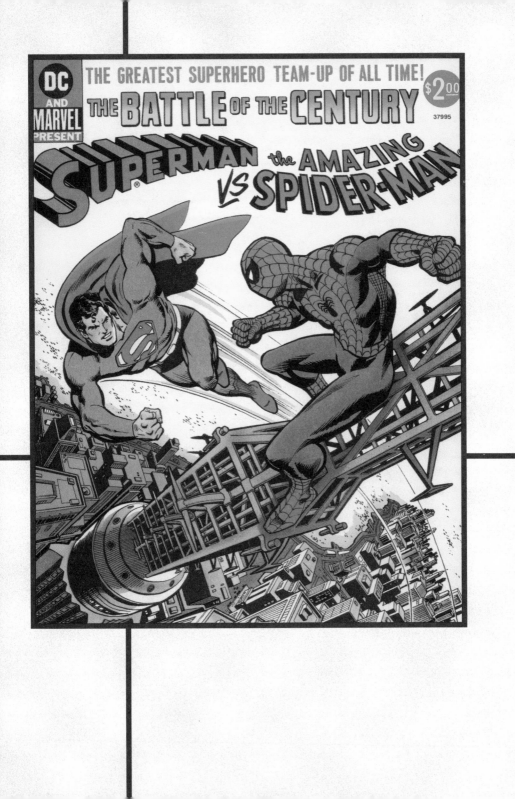

## THE GER SHEKER

# CHRISTOPHER SORRENTINO

I.

We moved when I was seven, to an artists' housing complex in Greenwich Village that had opened its doors maybe six months earlier, ample time for the kids who first dwelled within the boundaries of its award-winning design to construct an intricately petty social system from which, as a new kid, I was inevitably to be excluded. This brought a kind of malefic perfection to my discontent: I'd taken a dim view of the move to begin with, seen the whole idea as something of a downer. My parents had an abundance of reasons for leaving the old neighborhood, whose devastation during the 1960s was mild relative to that of some places but severe enough that before we left my father sometimes would hide silently in our darkened apartment, a homemade club in his hands, in an attempt to fool the burglars (who periodically made off with our TVs, jewelry, winter coats, blank checks, and spare change) into believing that the place was empty.   →

Luckily, they were never tricked. Reason Number Two for leaving was that unhealthy preoccupation with victimhood, Number One being victimhood itself. But I had quite a different viewpoint. The burglars terrified me; being mugged and robbed was not fun—but these were matters distinct from the neighborhood itself, which was *home*. I barely noticed that the school was failing, that stores along Avenue B were closing, that junkies nodded off in the entryways of abandoned buildings that grew in number each month. I didn't question why they put up sheets of plywood where there'd been the plate-glass windows of a corner saloon (someone had blown away everyone inside)— weren't, after all, a *lot* of windows covered with plywood? I had my friends, I had Tompkins Square, I had Mrs. Meller, whom I loved, for first grade.

Then, suddenly, what I had was this whitebread new group, all supremely at ease with each other and in their surroundings. Confident, well-adjusted, living in apartments that had in them, instead of stacks of cardboard boxes (or a crazed family man hiding in the shadows), furnishings and decorations, these young suzerains laid down the principles for living as a kid in the building—a male prepubescent kid anyway—laid them down simply so that there was no need to trouble oneself with nuance; so that, in their sheer, binary black-and-whiteness, the unsuccessful candidate for approval could easily spot where he had gone wrong. Some specific ways I fell short: they were thin, I was fat. They were right-handed, I was a lefty. They attended P.S.41, I attended P.S.3. They rooted for the Yankees, I was a Mets fan. See? I was sometimes reminded that I lived on the wrong floor, that my parents should have chosen to live on the *third* story, not the sixth. There were a dozen or so boys roughly my age—and they had constructed the world according to their own exacting and arbitrary standards.

## II.

But there was also Karen Barber. Karen lived across the hall in an apartment that would shortly be occupied by one of the building's typically calamitous families (the mother would die young of cancer; the father would attempt suicide; the son would be killed, crushed by a freight elevator in the warehouse he and his playmates had broken into; the daughter would grow up to be a prostitute). For the time being, however, Karen lived there with her parents, a mild-mannered couple with whom my mother and father got along, and so Karen and I fashioned our camaraderie on the coattails of the adults' friendship. She was a nice kid, and I think she felt as lonely and out of place in that building as I did. We spent hours together up in her loft bed, with stacks of comic books for company, fueled by snacks and sodas (Karen's parents allowed her a free hand in the kitchen), interspersing flurries of conversation with periods of quiet, concentrated reading. It was a puerile sort of heaven but it was heaven nonetheless.

And what we read was strictly puerile stuff, titles like *Casper* and *Richie Rich*, and the expansive Archie series: *Archie, Archie and Me, Archie at Riverdale High, Archie's Girls Betty and Veronica, Archie's Joke Book, Archie's Pals and Gals, Archie's Pal Jughead, Archie's TV Laugh-Out, Archie's Xmas Love-In, Life with Archie,* and the perhaps redundantly titled *Everything's Archie.* Even if our genre choices were regrettable, my lazy afternoons with Karen were excellent preparation for the intense comic book reading I would embark on, with great seriousness of purpose, within just a year or so; they had the effect of fully immersing me in the medium for the first time. Even the ads spoke of an exotic, hitherto undetected world, one encompassing not only pedestrian novelties like X-Ray Specs, sacks of foreign stamps sent, in that mysterious phrase, "on approval," and Sea Monkeys, but such extraordinary mail-order items as the "backyard Polaris Nuclear Submarine," from which you and your similarly equipped friends could lob nuclear missiles at one another after school. There were great prizes to be earned ped-

THE GER SHEKER

55

dling *Grit* ("America's Greatest Family Newspaper") and American Seeds, and perhaps I could carry with me for self-protection that Daisy air rifle I'd get for my birthday if I could demonstrate how responsible I was!

Ridiculous. Who did I know with a backyard? Could you own a personal nuclear sub *and* protest the Vietnam War? The family newspapers in our house were the *Times,* the *Voice,* and Dorothy Schiff's *Evening Post,* and anyway the only guy I'd ever seen selling newspaper subscriptions door-to-door came around once a year pushing *The Militant.* And the BB gun was something I knew not even to ask about. But that these revelations of middle America puzzled and exhilarated me far more than Archie & Co.'s weird composite lifestyle of surfing, snowmobiling, big-city adventure, and subdivision comfort, all apparently achieved within the city limits of "Riverdale" (which clearly was *not* the one in the Bronx), was a clear sign of dawning maturity of a kind. Effete, indecisive, impecunious Archie wasn't going to do it for me and so, Karen's good-natured disinterest notwithstanding, I began to incorporate DC superhero comics into our reading list.


Suddenly: a fellowship, or an adjunct professorship, and Karen and her parents were off to Woodstock or Santa Cruz or wherever it was that good fortune or karma or boredom guided them. I was back in the hands of the guys from whom I'd retreated up the shag-carpeted steps leading to Karen's bed and, deserted, avoidance was no longer an alternative. As beguiling as those fairy tales about spirited nonconformists can be, children simply do not perceive things that way. God knows, it may be that one day we'll all jingle in our pockets coins stamped with the image of that mythic loner, James Dean, but that is not what a kid wants to be, ever. And what an adult may view as puzzlingly self-denying behavior makes perfect sense from the perspective of the child who is expert at gauging his resources and chances, and what made perfect sense to me then was the zeal with which I sought to ingratiate myself.

About some of my defects, there wasn't much to be done. Some, like continuing unbroken a four-generation tradition of following New York National League baseball, were matters of quasi-religious significance. Others involved the gavel-stroke of heredity. But some were easily corrected. A pair of Pro-Keds to replace my unsightly "skips." A zippered, hooded sweatjacket instead of my grandmother's "bogus" sweaters. And then there were comic books. What kind of *pussy* was I to be reading *DC*? Suddenly, it was a very material question.

## III.

*In the beginning Marvel created the Bullpen and the Style.*

*And the Bullpen was without form, and was void; and darkness was upon the face of the Artists. And the Spirit of Marvel moved upon the face of the Writers.*

*And Marvel said, Let there be the Fantastic Four. And there was the Fantastic Four.*

*And Marvel saw the Fantastic Four. And it was good.*

—Stan Lee

Substitute "Stan Lee" for "Marvel" wherever the latter appears and you will more accurately capture the true, tenderly profane spirit of the exhibit furnished above.* It's generally accepted that the so-called

---

*There exists an ancient dispute over the principal authorship of many of Marvel's creations. Jack Kirby long asserted that he was the actual prime mover behind the creation of some of Marvel's most famous characters while minimizing Lee's involvement ("Stan Lee is essentially an office worker, OK?"). Lee himself has offered up equally self-serving assessments of his own contributions. It's not within the purview of this essay, nor is its author competent, to address this subject.

"Silver Age" productions of the Marvel Comics Group were patently superior to those of DC, their chief rival, but it's not too much of a stretch to suggest that this orthodoxy persists at least partly because of the tirelessly aggressive efforts of Lee—Marvel's impresario, editor in chief, head writer, art director, and, by the early seventies, publisher—to promote his comics and the roster of superheroes inhabiting them as preferable to those of DC not merely for some frivolous, kidlike reason, but because they were so innovatively written and drawn as to constitute a form of high art; they were socially aware and in tune with the zeitgeist; they comprised a modern mythology that in its scope and complexity reached back to that of ancient Greece; and they formed the basis for a secret society equipped with its own shibboleths and cognomens for initiates to memorize and cherish.

The force of Lee's splendorous bluster is such that even today I'm never completely sure when or whether this bullshit was written tongue-in-cheek. If anything, I'm understating the vehement razzle-dazzle with which he put forward his claims. Lee was fond of hyperbole, of alliteration, acronyms, and nicknames. He had the catachrestic knack of a dime novelist for deftly locating a ten-dollar word precisely where he could wring the greatest effect from it. He could maintain a straight face when he piously spoke of the "sophisticated philosophy" a close reading of Marvel was supposed to impart to its readers, while simultaneously making it sound marketably innocuous. And what's more, he took it all on the road, regularly speaking at the colleges whose students had begun to make up a substantial portion of Marvel's readership.

To a forty-year-old person who has spent his adult life *not* reading comic books, some of Lee's claims look pretty silly now, and his precious style can be grating. But give the man his due: Marvel transformed the medium in the sixties, starting with the elemental visual impact of Jack Kirby's drawing, which challenged the primacy of the paunchy heroes DC presented in their series of tiny, static tableaux (Jules Feiffer once dryly observed that ever since it had left Joe Shuster's hands, *Superman* looked as if it had been "drawn in a bank"). The scripts, building on the steady, accretive development of a vast narrative cosmos, were soon cross-resonating throughout the Marvel realm, so that to fully comprehend the action in a given issue of, say, *Thor,* you had to first read the prior month's issue of *The Avengers.* Consequent reader confusion was dealt with dismissively; an offhand footnote might stipulate, "If you've **forgotten** ish #45, you'll have to take our **word** for it! . . . Snide Stan." (DC, on the other hand, found continuity to be a bugaboo—or maybe it just didn't care: Were Superman's adoptive parents named John and Mary Kent? Eben and Sarah? Jonathan and Martha?) And the characters, if not the Sophoclean creations Lee suggested they were, were not the interchangeable hero-drone units inhabiting the DC universe, either.

The ineffable virtue that all of Marvel's wondrous qualities added up to was "hipper." Hipper than DC, to be sure, but the sense you get is that Marvel aspired to a startling magnitude of hipness, to hipness commensurate with that of the sixties itself, that strange decade that brought cosmopolitan otherness and an irresistible pop sensibility into alignment. Marvel zinged along strings the culture had pulled taut, drew from the same energy source that throughout the decade transformed similarly nebbishy, equally improbable entities into cultural conquistadors, from the Beatles to the VW Beetle, from Lenny Bruce to Leonard Nimoy, from Peter Sellers to Alexander Portnoy, from the SDS to the '69 Mets.

## IV.

The Comic Art Shop was located on Morton Street, just a few doors down from that enduring immigrant bazaar on Bleecker Street where, even today, amid fake trattorias and antiseptic shops selling six-dollar

59

ice-cream cones, remnants of my childhood such as John's, Zito's, Ottomanelli's, Faicco's, and Rocco's persevere, survivors of an Italian Greenwich Village that now exists largely in the imagination of the tourist trade. In this setting, the shop was probably as out of place as it sounds, but the Village, though rising fast, still had something of an improvisational, bohemian feel to it then. A business could still be run on a shoestring. People leased storefronts and gave it a go until the money ran out. The Village was dotted with places like this; esoteric places that gratified their proprietors' not-always-practical fixations on things like used books and houseplants and health food and gay pornography and, as one Hudson Street store put it, "Junque"; slightly squalid places run by youngish men and women who doubtlessly horrified their quasi-professional, vicariously ambitious parents by becoming the storekeepers their grandparents had been.

Even by these standards, the Comic Art Shop had a fugitive look to it, as if it expected to go out of business, to be hounded out of town, at any minute. It was an unadorned space, its bare walls destitute of the posters and other decorations now universally found in such stores. Remembering the austerity that heralded its single-mindedness of purpose, I'm reminded of the Harlem and Lower East Side "variety stores" where, a few years later, I'd go to buy nickel bags. But at that time, years before I required anything stronger than refined sugar to alter my brain chemistry, this was where I went for my shady thrills. This was where I went to educate myself in Marvel history and lore.

For the act of apostasy had come easily, occurring at the most private of levels and seeming to involve the most superficial of self-betrayals. It was my first conscious experience of a specific genus of cheating that I have since encountered many times, sometimes succumbing to temptation, sometimes not, and never being quite sure whether it's made any difference at all: *no one will ever know*. What a delicious secret. I could fob this off as a casual decision, made freely and independently—what a happy coincidence that for once my interests were in alignment with those of the majority! *No one will ever know*—is there anything *more* delicious? Anything that better offsets the everyday, quiet, automatic execution of what we know to be *right* and *just* and *necessary* (the return of the wallet to its owner, the proper disposal of the trash, the non-theft of the tip from the asshole bartender, the not rifling through the bureau drawers, the respected inviolacy of the personal diary)? Isn't it a rare pleasure when it seems *right,* and *just,* and *necessary* to tell the superego to take a hike and, without asking anyone's permission, to let the id step in and indulge itself?

Because I required social leverage and this was one way to obtain it. I needed it more than I needed some spurious self-fealty. Who would know? The real question was, who *could* know? Sure, I'd acquired a genuine fondness for DC's characters, but face it—it was exactly *nobody* I was being faithful to! Would Superman give a shit that I'd abandoned him? Would the Fortress of Solitude echo with more loneliness? Would my absence mark another traumatic loss for the Batman? Would there be a pregnant silence when they called the roll at the Justice League meeting and my name met with no response? With how much weight was I supposed to invest the decision? My parents didn't care. At school they wouldn't inveigh against it. My grandfather wouldn't shake his grey head sadly. This was just kid stuff—and the most important decision I had.

I'd found out about the Comic Art Shop from Kirk and Marco, two of the objects of my ardent pursuit, who deigned to tell me that the big distinction separating the callow juvenile who read the cretinous stories DC offered from the seasoned connoisseur who partook of Marvel's "sophisticated philosophy" was that the latter was also a commodity fetishist who carefully cataloged his collection and who paid not inconsiderable amounts for select back issues, which were then placed individually in special plastic bags and stored away in special cardboard boxes. Being the sort of kid who left his comics in the bathroom, tore off their covers, and clipped order blanks from them,

I'd had no idea. But it was pretty serious business: on Saturdays the shop resembled the floor of the Chicago Board of Trade, with kids milling three and four deep at the counter, hollering out orders at the clerk, usually the same guy in his early twenties with blond steel-wool hair, vivid acne, and an unfailingly patient attitude. You worked from a scribbled list. You had a price in mind. You tried to complete series, or to collect issues featuring particular artists; or you followed private criteria that would have been complicated and vaguely embarrassing to explain. You had an *idea,* in the Platonic sense, which is all collecting really is (whenever I'm in the presence of someone's array of matchbooks or shoes or 45s, I find myself imagining the pathology, the dream of order or comprehension or coherence it objectifies, for a collection is a snippet of dream-language, openly and inscrutably babbling away). In my case, the idea was simple: I was going to school myself in Marvel folklore, applying myself with the scholarly fervor of a convert, the Graham Greene approach—though, actually, the more appropriate analogy is that of the *Ger Sheker,* the mendacious stranger who converts to Judaism for ulterior motives or material gain. My scholarly aims derived from entirely unscholarly motivations—I stood in that shop, with its pleasant smell of moldering paper and cardboard, blowing my allowance and my birthday and Christmas loot because I'd started to make some progress, socially, and I wasn't about to lose any ground.

## V.

Still, it *was* a scholarly experience. To work my way back through Marvel was to grab hold of, understand, and form opinions about a literary canon. It was to intuit something about the nature of literary history; to see, literally graphically, the tumultuous effects of innovation on an art form. This was impossible to achieve reading DC alone because, as the megalithic presence Marvel was reacting against, DC had ceased to be fluid. Its here and now simply did not matter: its function, in view of Marvel's existence, was to be *of the past,* even as it ground out issues every month. Like the Washington Generals, the Harlem Globetrotters' perennial foils on the court, DC was there not merely to be defeated, but to be humiliated. DC's own history had become a trap; it was at best a historical artifact—"the way things used to be"—at worst an indication of how remote DC had become from its own days of excellence, innovation, and uniqueness of vision.

By the sixties DC had domesticated the superhero beyond any possibility of awe. He was as much a part of the landscape as the Bell Telephone System, a quasi-public utility in a cape. Superman was even once depicted using his X-ray vision to repair a cracked plate-glass window for a smug-looking storekeeper. How heroic, how astonishing, how splendid was *that?* Yet that's how it was—the DC squad cruised around like members of a tenant patrol, looking for action. Today you rescued an off-course dirigible. Tonight you tangled with a bunch of safecrackers wearing tight pinstripe suits. And if what you happened upon tomorrow was a broken window—well, you took what you could get. Only when someone like Luthor or the Joker turned up was there any hint of the sort of epic grudge match that fueled nearly every Marvel story. The DC hero was always accepting the key to the city; the Marvel hero was, at root, blithely unconcerned with law and order. He paid it lip service; there was always the obligatory panel depicting panicky civilians, or cops blasting away ineffectually at the menace du jour, but generally the well-being of civil society was merely ancillary to the psychodrama involving the principal players.

That DC was well aware of all this is evident from the slightly penitential tone taken by DC editor E. Nelson Bridwell in his introductions to the 1971 books *Superman: From the Thirties to the Seventies* and *Batman: From the Thirties to the Seventies,* compilations appearing just three years before Stan Lee's *Origins of Marvel Comics.* While Bridwell all but apologizes for DC's missteps with its two flagship characters, Lee's attitude is distinctly triumphalist. And why not? Marvel was Number One. *Origins of Marvel Comics* and its sequel, *Son of Origins,* marked a consolidation of the company's fortunes, while DC's clinically titled volumes seemed almost elegiac in nature.

## VI.

The question I seem to be moving toward is "Did DC suck?" but the more apposite question, perhaps, is "Was Marvel all that good?" Lee's two books are arranged according to a simple then-and-now schema, which contrasts, sometimes startlingly, the characters' original appearances with their later, presumably more familiar representations. Curious that, in the mid-1970s, Lee chose examples from the late 1960s to typify the "now" segments: the message coming through loud and clear was that Marvel had already peaked.

It had. Moreover, for Stan Lee the Peter Principle had obtained: as publisher, he'd clearly risen to the level of his incompetency and degraded the unique value of his flagship character by permitting him to play the Man of Steel's sidekick. Yes, in 1975 the two Great Rivals, DC and Marvel, shocked (and of course thrilled) purists on both sides of the divide by publishing a *collaboration*—the misleadingly titled *Superman vs. the Amazing Spider-Man* (actually, and somewhat disappointingly, the two heroes team up—as do, to much better effect, their arch-foes Dr. Octopus and Lex Luthor). In true détente-era spirit, art (Ross Andru and Dick Giordano) and scripting (Gerry Conway) assignments were carefully divided to suggest a parity between the two publishers, but my suspicion—then and now—is that this was strictly a Stan Lee project; that his personal green light had gotten the whole thing rolling forward—and for what? The script was no great shakes; I don't really remember what happens except that it ends—surprise!—with the two villains back in stir, hurling recriminations at one another. As to the art, the combined effect of Andru's ever-stilted pencilling and Giordano's lush Madison Avenue–style inking is of a Jess Collins comic collage constructed entirely from Saks Fifth Avenue and Lord & Taylor ads.

Mets and Yankees?

Christ and Moses?

P.S.3 and P.S.41?

*Superman and Spider-Man???* Well, of course I bought it—but the thing totally strained credulity. I mean, did Marvel think I'd forgotten Peter Parker's remark that he felt the way Clark Kent would if someone put Kryptonite in his phone booth? Now he's palling up to Kent and talking to him like he's any other mild-mannered reporter? Was this sort of lying revisionism what I'd bargained for?

When I wasn't hanging around the Comic Art Shop watching people handle old comic books as if they were fragments of the Dead Sea Scrolls, I was buying new ones at Andy's candy store on West 11th. I bought them, but I don't think I liked them a whole lot, because while I recall having been an RFO (a "Real Frantic One," in Lee-speak: the purchaser of at least three Marvel comics per month; the lowest rank of Marvel nobility), my interest in Marvel lasted maybe two years, tops. The Marvel books I bought then are mostly bloodless and derivative. There had been important personnel changes—most significantly, Kirby had departed and Lee, now publisher, was writing fewer scripts. Marvel was treading water. The stories became formulaic: for example, no installment of *Spider-Man* was complete now without Peter Parker cycling through recurring romantic, social, familial, financial, and academic worries. Every few pages he'd get into costume for some wiseass derring-do, but the rest was all a roiling soap opera.* When they tried to break out—killing off lover Gwen, making best friend Harry a psychotic junkie, introducing uninspired new villains, sending Peter to live in a lousy neighborhood—the title spun out. The last new issue I bought ends on a note of exhausted contrivance: Gwen has returned from the grave, as a clone.

*It's worth noting that *Spider-Man* artist John Romita, who had taken over from originator Steve Ditko and completely overhauled Ditko's grotesque vision, had extensive experience in romance comics (a genre pioneered, incidentally, by Kirby). A page of Romita's teen melodrama stuff beggars anything in Lichtenstein's canon.

65

What had drawn me in were the reprints Marvel put out, titles like *Marvel Tales* and *Marvel Triple Action*—that was the stuff that had started me throwing my dough around the Comic Art Shop each Saturday, buying up back issues. Such recycling saved some money, but it put Marvel in the position of competing against itself. It was like being given the option of watching Willie Mays at the end of his career or, simply by stepping through a discreet side door, seeing him as he was in his prime, and getting the Polo Grounds to boot. There is something urbane, something quickblooded and sophisticated, about those Marvel books of the sixties. You were given to understand that all those miniskirted bombshells on the streets, the guys in their Nehru jackets, had more important things to do than just stand there and gawk when superheroes sailed through the skies overhead. Consider the fact that all the Marvel heroes came from hither and yon to live in New York, the big time (just what were all those DC VIPs doing in bush-league burgs like "Central City"? Couldn't they hack it?). For me, it was a nostalgic glimpse of "Fun City," the chimera that the first Lindsay administration had celebrated. The nostalgia was illusory, of course: that was the decade through whose agency my old neighborhood had been destroyed, after all. But now the rest of the city had caught up; been enveloped in the sour funk that was the true aroma of those days, settled into a lingering fiscal and moral dilapidation: what better time for nostalgia, fake or otherwise?

## VII.

And a good time, too, for relevancy—which DC was embracing like a life preserver, pursuing Marvel and trying to shake off its own unquestioned *irrelevancy* of late. Its consequent jeremiads were typified by Denny O'Neil and Neal Adams's strident *Green Lantern/Green Arrow* series. Perhaps because of their lesser status in the DC pantheon, these characters were deemed most capable of shouldering the burden of relevancy and embarking on a journey through a landscape of racism, drugs, poverty, environmental depredation, and religious charlatanry. But nobody bought; the book was discontinued.

It's not hard to see why. The stuff is naked propaganda, ultra-naïve, paternalistic, and pretentious, from the overt Christ-figures Adams doted on to the literary quotations O'Neil threw in. If Marvel's "sophisticated philosophy" was a hodgepodge of pseudoexistentialist folderol ("With great power there must also come—great responsibility"), the philosophy of *Star Wars,* then DC's was the philosophy of *Star Trek*: idealized case studies in which right and wrong are laid out for all to see. DC missed the point. Sure, Marvel characters attended protests. Sure, Marvel talked about drugs. Sure, Marvel portrayed the inner city, and raised the profile of black people in their comics. Couldn't hurt. But what DC never got was that none of that was ever the point. The reason why, in the end, Stan Lee could get away with either taking blacks or leaving them, with either having characters protest or shipping them to Indochina, with either giving them drug problems or having them sip sodas at the drugstore, was because once the masks went on, Marvel heroes became *Other*. Out of uniform all the men may have looked as if they'd rolled off a Ken-doll assembly line; all the women like either Ann-Margret, Faye Dunaway, or Raquel Welch, but everyone *knew* that they were marked by an exotic ethnicity all their own. This was powerful—and undefined—enough for anybody to identify with. Marvel's "relevancy" was encoded in the implicit idea that any bunch of young people who looked different, who acted out the way Marvel's heroes did, would be regarded as freaks by all the straights scurrying around on the streets. DC's overt attempts at relevancy failed, finally, not because the posturing was less convincing than Marvel's but because the dramatis personae were so ill-suited to it. Suddenly, at midlife, its heroes were born again, sanctified by the gospel of centrist liberalism?

Well, maybe. It may just have been middle age, which DC was wise to acknowledge. DC wasn't in a position to start all over again, so it redrew what it could. Its stars handled change gingerly, but not completely unenthusiastically, and there is a persuasive feeling in these early seventies books of people facing a loss of potency, facing their own dwindling faith in authority, facing a growing sense of being out of touch—facing, finally, irrelevance. More than the "issues" themselves, a farrago of tepidly endorsed causes, what is intriguing is the sense you get of a mature soul being grafted onto the characters.

## VIII.

So—if Marvel was maybe not so good, if DC was maybe not so bad, was it worth it, was it necessary, to leave DC? I didn't know any of this history back when I started buying DC comics. If I made a conscious, uninfluenced, choice, it was based on the aesthetic appraisal of an eight-year-old: there they were—the famous Batman and Superman! They were, after all, on TV. But of their provenance, of their aesthetic rank relative to that of the competition, I knew nothing. I doubt that the juvenile commissars who suggested that I ought to watch what I read knew any of this either. And I doubt that it would have made any difference to claim that because its comics reflected the concerns of their makers at a difficult point in the country's history, because they represented a genuine search for a new creative direction, because as an American person you could do worse than to acquaint yourself with Superman and Batman, DC was actually pretty interesting. These were arguments that didn't even occur to me at the time. While my evaluation of the Fantastic Four, et al, was shrewdly political, it was still a relief to be told what to do. Marvel was a juggernaut then—it didn't matter that the drawing was often second-rate or that the writers aping Stan Lee's tone captured none of his flavor. It didn't matter that DC was putting out elegant, stylish books drawn by the likes of Neal Adams, Dick Giordano, and Jim Aparo and written by the likes of Denny O'Neil (who was OK when he wasn't saving the world), not to mention allowing Jack Kirby (who had defected) his head. It didn't matter that when it came right down to it, aside from Spider-Man (to whom I became emotionally attached), Marvel sort of bugged me. What did matter? DC was toilet paper on my shoe; someone was informing me—snidely, OK, but they were letting me know.

It's amazing to look back more than thirty years and realize how early received wisdom takes hold, and how tenaciously it retains that hold. I was wise, of course: I feel I have sometimes been astute enough to recognize the correct response when it looms before me. The corollary to this is that with the passing of each era of my life I've had to disentangle myself from one species of groupthink or another, but the key speculation is, from what would I have had to disentangle myself otherwise? Like no others, children provide you with the opportunity to give unambiguously correct or incorrect responses. The preservation of feelings is never of concern. They ask you openly: Do you want to belong—or not?

The fabulous appeal of Marvel heroes lay always in their isolation, their rejection of, and by, the worldly. And, through them, you may say, If I am alone, then I am a hero. There is a tremendous relief, a tremendous satisfaction in determining this about yourself. I am not *just* alone! Of course, that doesn't even begin to approximate the satisfaction of identifying with the lone heroes of Marvel, of embracing their stark emotional seclusion, shoulder to shoulder with a group of fellow adherents.

If there's a paradox here, it's not one into which I feel inclined to read a lot of meaning. It may simply be that no matter what their staunchest champions claim for them, comics really are intended for kids, who, whatever the quality of their social milieu, have yet to find their true lives, and who, in continuing to see things through a glass, darkly, when searching for those lives, see only themselves.

# STEVE ERICKSON

It was in the summer of 1983 that a friend called me and said, "Have you heard about this comic book *American Flagg*?" Comic book? At that point I hadn't read comics for almost twenty years. Of course I was obsessed with them as a kid; in my entire life, it may be my timing has never been so impeccable as it was when it came to comics. At the perfect age of thirteen I was there for the first Hulk and Spider-Man stories, the first Fantastic Four and the first X-Men; and if I had kept all of them, well, I would *own* Marvel Comics now. But in the spirit of a man setting aside ➜

childish things, out went the comics eventually, for two reasons: the first was the fateful intersection of adolescence and *A Hard Day's Night* in the summer of 1964, when suddenly the action was decidedly elsewhere and comics didn't seem so important; and the second, in tandem with the first, I suppose, was the realization that comics weren't paying off the way they were supposed to, that they always promised the imagination something they never delivered. Even among DC's best books—*Hawkman, Green Lantern, Mystery in Space*—the stories never lived up to the gorgeous covers, and in Marvel's new line that was just getting off the ground at the time, the Stan Lee shtick of neurotic, feuding superheroes constantly yelling "It's CLOBBERIN' time!" already grew wearisome. After years of reading them I still hadn't found the comic book of my dreams, the comic that completely performed up to its seduction of my twelve cents. Discovering Faulkner's "The Bear," my teen sensibility entered a new age of pretension.

So the comic book of my dreams didn't exist until I was in my early thirties, when I got that phone call—more good timing on my part, because Howard Chaykin's *American Flagg* definitely wasn't for thirteen-year-olds. Set in a time that then was half a century in the future and now is practically right around the corner, the scene was a Chicago-in-name-only that was half mega-mall and half madlands, in an America-in-name-only run by bureaucrats in the manner of a banana republic, their base of petty operations relocated to the moon and Mars. With a large dose of anarchy, and corruption as a way of life, the social order of *American Flagg* was libertarian at best, wherein the State's primary concern was whatever mass diversion it couldn't control, from organized sports to unsanctioned video entertainment; highly contraband tapes of everything from porn to old *Twilight Zone* episodes were at a premium. Otherwise, anything went. Guns in particular were rampant; everyone was armed to the teeth. Into this barely managed chaos bumbled Reuben Flagg, a naïve ex-actor turned cop and literally a Martian Jew who, having heard about "America" his whole life, was besotted with the idea of it. But for how he was distracted from his ideals only by his dick, his sanctimoniousness would have been insufferable.

The writing of *American Flagg* would be compared to Philip K. Dick and Raymond Chandler, although the more apt comparison was Alfred Bester crossed with Mickey Spillane. Visually, the book was positively Godardian: the pages seemed to barely contain panels that barely contained themselves; jagged dialogue spilled out of their word balloons and "sound" effects slashed across the page, which broke up behind the foreground like shards of glass or arctic ice. Several things were almost always happening at once, which gave some of the ongoing action and commentary an almost subliminal effect. *American Flagg* was a graphic explosion, and if you were truly intent on catching everything, you wound up reading a given issue three times—but catching everything was probably never the point. Once you learned to give yourself up to the stories' pell-mell pace and not worry about every detail, the comic actually came more into focus; the less you tried to make sense of every single thing, the more the whole thing made sense.

After almost fifty years of comic books, *American Flagg* was finally fulfilling the medium's potential, doing what comics could do that no other form could, acting as a kind of cinema for readers, every frame of the film subservient not to the chronology of the camera but rather to the human hand. And if *Flagg* was the *Breathless* of comic books, it was also the first Velvet Underground album, in the way it made explicit everything forbidden that comics had hinted at when you *were* thirteen: it was the comic book that lived between the lines of all other comic books, the comic book that mothers and fathers always worried that comic books were like, teeming with sex and violence except that, like no other mainstream book, *American Flagg* did teem with sex and violence, not to mention wit, cultural satire, a vaguely populist iconoclasm, a seething indignation that patriotism somehow had been requisitioned by the political right, and a talking cat named Raul.

Which is all to say two things. The first is that as Reaganism

73

flourished at its most bombastic and combustible, *American Flagg* was a wildly subversive comic, a taunt in the face of everything that conspired to make the 1980s an increasingly repressive decade. Besides the leftish subtext, Reuben Flagg's inalienable right to pursue happiness between the legs of every babe who came on to him—and that was every woman he met, particularly his main squeeze, Mandy— wasn't just an aside, it dominated the narrative as much as anything else. You would like to say the sex wasn't gratuitous and was part of some larger point, but really, gratuity was the larger point. An immoral hedonist by the standards of not only the early '80s but the early '00s, in fact Reuben was also the comic's conscience, a walking affront to whatever ideology insists on measuring morality purely in terms of sexual behavior while tacitly regarding CEOs bilking stockholders out of life-savings as righteous capitalism just getting a little carried away with itself. In 1983, with AIDS on the horizon, the sex of *American Flagg*'s 2031 was a Jeffersonian act by virtue of its humanity and insubordination, and the comic was eroticized from the opening pages of its premiere issue: the ambience pulsingly libidinal, the clothes stylishly fetishized, and feminism having reached a point where self-empowerment wore stiletto heels (all right then, a *guy*'s idea of feminism). And in part because sexual gratuity was the point, *Flagg* was also the fulfillment of our childhood taboos: I still have, for instance, an almost inexpressibly vivid memory from when I was a kid of an issue of *Mystery in Space,* with Adam Strange's unabashedly curvy, dark-haired girlfriend Alanna bestriding a full page (Jennifer Connelly, call your agent); it wasn't just hot, it was diabolical. This was the sort of image that launched tens of thousands of young male ids on their doomed voyages into the carnal oblivion called manhood, and *American Flagg* not only recalled every one of them but stripped them of all disingenuousness: Here, *Flagg* said, is what every comic has hinted at but could never show you.

Which is also to say that *American Flagg* was nothing if not the highly personal endeavor of its creator. An illustrator from New Jersey and a longtime comic fan himself, by many accounts something of a raging hothead and egomaniac, Howard Chaykin in the 1970s translated the work of science fiction authors like Bester, Samuel Delany, and Michael Moorcock into graphic novels before they were called that, and came up with an intergalactic adventurer named Cody Starbuck about the same time he was drawing the comic of *Star Wars*, before the movie was even out. It's been pointed out that Han Solo bore more than a passing resemblance to Starbuck. Nothing, however, that Chaykin had done before or would do later approached *Flagg*'s level of invention and inspiration, and it took the comic world by storm.

Published only months after the release of *Blade Runner* and *The Road Warrior*, it not only anticipated Gibson and cyberpunk, Tarantino and the postmodernization of pulp iconography, but more important—from the standpoint of this anthology—it kickstarted the independent comics movement, and also provided the door through which the medium rushed to the likes of such eighties landmarks as Alan Moore and Dave Gibbons's *Watchmen*, the Hernandez Brothers' *Love and Rockets*, Frank Miller's *The Dark Knight Returns*, and Neil Gaiman's *Sandman*. In its first year *American Flagg* swept all the comic book awards and was the first comic ever nominated for a science fiction Nebula award.

Then, almost as quickly, it was over. After twelve or fifteen issues, *American Flagg* ran out of steam. For starters, the independent company for which *Flagg* was the flagship book, First Comics, teetered on the edge of survival, finally going out of business. Also, plot was always Chaykin's least convincing talent; once the form of his comic was no longer a revelation and other comics made their way across the rubble of the barricade Flagg had stormed, fickle readers—like me—strayed. Researching this piece, I was startled to find the series actually persevered all the way up to #50, and you can't help wondering if that wasn't how Chaykin planned it all along: one issue for every forsaken star on what Chaykin clearly considered a blasphemed flag. Chaykin himself bailed, moving on to a graphic novel called *Time²* that, in a heroic but ultimately failed effort, squared all the audacious experiments of *Flagg* to the point of general impenetrability; and then, beyond that, on to a nasty noir work called *Black Kiss* (later collected in a single volume called *Thick Black Kiss*) that squared *Flagg*'s sexual outrage, what with cavorting gangsters and hermaphrodites. Today we would call it "transgressive"; then it was just good old-fashioned pornography, and its bracing sensual nihilism notwithstanding, without Reuben Flagg's passionate naïveté it was without heart. In the nineties Chaykin wrote more and more for television, and just in the last few years created for Vertigo a comic called *American Century*; though not drawn by Chaykin, its Steve Canyon–like character, Harry Kraft, definitely recalls one Reuben Flagg, perhaps his great-grandfather, and with what you have to figure are all the intentional echoes of the earlier comic that the title suggests, tries to wreak the same havoc on the mid-twentieth century that Flagg did on the mid-twenty-first.

Now *American Flagg* is forgotten. It may have been the *Breathless* and *Velvet Underground & Nico* of comics but only if you turn them on their heads: whereas their fame and influence grew over the years to far exceed their initial impact, *American Flagg* was a phenomenon at its inception and then exhausted itself. Just to make sure my memory wasn't playing tricks on me, I called the manager of the biggest comic book store in town, a guy who was unpacking comics as an assistant in the same store twenty years ago when I first began shopping there, and we talked and wondered how it was that arguably the single most influential series since *Fantastic Four* could have passed from recollection so easily. Go online and, even with it long out of print, you can snare a copy of *American Flagg* #1 for about three bucks. So it wasn't only the comic book of our dreams, it's the Great Lost Comic Book as well, the nova that illuminated the future of comics before imploding—and what does *that* say about our dreams? We won't even get into what it says about the culture. Maybe it means that comics are for thirteen-year-olds after all. I would like to think that Reuben Flagg so resisted the pernicious commodification that might have turned him into an action figure that there was only a place for him in his own future and his own America—trashed though it might be—and no place in ours. I would also like to think that, one of these days, I'll get another phone call like that one in the summer of 1983 and discover comics again. But I don't think so.

# The HOUSE of the SEVEN GABLES

*Illustrated by Harley M. Griffiths*

*By Nathaniel Hawthorne*

HALF-WAY DOWN A BY-STREET OF A NEW ENGLAND TOWN, STANDS A RUSTY, WOODEN HOUSE, WITH SEVEN ACUTELY PEAKED GABLES, FACING TOWARDS VARIOUS POINTS OF THE COMPASS, AND A HUGE CLUSTERED CHIMNEY IN THE MIDST. THE STREET IS PYNCHEON STREET; THE HOUSE IS THE OLD PYNCHEON HOUSE; AND AN ELM-TREE, OF WIDE CIRCUMFERENCE, ROOTED BEFORE THE DOOR, IS FAMILIAR TO EVERY TOWN-BORN CHILD BY THE TITLE OF THE PYNCHEON ELM.

# SEDUCED BY CLASSICS ILLUSTRATED

## GARY GIDDINS

I.

*I have never seen any good effects from comic books that condense classics. Classic books are a child's companion [sic], often for life. Comic-book versions deprive the child of these companions. They do active harm by blocking one of the child's avenues to one of the finer things in life.*
— Fredric Wertham, M.D.,
*Seduction of the Innocent*

On Sundays in the middle and late 1950s, we often ate dinner at an Italian restaurant near our home on Long Island's south shore. While our parents lingered over coffee and cigarettes, my sister and I would scamper to the bar to vote for Miss Rhinegold, stuffing the ballot box for our mom or my sister. Then the four of us would stroll to the corner candy store, where my father loaded up on Tootsie Rolls, Goldenberg's Peanut Chews, Spearmint Leaves, and Bonomo's Turkish Taffy, to be dispensed during the drive home, and I would wheedle—they never refused, but I always felt I was wheedling—two or maybe even three *Classics Illustrated* comic books. I'd promise not to read all of them that night,  ➔

but, if necessary, I had a flashlight ready under the blanket. I wasn't big on patience, and those comics quelled apprehensions of the Monday morning ordeal, for which I was never prepared.

The *CI* bug had bitten me at age six at the local synagogue's annual bazaar, where neighbors unloaded curios they had relegated to attics and basements. Someone had donated a pile of *Classics,* and the anomalous covers combining historical costumes and gruesome violence held my attention like a hypnotist's swinging watch-fob. I managed to acquire the pile. So by the time of our Sunday evening ritual, I was familiar with The List, an ever-changing guide to available titles printed on the back of each issue. Unlike other comic books, *Classics* were prominently numbered and irregularly reprinted and published— or so it seemed to those of us who read and collected them (one activity mandating the other). What did we know or care of the Gilberton Company's commercial considerations? All we knew was that the lists tweaked our curiosity about missing numbers, and that the earliest issues listed titles like *Mr. Midshipman Easy* and *The Black Tulip* that were practically impossible to find. One might search in vain for months, and then—oh, joy!—locate an obscure *CI* gathering dust in a Brooklyn store or in the home of a DC addict who was happy to trade it for a couple of tepid *Jimmy Olsens.* Cultural considerations aside, comics inducted us into the art of laissez-faire trade. Eventually I found all 169 titles, many in multiple editions. I have them still, though until now I had not looked through them in thirty years, beyond an occasional peek, like driving by the old homestead.

William Gass has written that "lists are juxtapositions, and exhibit many of the qualities of collage." They may, in fact, offer the primitive pleasures of serendipitous art. A computerized list, for example, of the popular songs published during the first half of the twentieth century reveals an infinite treasury of found poems: Flip to any page, put your finger on any title, and track the first ten songs upward or down, and voilà, instant lit. Lists of artworks are serendipitous and canonical, too—not just the pompous-ass variety (Famous Authors Choose the 100 Best Novels of the Century by Dead Persons and Themselves) but also publishers' catalogs and individual work-lists. The most influential film book of the 1960s, Andrew Sarris's *The American Cinema,* is little more than an annotated list. In subdividing, by director, a comprehensive selection of movies, he offered a more sophisticated canon than those built around movie stars to a generation raised on *The Early Show, The Late Show, The Million Dollar Movie, Shock Theater, Saturday Night at the Movies,* and the rest of TV's cinematic windfall. My first jazz canon consisted of ten-best lists volunteered by critics for a middlebrow magazine called *Cue*; my first classical music canon was edited and boxed by *Reader's Digest.* Preliminary literary canons included the catalogs printed on the inside jackets of Landmark Books and the Modern Library and the roll of prize-winning books in the almanac. But in the beginning, there was that curious collage, *Classics Illustrated.*

The back cover of each issue included the Gilberton Company's yellow order form—matching the yellow *CI* cover logo—and advice: "Mail coupon below or a facsimile." (*CI* fans had "facsimile" in their vocabularies before reaching adolescence, though my recollection is that none of us knew how to pronounce it.) On two occasions I tried to outsmart Gilberton by making a facsimile of old coupons with deleted numbers; the company flouted my desire by sending me whatever issues were at hand, always those I already owned. I had an image of a mailroom clerk, an ancient twisted harridan as drawn by *CI*'s Henry Kiefer, a master of the woodenly grotesque, bellowing "Ha! Ha! Ha!" while sending off yet another copy of *Caesar's Conquests* when I had optimistically paid my fifteen cents for *Two Years Before the Mast.* My frustration wasn't merely that of a completist with missing numbers to fill, but of an avaricious reader (albeit mostly of comics) besotted with the very idea of "classics" and the historical claims they represented. It was easy to figure out the reasoning behind a nineteenth-century ragbag such as could be found on any *CI* printed around 1958:

42. *Swiss Family Robinson*
46. *Kidnapped*
47. *Twenty Thousand Leagues Under the Sea*
48. *David Copperfield*
50. *The Adventures of Tom Sawyer*
51. *The Spy*
52. *The House of the Seven Gables*
55. *Silas Marner*
57. *The Song of Hiawatha*
58. *The Prairie*
62. *Brett Harte's Western Stories*

But what of those missing numbers? What were they and why were they deleted? Had certain classics been demoted from the rank of classics? Obviously not, as a comparison of various *CI* lists made clear:

43. *Great Expectations*
44. *Mysteries of Paris*
45. *Tom Brown's School Days*
49. *Alice in Wonderland*
53. *A Christmas Carol*
54. *The Man in the Iron Mask*
56. *The Toilers of the Sea*
59. *Wuthering Heights*
60. *Black Beauty*
61. *The Woman in White*

In time one would hear a variety of explanations, including poor sales, forthcoming revised versions, and censorship by a kind of HUAC for kids, the House Un-American Accursed Comics tribunal stimulated by the wannabe Dr. Spock of mental hygiene—the former director of Bellevue Hospital, Dr. Fredric Wertham. To its great credit, the Gilberton Company refused to sign on to the Comics Code Authority. On the other hand, it didn't want to press its luck. The opening graveyard sequence in Kiefer's 1947 *Great Expectations* was singled out as especially vile, though it was obviously influenced by David Lean's film of a year earlier. "You bring me a file and vittles," Magwitch threatens Pip. "Bring 'em both to me or I'll have your heart and liver out!" Today that reads like a droll moment from the Hannibal Lecter franchise, except for *CI*'s assumption that kids could make sense of "vittles"—just as it assumed kids would go for adaptations of Shakespeare that were far more authentic than, say, the retellings of Charles Lamb.

## II.

*I have yet to see a child who was influenced to read "classics" or "famous authors" in the original by reading them in comic book versions. What happens instead is that the comic book version cuts the children off from this source of pleasure, entertainment and education.*
          —Fredric Wertham, M.D., *Seduction of the Innocent*

Most issues of *CI* ended with the motto: "Now that you have read the *Classics Illustrated* edition, don't miss the added enjoyment of reading the original, obtainable at your school or public library." Always a sucker for added enjoyment, I did or tried to do just that, as did everyone I know who grew up with *CI*. When I mentioned to an editor of the *New York Times Book Review* that I was writing this essay, he broke into a wide smile and said, "I love *Classics Illustrated*. They introduced me to Dostoevsky"—or Dostoyevsky, as *CI* preferred. Me too. The only *CI* with a more urgent endnote than the one about added enjoyment was *Crime and Punishment*: "Because of space limitations, we regretfully omitted some of the original characters and sub-plots [like Sonya and Svidrigailov] of this brilliantly written novel. Nevertheless we have retained its main theme and mood. We strongly urge you to read the original." Maybe artist Rudy Palais felt guilty, though he had no cause. Other *CIs* were far less faithful, and his rendering of the murder, and the mounting hysteria of Raskolnikov (drawn to resemble Peter Lorre), and Porfiry's inquisition were expertly done. Yet who could resist "strongly urge"?

The only things harder to find than deleted *CIs* in small Long Island villages of the 1950s were genuine book stores. But it was not uncommon to find display cases of the Modern Library, Landmark, or Signature Books (rival nonfiction series for young readers), and paperbacks in supermarkets, drugstores, and stationery stores. My dad drove me to the latter when I begged him for *Crime and Punishment.* We were standing before a counter taller than I while the storeowner looked through the Modern Library behind him, only to report that he must have sold it. He did, however, have *The Brothers Karamazov* by the same guy. When my dad turned and asked if I wanted it, the storeowner, who hadn't noticed me, peered over the counter and said, "It's for *him?*" This inclined my dad to ask, sotto voce, if it was a dirty book. I carried it around for months, reading and rereading the first hundred or so pages until it dawned on me that Alyosha and Alexey were the same character, same for Dmitri and Mitya, whereupon I gave up, hoping in vain that *CI* would get to it. On another occasion, I searched everywhere for the "original" of Eugène Sue's *Mysteries of Paris* and reluctantly settled for *The Wandering Jew,* an even more horrific farrago of malignant plots and tortuous intrigue, set in motion by Jesuits who would have scared the pantaloons off Torquemada.

*CI* never tackled the 1,350 pages of *The Wandering Jew,* but it did briefly risk accusations of anticlericalism with its 1947 edition of *Adventures of Cellini,* which had enjoyed a revival of interest the year before in a volume sexily illustrated by Dalí. Cellini's rant against a succession of shortsighted and dim-witted popes is fully intact in the

*CI* adaptation; though dull in stretches, August M. Froehlich's primal art emits a claustrophobic feeling for the Renaissance absent from the more briskly paced and vividly narrated 1961 version (artist unidentified). The popes are just as corrupt and avaricious in the toned-down remake, but less stupid. The narrative strategy is also different. The first version shows Cellini dictating his story to an apprentice (as, in fact, he did); the second recapitulates the memoir's actual first-person telling. All *Classics Illustrated* comics included page-long bios of the authors, and the 1961 account forestalled criticism by describing Cellini as a liar and a rogue.

One of those Eureka moments when I knew I'd be a writer, no matter how little talent I had, occurred in fourth grade when I leaped from the *CI* version to the Hawthorne version of *The House of the Seven Gables,* a novel with which I remain obsessed. The *CI*, despite its splendidly horrific opening exposition, is better and more accurate than either of the two Hollywood travesties, and served as a stirring prelude to the real thing—the definitive American assessment of inherited sin. The *CI* splash page depicts the greenish, hairless, disembodied head of Matthew Maule (note the slightly pointed ears, a *CI* trope), hanged for witchcraft through the conniving of Colonel Pyncheon, while the colonel cowers in a chair, soon to drink blood in fulfillment of Maule's malediction.

Soon I was devouring "originals." After reading Verne's *From the Earth to the Moon,* I was moved to compose a short story and submit it to my teacher. It concerned a pack of scientists who launch themselves beyond Earth's gravity in a giant bulletlike projectile; the plot focused on the apparent murder of a passenger haunted by his ancestor's crimes. A detective who happens to be on board discovers that the fellow had accidentally killed himself by falling against a broken coathook. (The story remains unpublished.) *CI* led me to Robert Louis Stevenson, Mark Twain (including *Pudd'nhead Wilson,* not often recommended to young readers), Doyle, Poe, Cooper, Wilkie Collins, *Jane Eyre, Frankenstein, Lord Jim,* the *Bounty* trilogy (when I matriculated at

Grinnell College, all I knew of the place was that James N. Hall had gone there, though that wasn't my motivation). Before long, I had abandoned *CI*. But The List remained imprinted on my brain, an abiding source of curiosity and bemusement.

I continue to find myself grabbing at obscure *CI* source material when I come across it. Twenty years ago, while lecturing in Philadelphia, I found a 1902 edition of Edmund About's *The King of the Mountains*, and delighted in its brisk, funny narrative—a satirical, politically astute kidnapping story. It's probably safe to assume that no one beyond *CI* readers and French lit scholars know of it or About, which rhymes with Camus, since a web search shows no American edition in the last ninety years. Honored in France as the equal of Hugo (himself represented with four *CI* titles, including *The Toilers of the Sea*, originally done in the stark, faded, newspaper style of August Froehlich, and then updated in the more conventional and intimate manner of EC Comics veteran Angelo Torres), About is one of the mysteries of the canon; so far as I can tell, *The King of the Mountains* is the only one of his books to be translated and published here—its renown peaked between 1900 and 1910. I thank *CI* for the tip and heartily recommend it. A few years later, I finally found a UK import of *Mysteries of Paris*, and searched out the gory parts. More recently I've derived simpler satisfactions from *The Black Tulip* and the surprisingly mirthful—the *CI* version had revealed no such comedic spirit—*Mr. Midshipman Easy*. A fascination triggered by *CI*'s *The Oregon Trail* (not a single dialogue balloon) and *The Conspiracy of Pontiac* inclined me to tackle the three volumes of Francis Parkman published by the Library of America— another odd canon in the making.

Many of the 169 *CI* titles are now unread, including a good many copyrighted (twentieth-century) titles. But The List abides as a fair and appropriately idiosyncratic reflection of the old-school literary canvas as inherited by American-born and immigrant readers in the early years of the bygone century. The series, which began in 1941 as

*Classics Comics* and changed its name to the snootier *Classics Illustrated* in 1947, was largely a postwar phenomenon. Its canonical vision, however, was established before 1925. The personal and sometimes peculiar tastes of *CI* founder Albert Kanter and his staff embodied the reading habits of our grandparents, which proved readily accessible to children of the 1950s. Few of those books are as enthusiastically embraced today, beyond a small forest of evergreens like *The Three Musketeers* (issue #1), *Treasure Island, Tom Sawyer, A Tale of Two Cities, The Count of Monte Cristo,* and *Twenty Thousand Leagues Under the Sea,* and, to be sure, even some of them are shunned as creaky, remote, and pitilessly long. Besides, the thriving kiddie-lit industry knows better than to look to the public domain for serious profits.

So the canon appeared far more settled in Kanter's day, with confirmations everywhere. One measure of stature was inclusion in Scribner Illustrated Classics (and similar series), now remembered mostly for N. C. Wyeth's paintings, introduced before the First World War and cheaply reprinted in the 1940s. In addition to the usual titles by Stevenson, Verne, and Cooper, *The Boy's King Arthur,* and *Arabian Nights,* Scribner and other publishers offered minor works by the same writers (*The Black Arrow, Michael Strogoff, The Pilot*), and other volumes bound for obscurity, like *The Scottish Chiefs, The White Company,* and *Westward Ho! CI* did them all. Do kids still read *Men of Iron?* The last generation to seek out Howard Pyle's story may have been primed by *CI.* The same may be said for *The Last Days of Pompeii, The Cloister and the Hearth, Soldiers of Fortune, Waterloo, King—of the Khyber Rifles,* the collected works of hunter Frank Buck, *The Crisis* (by American novelist Winston Churchill, born three years before the PM)— erstwhile classics at best, given one last shot at a mass audience by *CI.* Ouida's ponderous *Under Two Flags* must have disappointed many who gasped at the comic's climax, in which raven-haired beauty Cigarette gallops into view bearing a pardon and throws herself before a firing squad to save her lover:

Cigarette: Stop! In the name of France, STOP!
Evil Legionnaire: Aim!
Cigarette: Do you not hear me? Stop!
Evil Legionnaire: Fire!
Cigarette: Read! Read! AH-H-H-NNN . . .

*Classics Illustrated* extended the lifeline of the late-nineteenth-century middlebrow canon much as early TV extended the life of old Hollywood. Indeed, hit movies sanctioned and influenced The List. Within a decade of *CI*'s start-up, the founder's son, Hal Kanter, succeeded as a Hollywood comedy writer (he eventually wrote for Bing Crosby and Bob Hope and directed Elvis Presley), and he would alert his old man when a public-domain classic was in one of the studio pipelines. What a coincidence that the movie *Master of the World* was released the same year *CI* issued that title and its companion piece, *Robur the Conqueror* (*CI* turned to Jules Verne ten times, more than to any other writer). Same thing with *The Red Badge of Courage, Knights of the Round Table, Rob Roy, Ben-Hur,* and *The Cossack Chief* (*Taras Bulba*), among others. When *The Hunchback of Notre Dame* was filmed anew in 1956, *CI* outfitted their 1944 version with a new cover depicting a couple not unlike Gina Lollobrigida and Anthony Quinn; the comic itself showed its age with a caricature of Hitler in the Feast of Fools episode, and a semi-happy ending in which Esmeralda lives (as in the movies) while Quasimodo plummets to his death from the bell tower (an original touch from *Classics Illustrated*). Sometimes *CI* outpaced the pipeline, hitting the mark a couple of years before the movie, as happened with *Cleopatra, Lord Jim,* and a couple of H. G. Wells stories. Sometimes the series took cues from TV, as with Wild Bill Hickok and Davy Crockett (*CI* did several biographies, usually of western heroes, but also Lincoln and Joan of Arc). Only once did Hal Kanter broker a direct movie tie-in; unfortunately, it was for the lumbering 1959 remake of *The Buccaneer.*

In the early years, *CI* artists often relied on their memories of old movies for treatments as well as titles, producing an inconsistent fidelity to the books. *Frankenstein* is true to Shelley; Dr. Jekyll's girl-friend is pure Hollywood. Usually fidelity won out, even regarding the incomprehensible *Last Days of Pompeii*, which has more characters than the phone books of small cities. Ah, but there were howlers, too. In the last panel of the 1942 edition of *A Tale of Two Cities*, Sydney Carton doesn't get the last line; no sooner does he ponder a far better rest than the executioner adds, "Put your head on the block Evremonde!" A far, far better version was prepared in 1956 by former EC regulars Joe Orlando and George Evans. At the close of *Robinson Crusoe*, Friday waves at the reader with a big smile and says, "Me like big city!" For *Cyrano de Bergerac*, the company's most prolific and characteristic artist, Alex Blum, added a childhood scene you don't find in Rostand. Blum also concluded *The Iliad* with a flash-forward of Achilles' death from an arrow in the chest—the source of that familiar phrase, "He has an Achilles chest." To be fair, Homer didn't use the heel business either.

## III.

*There is a high correlation between intelligence, vocabulary and reading. Comic-book readers are handicapped in vocabulary building because in comics all the emphasis is on the visual image and not on the proper word. These children often know all that they should not know about torture, but are unable to spell or read the word.*
    —Fredric Wertham, M.D., *Seduction of the Innocent*

Dr. W had a point, if you believe that the generation bred in the era of silent movies could not speak and was forced to communicate in mime. He was undoubtedly correct, however, about torture, primers in which were offered by such issues as *Two Years Before the Mast*, *Mysteries* ("The Pit and the Pendulum"), *Mysteries of Paris*, *The Man in the Iron Mask*, *The Man Who Laughs*, *The Last Days of Pompeii*,

*Uncle Tom's Cabin, Pudd'nhead Wilson,* and others, not least *The Spy,* in which English officers are shown whipping bare-bottomed men strung up by their wrists, bleating, with rather finicky punctuation, "Help, help!" while a limey bastard snarls, "Ha, ha! Give it to 'em boys." The myth of *CI's* high-mindedness tends to obscure its place as the primeval modern horror comic. The great Swiss playwright and novelist Friedrich Dürrenmatt, whose work would have made splendid additions to The List, once referred to fright as "the modern form of empathy." Fright is also the eternal mode of empathy for young people unafraid to admit the compatibility of curiosity and terror; most middle-class children don't get the chance to experience many other frissons.

Intensely conscious of its socially redeeming qualities, *Classics Illustrated* was forever touting itself as an educational tool. In the 1948 issue of *Twenty Thousand Leagues Under the Sea,* it had the moxie to run a feature called "From Our Mail Sack": "We are brother and sister in High School," one letter begins, "and we read many of your CLASSICS *Illustrated* in our classes." This probably didn't play well with critics who feared that students would use them as cheats, though it's hard to imagine anyone in the age of Cliffs Notes trying to fob off a book report based on a comic. The letter is illustrated with a Kiefer drawing of tousled-hair Junior, pencil in hand, his sexy mom right behind him, her fingers proudly squeezing his shoulder, while his cross-eyed dad— a double for Alexander Woollcott (thick glasses, square face, mustache) holds up a copy of *Classics Illustrated.* But kids didn't buy *Twenty Thousand Leagues* to improve their marks; they bought it for the attack of the octopuses (the lonely giant squid exists only in Disney). The jokey villains in *Superman* and *Batman* were fruitcakes compared to *CI's* monsters, human and otherwise, which prefigure the Iron Age of EC.

A very freely adapted *Dr. Jekyll and Mr. Hyde* (#13, 1943) started the *CI* horror line; it ends, presumably for moral instruction, by depicting a green, pointy-eared devil with a white beard and a steeple sprouting from its head, carrying a triton. A calmer 1953 version, drawn by science fiction specialist Lou Cameron, cagily evaded the censors and evidently stayed in print till *CI*'s demise. Not the case with the infamous *3 Famous Mysteries* (1944, wiped out by HUAC-for-kids in the fifties), which ends with a wondrously inept and scary riff on Maupassant's "The Flayed Hand." The hand is terrific: long bony fingers with knuckles you can almost feel. The Frenchmen are something else, with their narrow faces and uniform open-mouthed expressions, as if they had all sat on whoopee cushions. A good artist, like Robert Hayward Webb, could generate genuine fear, as in *Kidnapped*, when Balfour mounts the dark stairs and emerges from two mostly black panels onto the exposed parapet, illuminated by a triple-branch of lightning bolts. Too bad N. C. Wyeth didn't think of that.

My favorite *CI* artists were stylistically unmistakable: Henry C. Kiefer and Rudy Palais. Kiefer was pushing sixty when he began bringing his nightmares to *CI*. An old-fashioned hack trained in the age of woodcuts and profusely illustrated novels, he was a true primitive, his art often stiff and looming, with an eye for theater and pageantry. William B. Jones Jr., whose *Classics Illustrated: A Cultural History, with Illustrations* (McFarland & Company, 2002) is definitive, writes of Kiefer's "willful antiquity" and "an air of historical accuracy and almost metaphysical mystery not found in any other comic book line." Kiefer's heroes and heroines look disconcertingly alike, except that the men have facial hair and the women wear lipstick. (If you've ever defaced a drawing by adding a goatee, you qualify for the Kiefer School of Fine Art.) His villains are inspired: lumpy morons, maniacal savages, and calculating hags—obvious predecessors of EC's Old Witch. He was not great at children: on the cover of *A Christmas Carol*, Tiny Tim looks slightly psychotic. Kiefer's backgrounds employ elaborate waves of smoke, rain, and fog that unite multiple panels. Yet it was also Kiefer who adapted "Hans Pfall" as a comically ribald jaunt, including a depiction of the universe with several ringed planets.

Kiefer did twenty-four titles in six years, including *Great Expectations, David Copperfield, Pudd'nhead Wilson, King Solomon's Mines, The*

*Prisoner of Zenda, The Oregon Trail, Twenty Thousand Leagues Under the Sea, Around the World in 80 Days, Wuthering Heights, The Cloister and the Hearth, The Lady of the Lake, Western Stories,* and the ineffable *Mysteries of Paris.* Here we meet the deadly Schoolmaster, with his porcine nostrils, yellow hair, and acid-scarred face. The do-gooder hero straps him to a chair and burns out his eyes, hoping that will reform him—fat chance. Then there's the one-eyed witch Screech-Owl, who tries to pull little Marie's tooth out with her fingers and threatens, "If the girl sings out for the police, I'll break my bottle of acid across her snout!" Nights are blue-black, days are saturated with reds and greens, and the many flashbacks are pale-blue pen sketches; varied frames, heavy dialogue, and a complicated plot suggest the density of a novel. One four-page section includes the following notices: "We leave Rudolph and go back several years"; "Getting back to the present"; "We leave Marie in the hands of her abductors for the present and return to No. 25 Rue Du Temple." The *CI* biography of Sue says his books "have many technical faults" that are overlooked because of the good stuff. "He became imbued with the socialist doctrine that influenced his most important works," and though he is "rambling and diffuse," he has "something of the narrative gift of Dumas and something of the ethical earnestness of Hugo." This was for nine-year-olds?

Rudy Palais didn't do horror per se, though the old pawnbroker in *Crime and Punishment* might disagree. Yet his characters are so intense, so wired, and so damned pissed off that sequences another artist might pass off as tea-and-crumpets become in his hands cruelly volatile. His years at *CI* overlapped with Kiefer's, but he came from another world, having made his way through the Depression designing posters for Hollywood studios. His credo was action: instead of stick figures, you find characters caught unawares, shot from weird angles, moving from frame to frame with sweaty resolve. His gnarly, livid faces are never merely misshapen; they are contorted by meanness and fury, often exemplified in distended Adam's apples. Palais did only eight *CI* titles—small potatoes compared to Kiefer, Blum, or the most prolific of the later artists, Norman Nodel—but they are among the most memorable, including the best of Cooper, *The Pioneers* (configured more as a mystery and revenge story than the novel, which gets bogged down in feats of pioneering) and *The Prairie*; the second and third parts of the Bounty trilogy, especially *Pitcairn's Island,* a tour de force of paranoid duplicity; and *David Balfour,* in which every minor character is distinctive.

Not surprisingly, when the censors buried EC, many of its writers and artists found work at *CI,* invariably in mainstream titles—Graham "Ghastly" Ingels bided his time with *Waterloo,* though *The First Men in the Moon* looks like what it is, a collaboration between *Mad*'s George Woodbridge and *Weird Fantasy*'s Al Williamson. George Evans became a regular, and one of the best pages he ever drew depicts with striking economy the death of Lord Jim. Racial horror was also on the *CI* agenda, despite stock natives found in many issues and a 1944 pass at *Huckleberry Finn* that depicts Jim as a simp; the 1956 version restores his and Huck's spunk, but it misspells "sivilize" with a *c.* Topsy is more of a minstrel stereotype than was necessary in *Uncle Tom's Cabin,* yet *CI*'s 1943 rendering was uncompromising and timely, with pointed references to the Constitution and Exodus and a line about religious persecution; the angel coming for Eva is a bit much (in the Stowe bio, we learn that she too was taken by "a force from beyond"), but Legree and other slave traders are as nightmarish as anything in the horror genre, and the characterization of St. Clare's dreadful wife is no less merciless. In 1946, *CI* hired black artist Matt Baker, who died young, after creating a gorgeous Lorna Doone that made Betty Page look like a Chihuahua; Lorna rivaled Uncle Tom as an all-time bestseller. *CI* closed shop in 1969, after issuing *Negro Americans—The Early Years,* accounts of a dozen or so luminaries from Crispus Attucks to Matthew Henson. By then, *Classics Illustrated* had gone soft (Nodel's 1962 *Faust* excepted), returning over and over to animal adventures, Verne, and Dumas. Its day was over: What's the point of comics, classic or otherwise, if they're shorn of the sensational?

## IV.

*Radio, movies and television are considered worthy of regular serious critiques in newspapers. Nothing like this exists for comic books. Nor is it even possible, for the few critics who have written about them find them subjects for toxicology rather than criticism.*
      —Fredric Wertham, M.D., *Seduction of the Innocent*

When I headed for college, I knew my mother would visit retribution on the comics stacked in my closet, and I didn't much care, except for the *Classics*. So I wrapped them in my late grandfather's tallis and squeezed them into his tallis bag and hid them under cushions and in game boxes. Sure enough, they alone survived the comics holocaust. Now they are simply relics; in the course of writing this essay, I've come to admire again what they were and what they did for me, but have lost the emotional attachment that had waxed in memory. They are, after all, childhood pulp, and one wouldn't go home again even if one could. They will go back into storage and someday my daughter, who has no interest in comics, will deal with them as she sees fit. Maybe she'll get a lot of money for them, or donate them to a bazaar, where some young antiquarian will take them to heart and make the mistake of trying to read *The Cloister and the Hearth*. And maybe she'll close the circle I prevented my mother from closing and throw them out. That's jake with me. I just don't want to be there when it happens.

BY THE WAY, YOUR CONTACT LENS-CAMERA'S NOT TOO SHABBY. YOU'D MAKE A FORTUNE SELLIN' 'EM TO SPIES.
I KNOW. WHAT DID THE TITANS DO NEXT? I NEED TO KNOW EVERYTHING.

# HOW I SPENT MY SUMMER VACATION WITH THE JUDAS CONTRACT

## BRAD MELTZER

I was fourteen. She was sixteen.

I had a long, shaggy bowl cut (feathered on the sides, natch). She had a blond Dutch-boy hairstyle.

I was at the height of puberty. She was far more experienced.

I was an innocent. She was, too (or so it seemed).

Her name was Terra (aka Tara Markov). And she was the first girl to break my heart.                    →

Simply put, she lied to me. And I'm not just talking about the standard grade-school lies ("You're *definitely* my best friend" or "I never told Julie Lerner you were fat"). I'm talking about something far more sinister. Terra betrayed me. She deceived me. She shoved a knife in my belly and sliced upward all the way to my heart. And at fourteen years old, I loved every minute of it.

To back up a bit, and to give a little background in the hope that, when my mother reads this, she won't feel the parental guilt that will cause her to spend the next year of my life asking, "Who's this Tara Markov, and how come you didn't tell me about her?," here's a quick primer. In December 1982, *New Teen Titans* #26 was published, introducing Terra, a troubled fifteen-year-old who became the first new member of the Teen Titans. Let me make one thing clear: this was a big deal to me.

In 1982, *New Teen Titans,* written by Marv Wolfman, and drawn oh-so-exquisitely by George Perez, was easily the best book on the market (that's right, I said it—and yes, smart guy, I'm well aware that the Byrne-Claremont *X-Men* was being published at the same time). Made up of the "junior" superheroes of the DC Universe, the Titans brought together such mainstays as Robin, Kid Flash, and Wonder Girl, with the new characters Cyborg, Starfire, Raven, and Changeling, a young, green (yes, green) fifteen-year-old class clown who could change into green animals (yes, green, and yes, animals). As I type those words, I'm reminded that comics always suffer in the retelling, but take my word for it, the alchemy between Wolfman and Perez created a vehicle for stories that redefined what comic book characterization was all about. Sure, the Titans beat on the bad guys, but the book was first and foremost about the relationships between these young kids who were saddled with enough power to knock down a mountain. And you thought *your* puberty was tough.

Which brings us back to Terra. At the time she was invited to join, the Titans were a family. Seven members. And now there was an eighth. As I said, it was a big deal—imagine Ringo telling the other Beatles, "Hey, blokes—I got a great fifth to play tambourine!" Still, it was accepted without much fuss. Let's not forget, that's how super-teams work. Members leave . . . members join. Even Batman and Robin parted ways (the original Robin, fanboy). There are no Beatles in comics.

As Terra spent time with the group, there were definitely a few doubters. Would she fit in? Was she joining the team with the right intentions? But me? I was like Changeling—simply smitten.

I'm not ashamed. I was twelve when she first appeared. Wonder Woman was far too old, and Wonder Girl was mature enough that she was dating a guy with a beard. Dammit, where were the teenage girls who'd like insecure, loudmouthed boys wearing Lee jeans like me? And then, out of the George Perez blue sky, comes this fifteen-year-old fast-talking blonde with superpowers who could control the Earth itself. You better believe the ground quaked beneath my feet. Sure, she was trying to blow up the Statue of Liberty, but that was only because terrorists were threatening to kill her parents if she didn't take Lady Liberty down. She didn't want to do it, though—remember her words? "I don't want to do any of this!" Look at the back issues. There were tears in her eyes as she begged Changeling to stay away. "Don't make it harder on me," she begged. "Please!!" No question, this was a girl who needed help. She needed someone to come to her aid. She needed me.

Fast forward to issue #28. Terra was robbing a bank. Like before, her heart wasn't in it. She even apologized to Changeling as she attacked him. ". . . I'm really sorry I have to do this—" And again, there were the tears. Curse those tears! They melted my pubescent heart like Fire Lad tonguing a Klondike bar. Dammit, world, can't you understand she's only doing it to save her parents!?

Of course, the Titans understood, and helped her track down the terrorists, only to find that her parents were already dead! Raging out

99

of control, Terra screamed for revenge, gripping the terrorists in an enormous fist made of rock. As the villains begged for mercy, my girl squeezed them tighter. The Earth was shaking. She was so powerful, she started an earthquake. My young eyes went wide as the stone fist tightened—I couldn't believe it—she was really gonna kill 'em. But like all true heroes, as Terra peered into the abyss, she didn't like what she saw. Crumbling to her knees, she showed the villains the mercy never given to her parents. Again, my heart plummeted—Terra was fifteen and all alone in the world. Didn't anyone hear what she was saying on the final pages? "I . . . feel so alone." And then, Changeling looked into those sad, newly orphaned blue eyes and said exactly what my twelve-year-old brain was thinking: "You don't have to be, Terra. *I'm* here." (Emphasis not mine, but man, it could've been.) The teaser on the cover of the issue said, INTRODUCING TERRA! IS SHE FRIEND—OR FOE? "Friend!" I shouted. "Friend!"

I have to hand it to Wolfman and Perez. They knew what they were doing. Preying on the knight-in-shining-armor gene that's inherent in every male comic fan (oh, c'mon, why do you think we read this stuff in the first place?), they conjured the perfect young lady in distress, then stepped back to watch us put our legs in the metal trap. The first step was done. By introducing her as a victim, they made us feel for her. But then they raised the stakes. Sure, she was in pain, but she was far from helpless. In fact, when Changeling tried to come to her aid, she not only refused it, she actually punched him in the face, called him a "nerd," and flew away. Think about that a moment. Do you have any idea what a strong female character like that does to a thirteen-year-old psyche? No? Then let me back up even further and explain.

In 1981, in the heart of New York–accent Brooklyn, my biggest social dilemma was deciding between Karen Akin and Ananda Bresloff. The slam books ( *popularity ratings* passed around to decide our social fates) were clear: given the choices "Good," "Fair," and "Yuk," both Karen and Ananda had ranked me as "Good." Even in fifth grade,

"Good" was a good sign. Now the ball was in my court. How would I rank *them*? Sure, we had traded slam books at the exact same time, but only a fool ranks someone before they see how that person ranks them. Make no mistake, I may've been dumb enough to think my knee-high tube socks were cool, and even insecure enough to want to wear a gold Italian-horn charm around my neck although I was Jewish, but I was nobody's fool. And so, I handed Karen and Ananda their respective slam books.

"Did you do the chart?" they asked.

"Of course," I said.

But when they checked inside, here's what they saw:

| GIRLS | Good | Fair | Yuk* |
|-------|------|------|------|
| Darlene Signorelli | | x | |
| Randi Boxer | | x | |
| Danielle Levy | | x | |
| Ananda Bresloff | | | |
| Karen Akin | | | |

That's right, bubba. I left it blank. Who'd they think they were dealing with? I had read far too many Lex Luthor stories—every single *Adventure Comics* digest *and* the oversized maxi-books—to fall for some simple trap. I wasn't putting my heart on the line until I knew it was a sure thing. And so, armed with my recent "Good" ranking, I knew who I was deciding between. Time to make a choice.

Here's how it looked to me in fifth grade: Ananda was really cute, nice, soft-spoken, and really cute. Karen was loud, had a face full of freckles, and thanks to her older sister, seemed to have far more expe-

*Author's note: Every one of these girls was outrageously cute. But in fifth grade, only a schmuck would throw a "Good" to everyone. A few years back, I heard Danielle became a model. Who's the schmuck now?

rience than everyone else in the class combined. She knew how to write in cursive before anyone—and told us all what a *blow job* was. She was tough, too. More important, she made fun of me and pushed me around. Even back then, the choice was clear. Now I just had to break the news.

It was the last day of school in fifth grade at P.S.206. I'd spent weeks going through slam books and leaving Karen and Ananda's rankings blank. But today was the day that would all change. In fact, if I summoned the strength in time, I might even be picking my first girlfriend. The clock was ticking toward three. The school year was almost gone. Forever melodramatic, I waited until the final bell rang. I remember putting my little checkmarks in the appropriate columns, then slamming the book shut before anyone got a peek. As we all ran for the doors, flooding into the schoolyard, I handed the book back to its owner. I still remember her flipping through the pages to see my answer. She looked up when she saw it: Karen—"Good"; Ananda—"Yuk."* Yet before anyone could even react, I—being the brave young soul that I was—darted from the schoolyard and ran straight home without talking to anyone. The next morning, I left for camp. Two months went by before I'd have to face my decision. Was I a puss or a genius? All I knew was, when I returned to Brooklyn in early September, Karen was my girlfriend, even if she did push me around and completely intimidate me.

So what's this have to do with Terra? Simply put, I was a Karen-guy, not an Ananda-guy. Maybe it was young masochism; maybe it was just a love of being dominated—but when it came to choosing sides, back then, I wanted the tough chick. Karen was tough—which is why we broke up soon after. Then, in June of 1983, my dad lost his job and my family moved from Brooklyn to Miami, Florida. When we first arrived, I didn't have a single friend, much less a girlfriend. No

---

*Ananda was *so* cute. No doubt about it. I today blame my choice on my need to see things in black and white.

Karen . . . no Ananda . . . nothing. It was right around the time Terra joined the Titans. At first glance, she was tough, too. And she had superpowers. She mouthed off at Changeling and definitely pushed him around. No doubt, she could kick Karen Akin's ass. Truthfully, she could kick my ass. And with that soft spot she had from her parents' recent death . . . it didn't take three issues for Wolfman and Perez to achieve their goal . . . I was now a Terra-guy.

Laugh if you must, but it was a great infatuation. My father's generation loved Lois Lane, who always needed her Superman. I loved Terra, who didn't need me, didn't want me, and could pummel me with fifty tons of rock if I really pissed her off. Forget Black Canary in her fishnets. Here was someone my age, wounded by the loss of lost parents and searching for a soulmate. It was a potent combination for us young comic readers. Before Madonna made strong women cool and Gwen Stefani made them hot, Terra was the first official grrrl for the new generation. True love indeed.

For the next six months of my life, I watched as the kind, happy family of the Teen Titans welcomed this hardened orphan into their midst. She helped them fight the Brotherhood of Evil, Thunder and Lightning, and even the Titans' most feared enemy, Deathstroke. Whatever concerns they had about her were quickly silenced. Month after month, Terra put her life on the line for the team. Within six issues (a lifetime in comics, or a day, depending on the storyline), she was one of the Titans' own, enmeshed in their personal lives just as much as she was enmeshed in my own. Then came the final pages of *New Teen Titans #34*.

I'll never forget—it was a right-hand page, perfectly placed so the surprise wouldn't be revealed until we readers casually flipped past the DC house ads. I turned the page and there it was: in a rundown tenement, Terra was secretly meeting with *Deathstroke*! Her face was lit with a dark grin I'd never seen on her. *My God, they were working together!* My eyes stayed locked on her mask, which she twirled carelessly around a come-hither pointer finger. My world was spinning just as fast. It was like Batgirl sleeping with the Joker! She was plotting the Titans' downfall with their greatest enemy. I trusted her! I was there for her! And unlike any other comic creation I'd ever read, and I say this in the least creepy way possible, *I loved her!* And now she was reaching down my throat and ripping my heart out for her own enjoyment! *Terra, how could you betray me like this!?*

And now, a word from reality . . . Okay, so it wasn't that bad—but I also don't want to undersell the moment. I can still remember my stomach sinking down to my testicles. In the world of comics, nothing like this had ever happened. Sure, there were always heroes who were later revealed as villains. At Marvel, the Avengers did it every week: "There Shall Be . . . *A Traitor Among Us!*" Both Black Panther and Wonder Man were originally there to infiltrate the Avengers . . . The Falcon was created by the Red Skull to kill Captain America . . . even Snapper Carr took a potshot at the Justice League. But the end of those stories was always the same: the so-called "villain" (Black Panther, Wonder Man, Falcon, Snapper) came to his senses and saved the day. In Terra's case, however . . . this girl didn't just infiltrate the Titans—she really wanted to kill them. And best of all, as the months wore on, Wolfman and Perez never backed away from the decision. Indeed, issue after issue, they kept turning up the despicable meter on Terra's actions. By the time they were done, Terra wasn't just working with Deathstroke, she was *sleeping* with him. Let's see Black Panther do that.

For my now-thirteen-year-old brain, it was all too much. Don't get me wrong, I wasn't turned off by what she was doing. C'mon, I was thirteen. She was the first true femme fatale in my life. I was turned *on.* I can still remember the slutty eye shadow they put on her when she was in villain mode, smoking a cigarette like a young blond Britney Spears doing Marlene Dietrich doing bad eighties porn. There were even high-heeled pumps scattered across the floor by the (wait for it) beanbag chair. So scary . . . but somehow . . . *so naughty.* Which brings me back to my old girlfriend, Karen Akin.

In August 1984, I'd been living in Florida for over a year. I was

BRAD MELTZER

now the new kid who sat silently in the middle row of the class. No one knew my name. Sure, I'd made a few friends, but it was nothing like Karen, Ananda, or any of the other girls from Brooklyn. All I had was Terra. The only question was: *How was it all gonna end?*

The final chapter of *The Judas Contract* was published in *Tales of the Teen Titans Annual #3* during that same summer of 1984. It was titled *"Finale."* By then, all the cards were on the Titans Tower table: Terra was working (and sleeping) with Deathstroke, all the Titans (except for Dick Grayson) were defeated and captured, and Nightwing and Jericho were in the midst of a near-impossible rescue attempt in the heart of H.I.V.E. headquarters. No doubt, it all came down to this: Terra would either remain the villain, or come to her senses and save the day. I still remember looking at the cover, trying to guess the answer. Perez made the choice clear: on one side were all the Titans, on the other was Deathstroke and the H.I.V.E. Terra was in the middle, her head turned back slightly toward Changeling, who seemed to be pleading for her redemption. To play with our heads even more, Perez added two "worry lines" by Terra's face, as if she, too, were struggling with the decision. I made my guess. There was no way Terra was truly evil. Redemption was a few pages away.

Forty pages later, Terra was dead. I shook my head as the scene played out. Changeling begged her to come to her senses . . . he pleaded and prayed . . . but Terra's rage was all-consuming. Remembering the cover, I kept waiting for her to look back at him and see true love. Or hope. Or the family who loved her. But it never came. Eyes wide with insanity, she attacked with a ruthlessness I'd never seen in a comic—and in the end, as a mountain of self-propelled rocks rained down and buried her, that rage—literally and figuratively—killed her. I shook my head. *There's no way she's dead,* I told myself. I don't care what the omniscient narrator said. I know my comics. Hero or villain, Terra was too good a character. Until they find a body—

". . . We found Tara's body," Wonder Girl said one page later. I turned to another right-hand page and there was Changeling . . .

down on his knees, clutching Terra's broken corpse as her arms sagged lifelessly toward the ground. Self-destruction complete.

I still can't believe they went through with it. A few years ago, I read an interview with George Perez that said Terra was created to die, and they never planned on taking the easy way out by suddenly writing a happy ending. I hope they know how much that decision affected me as a writer. Old girlfriends and teenage fetishes aside, it was one of the most heartbreaking stories I'd ever read. They took people in capes and utility belts and made them real—and just when we loved them most . . . just when we opened our arms to embrace them . . . Wolfman and Perez stabbed icepicks into our armpits and did the one thing neither Marvel nor DC ever had the balls to do—they kept her as a villain and slaughtered her. She was sixteen. No redemption. No feel-good music during the end credits. The pulp side of the genre has it right—it's always best when the femme fatale buys it in the end— but in comics, it'd never been done. And the traitor side of the story? Wonder Man, Falcon, Black Panther, and even Snapper got honorary memberships. Terra got a headstone with her name on it.

To this day, *The Judas Contract* is one of the few stories that actually surprised me—not just in its ending, but in how it plucked at my emotions. As I said, Terra lied to me, betrayed me, and stomped on my trust with her six-inch heels. Without a doubt, I loved every second of it.

# THIS WORLD, THAT WORLD, AND THE INVISIBLE HINGE: THE WORDS & PICTURES OF JIM WOODRING

## JOHN WRAY

Reading a comic by Jim Woodring is like waking up in an abandoned cult compound and gradually discovering, as you move from room to room, that the religion that once flourished there was a beautiful one and that each member of the cult was one of your own family. The five-to-ten-page stories, as distinct from one another as sets of false teeth, trigger a greater variety of emotional response than anything else I've read. Wonder and horror, nostalgia and guilt—guilt perhaps most of all—chase each other from panel to panel like dragonflies. You yourself were the leader of this cult, it seems, or at least responsible for its safety, and in some indefinable way you failed. The beautiful compound is empty.                                             →

I was turned on to *JIM* by a friend in the early nineties. My first reaction was not the complicated one described above, but one of simple shock: the pages are packed with renderings of the author's nightmares and hallucinations, and the power of these drawings (usually not the least bit "graphic" in the PG-13 sense) to worm their way into the reader's subconscious and pry open hidden airlocks of terror there is equaled in my experience only by the sketches of Alfred Kubin. *JIM* is not for the wee ones. There'd be something almost pornographic about its obsession with things the sane mind turns away from were it not so obviously a matter of life or death for Woodring to explore them, and if the world that resulted were not so strange and wonderful and convincing. Woodring is less a comix guy than some sort of downscale self-proselytizing prophet, and in his own modest and incurably human way, his work bares the scarification of his genius.

My second reaction to *JIM* was so different from the first that it brought on an identity crisis (not, admittedly, a rare event in my mid-twenties). Returning to the comic after a couple of years—a safe enough interval, I thought—I discovered that it was a deeply funny book, though funny in a way that had nothing in common with the Crumb-inspired satire of other comic artists of the day (Daniel Clowes, Peter Bagge, et al). The humor in *JIM* gives reason, and as a result society (in the simple sense), a Charles Dodgson–sized berth. Woodring's alter ego suffers humiliations no less severe than those of Joe Matt's or Chris Ware's or Robert Crumb's, but they always proceed directly from his own psyche and are therefore somehow just, neatly avoiding the whiny self-pity that has kept indie comics in a state of arrested development for as long as I can remember. Woodring is, in fact, grateful for the terrible visions his brain sics on itself: as he writes in a letter to God in *JIM* vol. 2, #2:

Dear Supreme Altruist,
Thanks very much for placing within me the bomb that never stops exploding.

The landscape Woodring's characters inhabit is not simply that of a dream (as in Chester Brown's *Underwater* series, for example) but of a lucid dream; and the distinction is an important one. In most dreams the dreamer is passive, alone in a darkened theater with no responsibility for what is happening onstage. In a *lucid* dream, however, he has full control over his actions, with all the moral and psychic baggage that such agency brings with it. The characters in *JIM* do deeply frightful things, and frightful things are done to them; and they are horrified by both in equal measure, because they have called both into being. As a result of this, each episode, no matter how grotesque or laughable or surreal, lays bare the author's nature to a degree no other device could match, straightforward biography included. Nightmares, after all, teach us far more than wish-fulfillment dreams.

Does none of this sound funny to you? It is.

Consider the untitled story that opens *JIM* vol. 2, #3. Woodring's alter ego (a man who looks more or less like him, named Jim) has been led to the edge of a river at night by a girl he's met at a party. The girl looks about four-foot-two and is cute in a vaguely Florence Henderson sort of way; Jim is drawn the way he always is, huge and oafish and perturbed.

"Do you see that raft?" the girl says, pointing into the blackness with her eyes open wide. The next panel shows the river from their point of view; far out, almost too far out to see, a small square raft is floating with a man standing on it.

"Yeah," says Jim.

"The man on that raft is dead," says the girl. "If you swim out to the raft and assert your rights as a living man and take the raft away from him, then the raft will be yours—but if you are weak-willed and do not assert yourself he'll capture you."

"That sounds rather awful," Jim says timidly. (We can always count on our hero to wear his frailties stapled to the front of his shirt for our amusement.) The man on the raft seems to be drifting closer over the next few panels; we now see that he's completely naked.

"Oh, it is," says the girl. Her face grows grave. "But a living man who allows himself to be captured by a dead one deserves what he gets."

Jim is not convinced. He and the girl look out at the river; the man on the raft, still too far out to see clearly, appears to be looking back at them. "Why would I want to take the raft from him in the first place?" Jim asks. "What would I do with the cumbersome thing?"

The girl looks up at him sheepishly. "Well, you could . . . you know, float around on it . . . fish from it . . . like that." Then, as if embarrassed by her own answer, she turns to head back to the party.

"I bet you think I haven't got the guts, don't you?" Jim blurts out. The panel is drawn so that the reader sees what Jim himself can't: that the girl's expression, hidden from his sight, has changed to a cunning, ghoulish leer.

With the grinning girl looking on, Jim dives fully clothed, head-first, into the inky water. Instead of being held up by it, he sinks straight to the bottom of the river, and the next three panels are devoted to his struggle to scramble forward through weeds and clutching, ghostly arms, presumably of other dead men, before finally reaching the raft and hauling himself aboard, soaked and sputtering for air. The naked man is waiting for him.

"All right, now, you just turn around and swim back!" the naked man hisses. "I don't need any more aggravation!"

"Swim back, huh! I'm here to take this raft away from you!" Jim shouts back.

The next panel brings the naked man into clearer focus, and we see that he's at least sixty years old, and about as threatening as a mailman. "Fine, you coward!" the naked man spits. "I may not be as tough as I used to be, but I'll still fight with everything I got!" He grits his teeth. "So c'mon! Make your move, tough guy!"

Jim is at this point visibly chagrined. "Um, are you, ah, dead?" he says.

"Dead!?" says the old naked man, making a fist. "Up yours! I'll show you dead!"

At about this point I noticed that the naked man was drawn in perfect seedy R. Crumb squiggles. He also happens, for some occult reason of the artist's, to be hung like a Texas mule.

Jim mumbles a further apology, and turns to look back at the shore, only to see the little Brady Bunch girl standing there with another guy lured down from the party. "Hey!" Jim shouts at them.

"They are dead," the girl says, pointing at the raft.

The true wonder of *JIM*, however, came to me only on the third go-round. I often find that I have a lot of resistance to exactly the things I'll come to admire most in time, and *JIM* was no exception. Something about the art, especially of the early covers, put me off; it seemed too clean to me, too "Disney," too much like the Sunday funnies. (When I learned, much later, that Woodring spent some very unpleasant years in indentured servitude to a certain large animation house that shall go nameless, it all made sense). It seemed incredible to me at the time that a guy who moved so easily between any number of styles would pick the most banal of them all as his standard setting. So intense was my contempt for/fascination with Woodring's pictures that it took me longer than it should have done to pay attention to the words that came with them. Finally, though, I did, and saw that they were artlessly articulate and lyrical and sly, and that the words combined with the pictures had a radically different effect than either taken on its own. It was the original epiphany of the comic nerd, of course, except that from that point on *JIM* seemed to get bigger and deeper and more transparent with each rereading, until I was no longer reading about Jim Woodring at all but about the cult that I was the leader of.

It was one particular story, I remember, that did it for me: a five-pager in *JIM* vol. 2, #5, called "The Stairs." The text in "The Stairs" is simple, and the images almost more so: two characters in conversa-

113

tion against a black background. The mode, as per usual, is that of the lucid dream, but the effect is truer somehow, more frightening, wider: the dream, in its conversion into comic form, has been fashioned into an emblem. The story begins this way:

Jim, in bed with his wife beside him, is awakened in the night by the sound of his name. "Who is it?" he asks.

"It is I," a voice answers.

Jim recognizes the voice at once. "Oh—it *is* you," he says. "You've found me." He sits up in bed.

"Found you? You've never been out of my sight," the voice replies.

A horribly disfigured little girl now comes forward into the light, with a tiny, skeletal body and a withered horselike face; or perhaps a very old woman in the costume of a girl. Instead of the fear and panic we expect, Jim gets out of bed and begins talking to the creature evenly and sadly, the way one might to a long-lost friend from childhood who'll be staying lost forever. What it is that happened between them is never said or shown, and as a result their conversation refers to every suffering, every crime. "What can I say?" Jim asks her. "You know . . . you must know that I'm tormented by remorse."

Now we know a crime has been committed, at least in the mind of the man, against the little girl–thing. But there is nothing threatening in her, or terrifying, or even out of the ordinary, other than her repulsive face and body.

"Can you find it in your heart to forgive me?" Jim asks.

"It is not for me to forgive," the creature replies, with a perfect Bible teacher's grin. She seems very much like an old woman now, though Woodring's way of drawing her has not changed.

"Bad things were done to me, you know," Jim says, hunching over.

"Yes, I know," the creature answers, laying her shriveled hand reassuringly on his knee.

As can only happen in the world of comics, we are in the middle of a straightforwardly supernatural story but also seeing past it to the real life of Jim Woodring; being brought painfully close, in fact, to events that Woodring himself can perhaps only give voice to through his art. Again, however, the "bad things" are never described or shown, and therefore become every bad thing imaginable.

"The Stairs" finally helped me to understand Woodring's choice of style. In representing his human characters (especially himself) in an unremarkable, almost generic style lifted from newspaper strips, a style every reader is familiar with from childhood, Woodring renders the presence of the fantastic when it arrives (either in images or in text) as jarringly and unsettlingly as possible. And when Woodring shifts gears to a style more suitable to drawing the stuff of nightmares, his pictures have all the more power for still harboring traces—in brutally mutated form—of the vocabulary of Saturday morning TV. If Mickey Mouse's intestines were given their own comic book, the result might look something like Woodring's recurring visitors. But this again is only one of many modes: the girl-thing in "The Stairs," for example, has an understated horror all her own. In fact, Woodring makes use of the built-in limitations of comic art to make her image even more disturbing: Her long bony face might be the result of a childhood burn, or advanced old age, or something outside the realm of human experience altogether. She might not even be a "female" thing at all. Her voice is left up to our imagination; so is the color of her skin. No film or photograph, or even text alone, could equal "The Stairs" for mystery.

True to the quixotic relationship between *JIM* and me, the author picked exactly the moment at which I was most excited by his word-and-picture combinations to flush the words—all of them—down the proverbial privy-hole. *JIM* was phased out and *FRANK*, an entirely textless comic starring one of *JIM*'s most popular stock characters, took its place. I had an even harder time coming around to this new book than I'd had with *JIM*, if only because I'd become such a rabid fan of the work that Woodring was now scrapping. I liked the idea of a wordless comic book, of course (just as I admired Chester Brown's beautiful *Underwater,* which is narrated in an invented language), but not if it meant the end of Woodring as a writer. I'm a writer myself, after all. It's just possible that I felt threatened. Whatever the reason, I went off into another huff, and ignored *FRANK* for as long as I could stand to.

Which wasn't long at all, as it turned out.

# GEOFFREY O'BRIEN

## I.

"Properly, we should read for power. Man reading should be man intensely alive. The book should be a ball of light in one's hand."

Thus Ezra Pound, speaking for a literature in which each word would represent a convergence of rays, a limit-point of compression and concision. I came upon that line at a moment in the late sixties when it seemed appropriate to be taking in everything with equal attentiveness: *The Cantos, Martha and the Vandellas' Greatest Hits, Pierrot le Fou, The Nutty Professor, Filles de Kilimanjaro,* John D. MacDonald's Travis McGee novels, Ralph Kirkpatrick's clavichord recording of *The Well-Tempered Clavier,* and, not least, Jim Steranko's graphics in *Nick Fury, Agent of* →

*S.H.I.E.L.D.* Wherever you looked there was the possibility of finding the aesthetic essentials—urgency, immensity of perspective, speed, depth, improvisational ecstasy, and unwobbling balance—if possible, all at the same time, packed into a single image or a single note.

"A ball of light in one's hand": Comics promised to be such books, except that in the realm of action comics the ball of light was usually on the verge of exploding. The spectacle was inevitably of a destruction experienced over and over, a death that finally must be nothing less than the death of the world. While you were at it, why not of all possible worlds? The little picture books of the apocalypse that beguiled our afternoons described a ripping asunder that was as harmless as music. It was as music that we apprehended the swirling and interlacing ink lines, punctuated by boldfaced, all-caps phrases that were like drum accents: "THE WORLD HAS ONLY **13 MINUTES** BEFORE THE **DEATH SPORE** EXPLODES!" (*Strange Tales* #158)

Everybody always got off the hook just in time. I can recall only one exception to that law, a story that appeared in *Strange Tales* #168, the last issue before Nick Fury graduated to his own full-length comic. The story—"Today Earth Died!"—bears all the signs of a bit of filler designed to mark time before launching into a new extended narrative. It is a slight tale, its minimal plot largely an excuse for Steranko to indulge in the graphic experiments that at the time seemed like a turning point, although looking back it's hard to say where that particular turn led. When Jim Steranko emerged as an important artist at Marvel—initially inking Jack Kirby's layouts for *Nick Fury, Agent of S.H.I.E.L.D.*, and eventually taking the series over altogether as artist and writer—it seemed like the onset of a new and much more self-conscious aestheticism, a kind of metafiction in relation to Marvel's by now familiar fictions.

Even when Kirby was still doing the layouts, Steranko's drawing was already proclaiming a deliberate design sense that made Kirby's art seem "realist" by comparison. Instead of looking at Nick Fury we were looking at Steranko looking at Nick Fury; everything was to be made as deliberately and flamboyantly unreal as possible, as if to acknowledge how humdrum the norms of comic book adventures had always been. Henceforth the pleasure implicit in storytelling was to be refined and intensified by paring away the story itself. Narrative was to be first unmasked and then discarded: "Isn't this what you really wanted, the ingredients without the husk?"

"Today Earth Died!" is pretty much the quintessence of Steranko. Every effect calls attention to itself: the magenta-tinged photo enlargement of Nick Fury's girlfriend and fellow spy, Valentina Allegro de Fontaine, the Eadweard Muybridge–like frame in which Fury's leap into his sports car is shown in six successive stages, the obtrusive shifts of scale and angle. Each page announced that this new formalism was going to be pushed as far as it could go. Meanwhile the story unfolded: Nick Fury was summoned to Times Square to investigate the landing of a golden-skinned, togaed extraterrestrial visitor in human form, looking something like an eight-foot-tall surfer. With one arm raised to signify "I come in peace," this entity extended with the other a peculiar prism-like object—"The Prism of Miracles, a cosmic gem of uncommon wonder!"—with an eye in its center: "Simply peer into the purple iris and your every wish shall materialize!"

But within a few frames things started to go horribly wrong, starting with Valentina's premonitions: "We'll call it a woman's intuition, but I have a feeling, Nick! Something's not quite what it should be!" A S.H.I.E.L.D. image scanner revealed that the celestial messenger's real form was monstrous, and seconds later Valentina and Fury's sidekick Dugan were reduced to charred ashes. Fury engaged in a quick desperate struggle with the alien—a struggle that involved appropriating a headband that turns Fury into something resembling one of *Dune*'s sandworms—only to learn that it was all too late: "The Prism of Miracles is a world-killing machine . . . and the purpose of my race is to eliminate all life—everywhere! Listen! Already greedy earthlings have turned on the machine and begun to upset the balance of the universe! It is all over! All over!" And indeed the opposite page showed a photo collage of collapsing skyscrapers, panicked crowds, immense piles of urban rubble, a dead Earth hanging in empty space.

On the eleventh and last page, a sleeping Fury is woken by Dugan and slowly comes back from his vision: "Man . . . what a dream! Must be these new cigars I been smokin'!" In the last frame Dugan remarks casually that "some kinda UFO or something's been spotted . . . probably nothin', though!" In the foreground Fury, just about to light his cigar, stares out with renewed terror, his face a precise homage to the horrified faces that once filled the pages of EC's horror comics in the fifties.

This gratuitous tour de force—a story that canceled itself out, not to mention canceling out Fury, his pals, and the human race—seemed, precisely, the comic book story to end all comic book stories. The doom always threatened had for once actually arrived, and even though the story was a joke, nothing more than an occasion for showing off Steranko's design concepts, it had the capacity to awaken a genuine sense of dread, no matter how fleeting. All the dread that had piled up in the course of a decade was ready to attach itself to a little novelty item in a comic book, a variation on the most tired of narrative conceits: "It was all a dream." The dream, it turned out, was one from which it was not finally possible to awaken; the world would find a way to infiltrate even that domain which had been explicitly set aside for harmless fantasy; and Steranko's formalism, which appeared to reduce all narrative tropes to mere fodder for abstract pleasures, became the vehicle for an apprehension that went deeper than his repertory of situations mined nostalgically from old issues of *Doc Savage* and *The Phantom Detective*.

To weigh the impact of that isolated episode, I find I have to go back through earlier layers of comic book reading. To reenter the world of comic books as experienced while growing up in the fifties and sixties is like tracing, through garbled lore and remnants of ritual life, a lost pastoral tradition. The particular mental space that comics offered was distinct; it's easy enough to talk about escape, but escape to what exactly? To something like a dream that could be shared, passed around, that did not dissolve on waking.

That the specific contents were perhaps not as interesting or unusual as those of sleeping dreams—that they were sometimes not interesting at all—mattered surprisingly little. We didn't really read comics to find out what happened—we knew very well, before long, what was likely to happen—but to enjoy a lucid detachment. Like those superheroes who were able to move through walls or become invisible to their enemies, we appreciated the liberty that comics gave us: we were free to move in and out of what we could see was an illusion. We could allow it to be as real as we wanted it to be; we could dissolve it at will.

## II.

Of the many distinctions that comic books seemed intended to dissolve—between word and image, between danger and pleasure—the most crucial was between the solitary and the collective. Even when alone, these librettos were read as if by a member of a chorus. No secrecy here: everything was laid out too completely, often too mindlessly bare for this to be anything but a shared text.

A comic book was, in the first place, easy. It was something that could be absorbed without effort, a book capable of reading itself. Where the page consisting of only words could seem opaque, these pages disclosed. A comic offered instant gratification of a longing for quick answers, passwords, shortcuts. It dismantled the narrative that kids didn't want—the narrative that was cumbersome, obstructive, an imposed duty, a deferral of pleasure—in order to get at what every laborious framework seemed to conceal within itself, the story that had already arrived at the place where we wanted to be. At every point it was visible, exposed.

If comic books dissolved words and pictures into each other they catered to an impatience that such separate categories should even exist. Not that we distinguished, at that early stage, consciously between words and pictures: the dialogue balloons were just as much part of the picture as any other element, the drawing was itself a kind of sign language, or rebus, or logo. What happened from frame to frame was always in transition, and one aspect of that transition was a sense of word and picture in turn handing off the burden of meaning to each other, like a ball kept constantly moving because if it stopped, the game would be over. You turned the page and there you were, without mediation, caught up in a movement that, without any particular effort on your part, would sweep toward some as yet undisclosed information.

The comic books of childhood passed from hand to hand and then disappeared beyond retrieval; and always, it seemed, with a crucial issue missing. The gaps were to be filled from memory or imagination, yours or someone else's. Comics always existed as much in the debates and speculations surrounding them as in those fragile and evanescent pages: evanescent for all but those actually rather rare individuals who made it their business to save the things systematically. For the rest of us they came and went like those otherwise uneventful summer afternoons that the reading of them so thoroughly occupied. What they were supposed to be about tended to dissolve if you thought about it too much: the mysteries of secret identities and secret origins, the mantralike comfort of the word "invulnerable" (a word that entered the common language entirely through comic books), the possibility of suddenly acquiring an alternate body or entering a parallel dimension.

There must somewhere have been a poetry in them, but it remained on the half-conscious margins: in the aura of religious scripture hovering around the birth of Superman and the destruction of Krypton, or in the oddly depressive concept of the Man of Steel retreating, when the sheer burden of being Superman got too much for him, to the well-guarded isolation of that Fortress of Solitude that seemed like a peculiar reward indeed for the rare good chance of being uniquely invulnerable. There was a touch of fear, too, in the mere thought of supercriminals plotting to turn the whole world to ice, or whatever the latest threat was. It was rare that anything less than the world was at stake.

It wasn't for long, though, that anyone read comics in a mood of reverence for the impossible premises that had drawn us in. After a while the question became not what would happen but what wouldn't: that is, how DC Comics would once again weasel out of the situation promised on their cover, in which Superman faced a firing squad equipped with Kryptonite bullets, or had his secret identity revealed on television, or stood by helplessly as Lois Lane yelled at him: "Superman, I hate you!"

From all such dilemmas, as even the most naïve reader finally accepted, the hero would extricate himself through a kind of legalistic sleight of hand that had less to do with brute force than with the parsing of definitions. Anyone who felt sufficiently passionate about these little casuistries (none of us ever did) could always write one of those letters that occupied one page of every comic book, laying out arguments that would then be patiently demolished by the editors.

## III.

It didn't take many summers to make us so expert in the scriptwriters' ploys as to feel a certain resentment when we fell once again for the same old bait and switch. At this point Superman and his colleagues in the Justice League of America became something to kick around, a point of departure for vulgar jests and obscene extrapolations. We lost our respect for superheroes so unapologetically predictable. We had, after all, grown up on *Mad,* and so DC's Superman had already been compromised by our awareness of his parodistic alter ego in the pages of Harvey Kurtzman's original comic book version of "humor in a jugular vein" (perpetuated for years thereafter in paperback reprints): the lecherous, swell-headed, muscle-bound cretin Superduperman of 1953, who in his incarnation as drooling assistant copy boy Clark Bent used his X-ray vision to peer into the ladies' powder room across the hall, and narrowly avoided arrest as a flasher when he did his quick change in a phone booth that turned out to be already occupied. *Mad* provided a lesson in reading, demonstrating that every comic book—for that matter every movie, sermonette, political plug, newspaper feature, mail solicitation, and public service announcement—could be read as a parody of itself.

At a certain point in our young lives, my friends and I pretty much stopped reading comics; Aquaman and the Green Lantern had come to seem childish alongside other popular entertainments (*The Twilight Zone, Alfred Hitchcock Presents, The Naked City*). Comics persisted as time-killers not too different in kind from paperback compilations of *Ripley's Believe It or Not* or the Bazooka Joe cartoon jokes that came with bubblegum; they offered, at best, an unconditional freedom from the pain of emotional reaction.

If, within a few years, Marvel got many of us back into the game, it was because at first we took their comics for parodies. We came for the wisecracks and stayed for the storylines; an appreciation of the artwork evolved gradually into an ongoing conversation about the relative merits of Kirby, Ditko, Romita, Colan, Wood, Trimpe, Buscema, and, ultimately, Steranko. What was most strikingly different from other comics we'd read was the sense that there was a conscious intelligence on the other side of the page (in those days, not knowing all the story, we identified that intelligence with the relentlessly self-advertising Stan Lee). Instead of the comic book being a naïve object that you could stand outside of and comment on, it was an object that had already incorporated that potential commentary. But if the Marvel team managed to work the jokes kids made while reading comics into the comics themselves, they managed the neat trick of doing so without betraying the values of naïve fantasy that remained the core of their work.

It was the revenge of the real pop artists, the underpaid artisans who'd served their time under the banner of Timely and National and Atlas and Charlton, against the intellectuals who, having just discovered pop culture, thought they had an instant franchise on the nuances of fractured awareness. If Marvel offered parody, it was a sort of utopian parody, a defensive weapon. In a fallen world (or so Marvel seemed to assert), heroes could remain heroes only by blatantly absorbing into themselves their own travesties. On one hand, the Marvel heroes weren't kidding. (Reed Richards of the Fantastic Four: "I wonder if the world will ever know how close it came—to an almost incomprehensible fate.") On the other hand, they were always kidding. (The Thing, in response: "Don't worry! there'll always be some loudmouth like you around to spill the beans!")

The characteristic Marvel mix—a combination of high-flown, pseudo-archaic rhetoric (especially if the speaker was Thor or the Silver Surfer), elaborately interlocking melodramas that might go on for many issues, suggestions of inner conflict (most notably in the cases of Spider-Man and the Incredible Hulk) that had not previously been typical of comic book heroes, and a constant leavening of good-natured silliness—created an impression of depth of characterization and density of plotting that may to some extent have been an optical illusion. Endless elaboration did not, perhaps, really equal complexity, but it certainly provided a jumping-off point for complex thoughts.

Unlike the cut-and-dried scenarios and simpleminded puzzles of older comics, Marvel's structures opened up spaces—whether literal (the various compartments of interstellar, suboceanic, and multidimensional geography) or metaphoric (the constant evocations of split consciousness and systematic social exclusion)—into which readers were free to pour whatever ancillary material they chose. By revealing so much of their own strategies, the Marvel gang seemed to hint that it was finally the comics' purely formal qualities that were pushing our buttons so expertly, making us actually suspend disbelief long enough to care about how Dr. Strange was going to manage the interdimensional jump in time to forestall a cosmic takeover by the Dread Dormammu. It wasn't about emotions or characters or motivations at all; it was pure abstraction, and whatever it was really worrying about was taking place maybe on the level of molecular structure. It was perhaps about nothing but the frame, the juxtaposition of frames, the suggestion of infinite depth and constant violent movement through means that were altogether transparent, consisting of nothing but inked lines and inked words. The rest of it was just standard repertoire, the furniture that happened to be in the room.

What is hard to recapture is the trancelike absorption with which these comics were read, a wide-awake dreaming in which disbelief was entirely suspended and the world consisted of nothing more than the frame-to-frame evolution of Jack Kirby's storyboarding. (Drugs helped, of course, but mostly by providing a model of attentiveness that could be honored even in their absence.) That state of mind, somewhere between profound stupor and meditative acuity, encouraged allegorical readings. The events depicted in those picture stories could easily be taken as emblems or portents, all the more disturbing for being encountered in such an apparently innocuous context. The secret is revealed where least expected: not in the *New York Times,* but in a comic book that can travel everywhere because no one would suspect it of carrying prophetic freight.

In the course of a celebrated run of issues of *Fantastic Four*—#48–50, encompassing the saga of the world-devouring Galactus and his herald, the Silver Surfer—we come upon an image of crowds running in all directions in a Midtown Manhattan whose skies are swept by rolling flames. The caption explains: "Quickly reaching the heart of the great city, the Human Torch sees a sight he is destined never to forget—the sight of a mighty metropolis in the dread grip of panic!" The scene, which just might have been an unguarded glimpse into the future, arouses a sense of dread that it immediately downplays, as the Thing remarks: "Mebbe they're just advertisin' some new Joseph E. Levine movie."

The context, as usual, is imminent apocalypse. In this instance the immense and amoral entity Galactus has come to devour all earthly life—as casually as eating breakfast—in order to sustain his own un-imaginably remote form of interstellar existence. This mini-serial was prized by many readers at the time for the exceptional solemnity of a passage in which the Human Torch (the literally and figuratively volatile teenager who was, roughly, Ricky Nelson to Reed Richards's John Wayne) was obliged, to thwart the Galactus threat, to travel to another dimension in order to bring back a tiny but apparently almost infinitely powerful object capable of cowing the world-devourer. The Torch took his instructions from a prehuman intelligence—a minor god along Gnostic lines, privy to the intimate secrets of creation but no longer intervening in the outcome of events—called the Watcher, depicted as bald, white-robed, and about twenty feet tall.

According to the Watcher's instructions: "You can serve them best by doing the unexpected . . . by fleeing this world! . . . We must force open the very fabric of time itself!" Nothing was more calculated to massage the notion that the young explorers of psychedelic inner space were not indulging in escapism but rather performing an invalu-able, indeed a necessary, service. Even more striking was the Torch's eventual return from his journey, materializing seemingly out of nowhere in a condition something like cosmic shellshock: "The delayed, stunned reaction begins to set in, as the teenager suddenly becomes aware of what he has done . . . what he has seen . . . where he has been! 'I traveled through worlds so big . . . so big . . . there . . . there aren't words!'" And then, unforgettably: "We're like ants . . . just ants! . . . ants!!" "Try not to remember," he is advised by Reed Richards. But there is no forgetting.

It was these moments that threatened to tear the fabric of the Marvel Universe that proved that the fabric existed in the first place.

129

We prized a resilience that seemed all the fiercer for passing itself off as a species of kidding around.

## IV.

The Nick Fury series, which shared *Strange Tales* with the continuing metaphysical predicaments of Doctor Strange, was an attempt to fuse James Bond–style spy adventures with the characters already developed for the World War II comic *Sgt. Fury and His Howling Commandos.* Sergeant Nick Fury, a tough-as-nails, unshaven, cigar-smoking leader of men seemingly modeled closely on the drill instructor played by John Wayne in *Sands of Iwo Jima,* led his wisecracking crew through an endless series of missions, often venturing into science fiction territory, while defending themselves against Fury's Nazi opposite number, the *Übergruppenführer* Baron Strucker. In his postwar incarnation, Fury was the director of S.H.I.E.L.D. (Supreme Headquarters International Espionage Law-Enforcement Division) and spent most of his time fending off the usual schemes to take over the world.

Jim Steranko, who had been a professional magician and escape artist before getting involved in comics, began working on *Nick Fury* at the tail end of a protracted saga about the secret organization Hydra ("Cut off a limb and two more shall take its place!"), dedicated to conquering the world by means of a weapon of mass destruction called the Overkill Horn. Revisited decades later, Hydra resembles, in terms of organization and tactics, nothing so much as Al Qaeda, and there is a kind of weary fascination in being reminded yet again of how thoroughly the rhetoric of the contemporary world can be found rehearsed in old comic books. (Consider the following, from *Strange Tales* #150. Fury: "It's up to S.H.I.E.L.D. to keep a death watch . . . until we find that horn—and destroy it!" Aide: "Begging your pardon, Colonel— but, how do we know it really exists?" Fury: "We got ways of findin' out, mister! I wish I wuz wrong—but, you better believe it!! It exists!")

The intersection of the generic paranoia of the Hydra story with Steranko's self-acknowledging pop formalism felt, in 1968, like the Spirit of the Age breaking out in four-color splendor. The total impact of the page triumphed over sequencing within the page: you saw everything at once, the larger shape within whose coils and branches narrative can be seen as merely a kind of ornamentation. We already knew the stories. We wanted to see the shape they made when taken together: the view from God's eye, where the future has already happened and the past is still going on. It was a way of rebelling against the slavery of time, of sequence, of patiently waiting for next week's exciting episode.

As Steranko took control not just of the art but of the plotting, it became clear that things were moving very far from Marvel's narrative formulas, very far from any kind of narrative. Pieces of existing stories, fragments lifted from other arts, were recombined, and could be imagined as functioning somewhat like the "radiant gists" of Ezra Pound's ideogrammic poetics: here was Sidney Greenstreet entering a dusty old shop out of film noir; here was a slice of Bridget Riley's undulating op art lines; here were recognizable shards of *King Kong, The Hound of the Baskervilles, The Mask of Fu Manchu*; here were those solarized Avedon photos of the Beatles, transmuted into the successive metamorphoses of the supervillain Scorpio; here were lovers drinking cocktails, a comedian trapped in an exploding phone booth, a lonely pier, a prophetic blind girl. This was perhaps what it felt like to be on the brink of a new story altogether, a story about simultaneity and randomness that would also be a wholly realized picture: and the more you were concerned with that picture, the less it mattered what was going in all those little episodes that made up the picture.

Finally it had the feeling of circuits being blown out. Narrative moving at such high velocity to escape from narrative produced an effect like those sports-car collisions that Steranko was fond of depicting. As it turned out, he only did four issues of *Nick Fury* before moving on to other things: painting book covers, editing magazines, writing historical accounts of the pulps and the early comics. Anyway, the world had already ended, back in the pages of "Today Earth Died!" Now we were simply living out the twilight of the comic book characters, watching the ghosts of Nick Fury and Dugan and the Countess Valentina go through the paces of a reality that had been blown to bits. Or had we simply gazed into the purple iris of the Prism of Miracles a little too long?

In the simple device of Nick Fury's dream, Steranko had isolated the nagging point where comic books come dangerously close to resembling life and life comes dangerously close to resembling a comic book: the point where the bubble breaks. At that moment one might snap out of the dream on either side of the page and achieve spontaneous Buddhahood, or else start looking for another line of work.

# OUI, JE REGRETTE PRESQUE TOUT

## GLEN DAVID GOLD

All stories of collecting are about self-loathing, self-love, and self-deception confused with the piquant cologne of loathing, love, and deception that drenches the object so desired. This is about one peculiar flame reaching out to me, just another hypergolic moth. It's a comic story, but it's not a happy story. →

When I was a kid, I collected comics, and a cousin of mine tipped me to the fact that artists *drew* them. "If you could have the original artwork to any of these, what would it be?" he asked, and the question got me so excited I spread out all my comics on the floor, stacking and restacking them, casting away discards, then reshuffling, a game of solitaire, until I came up with the *Incredible Hulk* #139 cover, which I learned was drawn by someone named Herb Trimpe. I started paying attention to the credits boxes, and soon learned that Trimpe drew not unlike a guy named Jack Kirby, whose work was so distinctive I would never again mistake it for anyone else's. Then I learned about the primitive Steve Ditko *Amazing Spider-Man* issues, in which the characters looked as famished and ill-dressed as refugees from Hungary. Then Gil Kane (the shiksa noses, the almost rabid sinews of his characters' arms, the repeated motif of a hero belted backward, into the extreme foreground, chest a distended horizon line, head kicked to the side like a broken balloon). And John and Sal Buscema, who drew similarly but could never be mistaken for each other, and Gene Colan, who always drew chiaroscuro as if it were itself a superhero with powers far beyond those of any piddling mortal.

Now, several decades later, I work in a Chinese pagoda–red office decorated with original comic book artwork. I subscribe to a Yahoo group that discusses original comic book artwork. I go to conventions. I read academic treatises on conservation, obscure inkers, companies long ago gone belly-up. There are shelves of auction and dealer catalogs going back to the 1970s. I've memorized which of my peers has what art, and who has had what, and who wants what, and what hasn't been accounted for. A friend of mine, who dabbles in comics, who likes comics, but who doesn't have this genetic malfunction, a guy who likes me pretty much always, *doesn't* like to see me when I'm at a comic book convention. "You have the fever," he said to me.

· · ·

As I'm writing this article, I'm pausing every few minutes to toggle my windows back to the Collectibles > Comics > Original Comic Art category of eBay, where there is an auction ending in a few minutes for a Dave Sim *Cerebus* cover. I don't collect Dave Sim. His storylines reflect a misogynist streak that makes Strindberg look like Adrienne Rich. But I'm curious what money the cover will bring, as one day, eventually, I might walk into a comic book shop and see a Dave Sim *Cerebus* cover, and knowing how much it brings on eBay might come in handy.

(The auction has just ended, and received no bids at $1,800, which I would find meaningful if, as I was revising this essay, a set of three covers hadn't sold for $10,099. The moral for most people would be "stop trying to make sense of this," but for me, it's "I don't yet understand the *Cerebus* market and I must study it more until I do.")

When I was a little kid, I collected coins with my father. Which seemed to generate, when I lay in bed, loops of dreams in which I found stashes of rare coins in abandoned buildings, and in examining their mint marks, their reeded edges, I felt relief and joy that would propel me awake. And then, realizing it hadn't actually happened, I would sink back into the dream, trying to make out the dates, the conditions, the variants of the stellas or strawberry-leaf cents.

When I started collecting comics, the dream shifted: now it was about walking into a thrift store and finding artwork. Once, and this is true, I was in a Vallejo, California, Goodwill, and propped up in the corner was what looked, from across the room, like a Jack Kirby *New Gods* full-color pinup. When I got closer, I realized it was a kid's drawing that some proud parent had framed. Only the love of a parent, or the blindness of a desperate collector, could have turned it into a Jack Kirby original, even from across the room.

. . .

I have a secret weapon as a collector: I can get along with the clinically insane. This manifests in supreme patience and the ability to jump through flaming hoops when a lesser man—perhaps that isn't the adjective I want—a *stabler* man—would turn away. Every collecting field attracts maniacal, paranoid tyrants, guys who cling to their moldering treasures as if they'd never read Greek legends about gold-hoarding kings whose stories never went that well.

But I have started to understand. There is a sorrow that blooms in your chest as your dreams of wealth are suddenly quantified—as long as you don't know what your trinket is worth, but you know it's worth something, it's like imagining Paris in the spring. But once there's a price, it's like actually stepping onto le Pont Neuf and discovering that the Seine smells terrible, there are tourists, and thieves, and shopkeepers who have prepared for you and all the people who, it turns out, are just like you, and your dream can be reduced to an off-center and ill-posed snapshot just like everybody else's in which you still have not been made happy. No one is ever really made happy by Paris in the spring unless they were at least a little happy beforehand.

Which leads us to comic books. Because the adventures are continuing, they beckon readers back month after month to find out what will happen next in this more perfect, simplified universe. Marvel Comics, which I started reading in 1973, had perfected the idea of continuity, meaning that there was a collective memory from comic to comic, title to title. You might understand, somewhat, if you jumped into the party with *Avengers* #127 and *Fantastic Four* #150, as I did, but you'd feel a little left out if you didn't know all the histories of all the cliques. It's a powerful drug, the urge to belong. I had to buy all the old issues of those titles, and then the adventures of the individual team members, the *Iron Man* issues, the *Captain America* and *Tales of Suspense* and *Tales to Astonish* and the *Hulk* and the *Defenders*, and so forth, because every story depended on every other story, and soon enough I knew everyone as they walked into the room, which made me feel as if I actually had friends, which, at age ten and eleven and twelve and thirteen, I didn't.

And, around the world, in pungent bedrooms, there were thousands of us, all alone, reading comics, dreaming in isolation of the unified world of superheroes and secret identities and the rescue of beautiful girls. It's no wonder that, grown up, some dealers at conventions treat every sale as if they're ratting out a best friend.

Three years ago, in what shouldn't really be a shocker to anyone who has read this far, the accumulation of body blows in this life had led me into therapy. At some point, my therapist had to change my appointment time and I was let out at rush hour. I took to turning off the freeway early in search of cafés or bookstores to browse, and then, rather quickly, everything changed.

There was a strip mall somewhere in Orange County, and I'm not being coy about the location so much as I'm being very precise—there are large areas that creep into each other, multilane boulevards that show no interest in the boundaries between cities, designed in the 1950s for the day that tanks could rumble six abreast toward the Communist menace. The recurrent Del Tacos, Ministorages, and third-rate burger stands make it seem like the laws of geometry are suspended. Like the old Flintstones animation in which a character runs through a house, passing the same window, potted plant, framed picture over and over and over, until the land feels empty and infertile, kind of a *No Exit* for the Hanna-Barbera set.

In the midst of this, there was a strip mall indistinguishable from any other, except for a word on a broken laminate sign in the parking lot: BOOKSTORE. So I pulled in for a look.

I passed a store that sold musical instruments and sheet music, and a mattress warehouse, and what used to be called a five-and-ten-cent store, and then a darkened, perhaps even abandoned storefront furnished entirely in original comic artwork.

It was such a startling sight that I felt the same kind of numbness that must have overcome the Conquistadors upon bumbling into a

139

room of Aztec gold. I remained utterly still, not double-checking, not believing I was in a dream, not even coveting anything yet, just living with my heartbeat (which was no faster, yet, than normal).

To my left was a display window, and a Chinese screen hung with framed illustration artwork from the pulps, and right in front of me was the cash register counter upon which were thumbtacked *Fiction House* war stories from the 1950s, single-panel cartoons from the *Saturday Evening Post,* a Nancy and Sluggo strip, a few unidentifiable nudie gags from some magazine like *Gent* or *Cavalier.* The bulk of the store was taken up with piles of books and magazines, and display counters, glass-topped, like aquariums long gone to seed, filled not with tropical fish but with brightly colored comic books. And way in the back, off at oblique angles so I could hardly figure out what I was seeing, were stacks and stacks and stacks of original comic artwork. There were also framed pieces of art on the walls, but no matter what angle I approached the storefront from, I couldn't see anything more than a faint impression of black ink splashed against off-white paper, some title lettering, a general suspicion that, for me at least, there hunched in the dark some fat, ruby-encrusted idol with spun filigree wings.

But have I mentioned that the store was closed?

I walked to the used bookstore I'd seen, and spent a few minutes browsing, trying to appear somewhat like a normal, jovial guy, before pouncing on a clerk who worked there. He knew all about the closed store down the way, which had been there for years, but which had, during his employment, never been open. The owner had personal reasons for staying closed—a messy divorce in progress—but the specifics of why exactly that should keep the store closed for years made little sense. Which was, if not my first warning, at least one that made its own little fanfare as I digested it: *This won't be easy,* I thought.

"Does the owner ever come by?"

"Sometimes."

"Cool. I'll leave him a note."

"I wouldn't do that," the clerk said. "He seems to think everyone is a private detective sent by his wife."

I had therapy once a week, which meant I returned to the strip mall every Wednesday night. I found out that if I waited around until six or so, a woman came by to feed the cat who lived behind the store, and so one evening I happened by to see a grey tomcat on the counter, eating wet food while a woman looked on approvingly.

Somewhat to my surprise, she answered the door when I knocked, and when I explained I collected comic artwork, she let me in.

I knew that it couldn't last, so I tried to memorize everything I saw: 1950s splashes to stories I'd never heard of, perhaps by Lee Elias, perhaps by John Rosenberger; a John Buscema *Conan* page leaning against a display case. I couldn't tell. On one wall, an enormous wall-length tablet with dozens of characters drawn by dozens of different 1940s artists as a get-well card. On another, a color Chester Gould *Dick Tracy*. I was talking to the woman, and she was talking to me, but I couldn't tell you what we said in the perhaps ninety seconds I was there—all around me were stacks of comic artwork, the aisles were full of it, but there were also books and comics and posters and newspapers stacked on the artwork itself, so I couldn't see a single image, just the telltale dog-eared edges of 22-by-15 three-ply Strathmore.

She was nervous to have me there. "The owner, he can't really open up," she explained, ushering me out, "but here's his card."

The card was colored gold, and I still have it here, right by the computer. The name of his store was vaguely familiar—I started looking through fan directories, and finally found it in a very old *Overstreet Comic Book Price Guide.* An ad in the yellow pages, illustrated with a Pre-Raphaelite kind of babe tossing you a wink and reading a comic book on the moon while weird EC creatures stalked her. "Mainstream . . . underground . . . ground level . . . sci-fi . . . original art . . .

pulps . . . Disney," it read, and for the hell of it, I thumbed through the other ads. It was a transition year for collecting, with hand-drawn fan art in about half the displays and the other half looking upright and professional. The hippies, in it for the love, and the speculators looking over the hippies' shoulders and toward the 1980s. Which was my guy? The girl in his ad was a beacon of free love, but the fine print, the promise at the bottom, "I treat this as a business, not a hobby, and will pay 65% of guide for the following books in VF++ condition" struck me as a crafty promise direct from his rapidly icing heart.

I called him, left a message, this time saying I collected artwork by Chester Gould, John Buscema, Lee Elias, and John Rosenberger. After I hung up, I realized I'd mispronounced Elias (it has a long "i"), which might make him suspicious, and then as I thought about it, I realized it would strike him as weird that the artists I liked the best were those he had in his shop. As if I'd been spying on him. Which I had. But for reasons other than his paranoia would allow. I could imagine him getting the message and saying, "What kind of a guy would claim to like those four particular artists?" No one. In fact, I didn't particularly love any of them, or anything that I'd seen so far. Instead, it was the *possibility* that drove me. I was sure that even if 99 percent of what he had was nonsense and meaningless to my own particular fetish—Marvel Comics artwork from the 1960s to the 1980s—finding even one piece I wanted among all the dross would make my phone calls and visits worth it. Sometimes I imagined turning through meaningless pages— the worst kind of artwork, funny animals you've never heard of—and then, as I would flip past some acid-burned fox and bunny page, revealing in all its majesty the cover to *Fantastic Four #39*, Jack Kirby pencils, Chic Stone inks, a deserted New York with the FF and Daredevil below a hulking, skyline-dwarfing Doctor Doom. "How much for this?" I would ask after thumbing through a few other stacks of art to show it didn't consume me that much.

He would hem and haw and shrug and be cagey. "That would be, oh, at least a thousand dollars." Trying to scare me off. At that point in my fantasy, I realized I should have money on me, so I rewound, and thought that earlier that day I would have gone to the bank and taken out at least a thousand dollars on my credit card. No, two thousand. Three. With the cash advance fee and the interest clock ticking, yes, I could just about justify that, just in case, just for emergencies, just in case I found something and loved it and if I left to get money, he might close the shop again and disappear. "I have three thousand dollars," I would say. "Let me buy a few things."

I, too, was dreaming of Paris in the spring.


Now would be the montage shot: me returning once a week through the fall, the winter, the spring—since there are no seasons in Orange County, there would be no falling leaves or snow drifts or crocuses bursting through the ice. But my therapy ended (let us all pause for a moment to consider the wisdom of that), and then I started going by the store only once a month, once every two months, and calling the answering machine perhaps quarterly. The woman with the cat never again let me in. No one ever returned my phone calls. And though the displays in the window kept changing, I never saw a piece of artwork I knew I wanted. But that didn't matter.

Two years went by.

One day, the clerk at the used bookstore (who had benefited from my orbits in that, frustrated by the truculence displayed down the way, I frequently bought old Rafael Sabatini novels from him) asked me what I knew about comic book artwork, anyway.

"Why?"

"The guy who owns the store, he's been selling stuff."

My heart started dragging downward. "What do you mean?"

"He was in here the other day looking to sell some things. But nobody knew what they were, so we just told him 'sorry.' "

I was horrified. Selling stuff? But not to me? Why wasn't he returning my calls? What had I done wrong?

I dropped another note through his door, and called the answering machine again. I paid visits more often, and each time I came by, with a queasy feeling accompanying my insights, I noticed less and less in the shop.

"He's taking stuff out," the used-bookstore clerk said. "Some of it he's selling, some he just seems to be packing up."

"When does he show up?"

"Anytime. No real pattern to it."

I couldn't stake the place out, though I considered it. If I just parked outside and stayed, I'd have to run into him eventually. Would he respect that? "Well, now that I've made you jump through so many hoops, I see you're a serious collector." Or would it just make him more suspicious? "You must work for my wife!" Or would he just not notice? Perhaps grudgingly talk to me, or just as grudgingly ignore me as I pounded on the window, begging to be let in: "I've been thrown out of my house, my wife left me, my friends think I'm a lunatic, I haven't shaven in a week, and I've been sleeping in my car for the last three days, bathing out of the sink at the McDonald's across the street, reading all these old comics that I have scattered across the backseat to prove to you that I'm really a fan, and I brought my cell phone so you can call all the dealers and collectors I know to prove I'm legit, and, hey, look, these aren't pajamas, I sewed this costume, do you like it, it's Spider-Man, sort of, only it's hard to see out of the eyeholes and I also like the Hulk and Captain America, heh, 'When Captain America throws his mighty shielllld,' I have all those old cartoons memorized, hey, don't go away, I've been counting and re-counting this three thousand dollars in cash I've brought you just to show you how committed I am to the possibility that one day you will open up your shop for me." How would that go over?

It is perhaps jarring to note here that I actually had a job. I had to go to Holland for two weeks in early December. When I called my wife to let her know I'd made it there safely, she said there was a message on my answering machine from some nutcase about being ready now to sell me some artwork, and he was waiting for my call.

She and I chuckled briefly over the ludicrous idea that he expected me to call him from Amsterdam, then after I hung up, I used my rented cell phone, at $2.40 a minute, to call for a conversation that even now, in retrospect, I can't quite believe I had.

The woman answered the phone. "Ah, Mr. Gold, thank you. I talked to the owner, and he's ready to sell things. But he's a very busy man and can only be bothered with this if you're ready to spend some serious money."

One of my fantasies had gone this way. Me, paging through my portfolio, showing off the artwork I had so that he'd know I wasn't a piker. So I was prepared. "Well, I'm calling you from Amsterdam," I began, pausing to let that sink in, and then I started listing some things I had at the high end of my collection, and then I paused, sensing it had done nothing, and I mentioned some things I'd owned, not mentioning I'd sold them because I couldn't really afford to keep them, and when I just got a terse "Umm-hmm" in response, I started lying. "And, of course, a couple of Frank Frazetta oil paintings. A pair of hand-colored *Krazy Kat* Sundays. Golden Age covers from *Action Comics*," and, as my knowledge of six-figure artwork dried up, I fell silent.

"I see," she said. "And how much did you pay for all those things?"

Because I'm slow, slower than even the average collector, it took me until then to realize she didn't know what I was talking about.

"Would you be willing to spend at least ten thousand dollars?"

"Yes," I said, hoping to rack up more points by my quick jump over the net. "Of course." As if she could see my hands, I made an expansive gesture: what's ten thousand dollars? And at the same time I was trying to figure out where I would get that kind of money, and what of his I would have to presell in order to make this deal work.

"Okay, Mr. Gold," she said. "The owner is right here. Please hold."

She put her hand over the phone. A moment later, he was on the line with me.

I was so shocked I hardly knew what to say. I don't even really know what I said at first—did I say again I was in Amsterdam? Maybe I told him I'd been by his store so often that it was funny we were talking now, ha ha. I didn't mention that I'd seen his old ads in the 1978 *Overstreet*, that I'd tried to imagine him along the continuum from being in it for the love to flinty-eyed capitalist.

Whatever I said, he didn't respond. Not a word. Until I asked him what sort of art he had, and then I heard him. It was a voice that sounded almost metallic: heavy, single, evenly spaced words dropping out with a clunk. He said, as if the effort to talk to me was costing him money, that I should be ashamed of myself, that he had so much artwork, so many different artists and genres, he couldn't possibly list it. Why didn't I just start naming things, and he would tell me what he had.

"Okay," I took a deep breath. "Kirby."

"Jack Kirby? Ahhh . . . no, none of that."

"Steve Ditko?"

"Hmm . . . no."

"Gene Colan?"

"No."

"Anything by Buscema?"

"No."

I'd seen a John Buscema *Conan* page in his store, so the "No" meant he'd started to lie at some point, perhaps even shortly after hello. And the thing to do, here in my hotel room in Holland, was to say goodbye. And yet. I had a vision of myself shimmying up a drainpipe outside a mental patient's window, whispering through his window. And hoping for some crucial information. I couldn't give up. "Well, I'm a Marvel guy, anything from Marvel at all?"

"Marvel? Well, let's see . . . I have . . . no, I don't have anything."

"Nothing at all?"

"No. What else do you like?"

"Well, how about DC art?"

"What kind?"

"The superhero stuff," I said.

"No."

"How about their mystery line?"

"No."

"Okay." We'd talked long enough, and clearly it was time to go. Instead, I kept clawing at my tremulous hold on the crumbling ledge. "Well, then, I like strips, too. Any classic strip stuff?"

"What sort of stuff?"

"Well, umm . . . say Milton Caniff?"

"Oh, *Terry and the Pirates,* that kind of thing?"

"Yeah."

"No."

"Eisner?"

"No."

"Herriman?"

"No. Nothing that high-end."

I started racking my brain. "Any Fiction House stuff?"

"Had some. Sold it."

"Any covers of anything, anything whatsoever?"

"Depends what you're looking for. What are you looking for?"

I knew that "covers" was too broad, and then I found myself saying "covers" again.

"No, no covers," he said.

"Illustration art," I said. "I'm looking for illustration art, too."

"Like who?"

I started naming names. Jeffrey Jones. Frazetta. Alex Raymond. Charles Addams. At some point, with each "No," it became musical, a duet for inquisitor and hostile witness, two tenors running up and

147

down some private scales. To keep the rhythm of the thing going, I started pulling names out of my ass, anyone I'd ever heard of in my life, and when I got to St. John, he stopped me.

"Yep, I have some St. John stuff."

"Oh! Really?"

"Pricey, though."

"Yeah, well it is."

"I mean, any *one* of those pages . . ."

"I know." J. Allen St. John was high-end, an illustrator from the 1930s whose work was both impressionistic and precise, not too distant from Henrik Kley, or any classical stylist. I imagined nudes, skulls, a tightly wound grotesque universe. "What do you have?"

He held on to the name for a moment like it was chocolate. "Dinky Duck."

Imagine on my end of the line a really, really, really long pause. The name meant as little to me as it probably means to you, and when I did finally research it, I confirmed what I'd thought: it was a funny animal comic, a fifth-tier Bugs Bunny, from the early 1950s. I was trying at that moment to imagine holding in my palm a J. Allen St. John Dinky Duck. It would be like a Paul Klee Dilbert. "Dinky Duck?"

"Yeah. That's what I have. Thousands of pages of it. Great stuff published by St. John Publishers."

"Funny animal stuff." The worst. To me, about as desirable as dryer lint.

"Yeah!"

"Just funny animal stuff is what you have?"

"Yeah." But, he reminded me with a note of caution, pricey. Really, really pricey.

There was some kind of conversation between then and when I hung up the phone, some sort of promise he would look for the artwork I liked again, me thanking him, and then, yes, hanging up, rubbing my temples, realizing how much I'd just spent on the phone call, and then me slumping into a chair and looking out across the canal at the ice and wondering what the hell I'd been chasing.

Or still was. Because, and though it shames me, I will tell you this. I said to him, before we hung up, I said, because I am a freak, I said Whenever You Can Work It Out I'd Like to See Your Dinky Duck Art. Because, of course, I was hoping that, oh, we might turn the pages of *Dinky Duck* #19 to find, oh, the cover to *Fantastic Four* #39.

That was a few months ago. And then, my calls went unanswered. I'm told by my friend at the bookstore, though I haven't seen it myself, that the storefront down the way is now empty.

And somehow the fever has broken for me. The mechanism is rather mysterious. I like the artwork and all, but right now I'm not feeling obsessed. How odd.

The piece of artwork I most want is from a comic book I saw in 1975, when I was eleven. This was an era of boundless energy in which characters routinely fought God, destroyed the universe, or fell into shaggy dog stories (there is, somewhere in the ether, a good essay to be written about Steve Gerber's Elf with a Gun character).

One of Jim Starlin's peak moments was his thirteen-issue run on the Adam Warlock character, whose dark narrative led to monologues on narcissism and soul-weariness and apotheosis, and whose climax was so riveting that I, as an eleven-year-old, read and reread his fate until I had every panel of that page committed to eidetic imagery. Warlock has discovered that he is doomed to become unspeakably evil; the only way around it is to follow one of his kismet lifepaths—since he is being pursued, he chooses the shortest—and then to kill his future self.

When he arrives on the scene of some horrible industrial devasta-

149

tion, he finds his future self, who mutters, bleeding and broken, "*Everything* I've ever cared for or accomplished has fallen into *ruin*! Everyone I've ever *loved* now lies *dead*! My life has been a *failure*!" And then, with tears rolling down his dirty face, he whispers, "I welcome its end," and then Warlock massacres him.

If it was unsettling to see the first time (as we followed his younger self), it was horrific two years later to see it unfold again and to realize he hadn't escaped his destiny, that he was now the older self, broken and damned. Further, this time, the inking was tangled with darkness, the backgrounds more start, the border panels black like a funeral announcement. This fatalism, the undiluted sense that Adam Warlock was born to be screwed, was more powerful to me than James M. Cain or Jim Thompson or Nathanael West—this was the story of Job unfolding before my eyes, on a monthly basis, and more important, it was the first time I was running into such a thing, and so it was almost overwhelmingly powerful to me. There is something in the eleven-year-old mind that romances the big flashing marquee lights of destruction. I was Adam Warlock. I could imagine my kingdom crumbled and my legacy destroyed, with no hope but death. To save yourself, you destroy yourself, and I felt like I'd already made that choice somehow, and that I would make it again, consciously, heroically, someday.

That page is high on a few collectors' want lists for reasons I can't quite explain. Obviously, it speaks to us, and I wonder if for all of us it's exactly the same way. We wanted to succeed at something, and we didn't, and we think that somewhere in our future is this awful demon we are cursed to become. What is *that* about?

I just looked through that old *Overstreet* comic price guide, the last I owned as a kid. This was when I gave up comics as reading material, when I discovered actual novels (who knows why certain books but not others lead us away from childhood? My gateway drugs were Vance

Bourjaily's *Now Playing at Canterbury* and Robertson Davies's *Fifth Business,* and the alchemy there is unknowable, but nonetheless I was no longer a committed comic book reader when I finished those novels).

The 1970s market report is hilariously out of date, the preservation articles are shockingly dangerous, but the dealers' ads are what catch my eye. What happened to Howard Rogofsky, who owned the first page of every *Overstreet* for years with his amateurish lightning-bolt-and-star-spangled hero carrying an ill-drawn woman before a field of benday dots, promising two massive catalogs for $1.35? What happened to the nameless coin, stamp, and comic-store owner who felt the best possible ad was a drawing—no, an eyes-closed scrawl-with-a-stick—of Howard the Duck sitting on the toilet? I'm touched by R. E. Winfree Jr. of Richmond, Virginia, who went the polite route: "If you desire to purchase better books at reasonable prices, I invite your inquiry. I think you'll find me to be a pleasant, honest person to deal with. Thank you."

The Internet helps me find some of them. A few guys show up in library holdings, special fanzine collections, something they wrote twenty years ago. Or in a comic book database, as an inker on a backup story for a company long extinct. Or on eBay, someone selling an old catalog, or in a newsgroup, asking, like me, whatever happened to . . . There are a few guys who thrived in the hobby, but for most of them, no, there is no legacy. One guy is a conspiracy theorist, and appears on a lot of JFK websites. A few of them are dead. There are blind links, 404 codes, GeoCities apologies for pages that no longer exist. Objects not found.

There is a strange twilight awaiting collectors. Your moment passes and what you are left with is stacks of whatever monstrous accumulations you so desired. And you fade by some mechanical, spiritless process, like that little blue dot at the center of the screen in the days of solid-state television.

I am feeling strangely generous toward the owner of the empty storefront—when you think about it, he wasn't the one who wasted my time for the past several years.

Now I imagine: it's nightfall at his half-abandoned, cluttered business, and the woman who feeds the cat has handed him the phone and she has gone home. He is talking transatlantic long distance to someone who doesn't know him, who hardly cares to know his actual daily life, who just wants something with an obsession he, the store owner, once saw, day in, day out, back in the 1970s. And at first, maybe he feels he could gather together his strength for one last deal, but as the voice burbles with tiresome excitement, no different in its eagerness than any other collector voice—except almost unbelievably persistent—the dealer begins to look around his stacks of artwork, the dust and the grime, the moldering carpets, the unpaid bills, and he thinks of how he has no one at home waiting for him, or if he does have someone there, he thinks of how there was an inevitable, tidal pull that drew him out to sea, away from human emotion, how he can barely even see the stone-slab jetty between himself and the rest of the world. He's divorced. He hates his business place so much he never comes here. And it's too late to save himself. "Everything I've ever cared for or accomplished has fallen into *ruin!*" he thinks.

And here, he makes a heroic gesture. As the voice—a younger voice than his own—begins to ask after all the artists he has once owned, and might currently have examples of, he finds himself hesitating. And then lying. "No."

It comes out at first from defensiveness, an unwillingness to give up what he has earned, bulked up with, the objects that both save him from and create so much despair in his life, but then, he begins to feel with each denial he might be saving someone. "No." And again, "No." It gives him strength and energy. In a way, he is killing himself, wiping a future self out before it can even develop. "My life has been a *failure.* I welcome its end," he whispers to himself, a dead receiver in his hand, and he feels he has succeeded in snuffing out a flame.

I believe in heroes, the quiet ones who find a way we hardly notice to live with their weaker selves.

The next day, he begins to clear out the store, participating in his own extinguishment with, for the first time in years, an untrained eagerness in his heart and the firm desire to investigate what, at such a late age, it would be like to drive at fine speed a sports car in clement weather along the boulevard whose name he would like to know, the one that passes by the Arc de Triomphe.

# LYDIA MILLET

I used to dream about a toilet.

It was a toilet like a fountain, with a stone seat around a vast basin and nothing unseemly visible in the sparkling water. This toilet-fountain was the central element of a main square in a quiet town, and all the townspeople sat along the edge of the toilet, facing outward. They talked to each other, read newspapers, ate croissants, and sometimes leaned down to tie their shoes. I was among them. The act of sitting was friendly. I don't remember whether we had our pants down around our ankles, but I doubt it. The dream was too genteel to be specific. →

That was back in the days when I had dreams all the time, when dreams were practically a dime a dozen. The toilet dream was recurring, as were dreams of flying above the trees by pumping my arms until I rose vertically. Our street was mostly old maples, lined up in front of fake-Tudor houses built too closely together. I remember how pliable the air was, tucked under my arms and pushed down beneath my palms like marshmallows. I remember how I ratcheted myself upward in the air bit by bit, gaining elevation through a combination of buoyancy and persistence. If there was going to be magic, I would have to work for it.

Or maybe the dream said nothing at all about me. Maybe the dream was just a piece of the world.


I got to know *Little Nemo in Slumberland* because of my father's toilet. Nemo lived on a bookshelf above the tank, sandwiched between dog-eared copies of forgotten classics like *Low Man on a Totem Pole* and *Waikiki Beachnik*. It was on the toilet that I first read the line *We have met the enemy and it is us*, and also there that I got my first glimpse into the fantastic landscapes of Slumberland.

When I was a kid, up until I went to high school, my family didn't have a TV, and all we ever did together was read. We would sit around the dining room table or line up along the living room couch in silence, each immersed in a separate world. In his armchair, my father might be boning up on the life of Joseph Bonaparte, Napoleon's loser brother, while kitty corner from him, on a couch stolen out of the neighbor's garbage, my mother laughed at Bertie Wooster the English upper-class twit. Beside her with my legs tucked beneath me I might be learning about Hermann Goering's oddly *piercing blue eyes* while my brother, Josh, studied the life of Joan of Arc and my little sister, Mandy, cried soundlessly over the death of Charlotte the spider, vowing never to admit to the tears.

But we all read my father's favorite comics. For one thing, they were near the toilet.

They were all hardbound books—some collections of comic strips, others what would later come to be called "graphic novels"—and were peopled with colorful adventurers who liked to solve mysteries. There was Tintin, the young Belgian reporter with a button nose, nutmeg hair, and a cowlick, who traveled throughout the European colonial empires solving mysteries. With his little white dog, Snowy, and his drunkard sailor friend, Captain Haddock, in tow, he did battle with bad guys and often *savages,* too. There were Asterix and Obelix, one a midget and the other a gigantic fatty, who lived in the backwaters of ancient Gaul under the Roman empire and spent their time foiling the Roman soldiers; and there was *Pogo,* which at ten I did not understand at all and at thirty-four understand even less. There was lowbrow, simpleminded fare, too, possibly for relaxing the brain after a hard day of thinking. (My father is an Egyptologist and studies an ancient language called Meroitic, about which little is known. For a man who spends all day trying to decode the opaque scrawlings of long-dead Nubians, perhaps the lapse in aesthetic rigor represented by *Family Circus* can be forgiven.)

And finally there was Winsor McCay's *Little Nemo in Slumberland,* in a class by itself.

What there were *not,* in our house, were comic books. There were plenty of comic strips made into books and published as treasuries, but there were no tawdry dimestore cheapies, with their shiny covers and soft paper, about superheroes or Richie Rich or Casper the Friendly Ghost or Betty and Archie, with their simpering smiles and simple bodies. Those, along with chewing gum, were banned. Whether it was because Casper and Richie were too witless, too soulless, too massproduced, or just too pop and modern, they were not considered appropriate fare for children. Neither were superheroes, with their bondage-and-domination undertones and large-breasted damsels in distress. Like candy, comic books rotted parts of you that were supposed to be pure and white. My father condemned comic books while adoring comic strips, and my mother's father, she recently told me, felt the same about comic books back when she was a child, in the forties and fifties.

Because of the ban on comic books we sometimes touched them with gentle, wistful fingers when we were at Green's Variety or Player's, the two corner stores close enough to our house to walk to. They were the pornography of our childhood, the objects of shameful and furtive desire. We knew there was something sordid in them, something easy and gratifying, something empty and sugary that dirtied you with its delicious grease and made you plump and lazy inside.

And we wanted to read them. We longed for that feeling of inner fat.

So we dreamed of comic books but read comic strips all the time, hardbound in collections and printed on thick, expensive paper. One of the world's first newspaper comic strips, *Little Nemo* began its run in the *New York Herald* in 1905, four years before Sigmund Freud's first trip to America. Week after week, for years, it told the neatly formulaic story of a young boy named Nemo—Latin for *no one*—who, in each strip, dreams an elaborate dream and is ultimately woken up by one of his parents (if the dream is a good one) or by falling out of bed (if the dream's a nightmare). In sleep, Nemo travels to majestic and fanciful places full of creatures both ferocious and serene, with colorful, soaring architecture and surreal, impossible settings: a field of thin mushrooms as tall as redwoods, or a flock of bright birds with twenty-foot legs. A tree is transformed into a rhinoceros as we watch; a rose in the hand of a mischievous street scamp turns into a bedraggled dead cat. There is little danger or drama, because even the villains are picturesque. And when Nemo wakes up, one of his parents usually offers a banal and predictable explanation for the intensity of his dreams: He ate too much raisin cake, huckleberry pie, or ice cream and raw onions before he went to bed.

Bad boy, Nemo.

The thing about Nemo is, he's the polar opposite of the comic book heroes that succeeded him in popular culture. Living in a world of observation, not action, he's carried along on the river of his dreams without propelling himself. His adventures are almost plotless, a series of static tableaux instead of stories, exquisite art-nouveau renderings of landscapes and palaces in which Nemo finds himself first and foremost an observer. Other characters in the series—Morpheus, the king of Slumberland; his young, beautiful daughter, the princess; and Flip, the annoying street scamp—decide what happens, and take Nemo along for the ride. All that he encounters is lovely, monsters and angels alike.

In *Nemo*, we're not tipped off to characters' innate villainy by their ugly faces or deformed bodies. We can't gauge moral character by attractiveness, because everyone and everything in *Nemo* is beautiful.

In Slumberland the threats are never felt, the victories never celebrated. Nemo's face never shows real fear, though he often says he's afraid ("Ooh! I was scared!"). And it's almost impossible to predict what will frighten him. A witch or a gigantic elephant with a raised foot may not bother Nemo, while pretty fireworks or gently falling snowflakes may terrify him. Like real children in waking life, he doesn't always know what he's supposed to fear and what he's supposed to love. Everything is cast in the same wonder.

In short, Nemo's dreams don't take you on an action-packed ride full of obstacles and events. They're not plot-based at all. They're pictures without much of a narrative—unlike later comics, in which art increasingly took a backseat to story.

Nemo, unlike superheroes and unlike even Casper or Archie, is not a problem-solver. He doesn't take care of business.

He mostly just watches.

· · ·

For a while, after I had grown up, I forgot about Nemo. But Nemo had never really left me, and the novels I write are haunted by him. In fact, the characters that fill my world are the ghosts of Nemo: passive like him, and like him, often ciphers. They're translucent but not transparent.

My impulse is always to write about people who are eternally childlike in the openness of their minds, whose judgment is either nonexistent or skewed. I like characters who either are incapable of doing battle with the forces that oppress them or don't want to enter the fray—protagonists who live in rich and veiled environments of their own imagination but who, in the social and political world outside, can do nothing.

In the outside world their hands are tied because they know that the world is not only about them. That kind of knowledge can humble a character.

What breaks my heart about people is the way they fill their own landscapes. Because we can't live easily with the fact that the universe is huge and we're tiny, we make ourselves enormous, we make ourselves into towering figures. We do this in the only place we can do it, the privacy of our own imaginings. To me, that impossible yearning to be a giant is the precise center of both human likebility and the tragedy of our selfishness.

So the antagonists in my books tend to have delusions of grandeur, whereas the protagonists see beauty in the world outside them instead of in themselves. What's most fascinating about these characters, to me, is their own fascination. Like children, characters I make up are compelled by the magical elements of the world around them, curious and titillated. Again like children, they don't always know their enemies from their friends. Instead of answers, their experience offers questions, and their inquiries into the nature of things are lacking a precise agenda. Because they can't tell what poses a danger to them and what might offer them benefits, they don't maneuver well in power. They imbue the whole universe with life; to them very little in the world is without personhood: personhood is in the world, not in the person. Ego is weak but love is strong.

Because they do not classify and categorize naturally, as most adults do, these people float forever in a sea of interest. They're not oriented toward conflict or domination, and so their purity—not any moral purity but a purity of hope and desire—leaves them without power.

To me the world of stories divides neatly this way: there are stories that presume humans are giant, and stories that presume humans are miniature.

Recently my husband and I got a small puppy named Bug. Bug is happiest when she's chewing on something, and she's not afraid of cars, people, cats, or other dogs. What *is* she afraid of? The answer is obvious. A stuffed rabbit with a mechanical voice that says in a French accent, "Hello my friend, my name is Henri!" and a can of shaving cream marked COLGATE.

She quakes in fear when she sees them. Then she falls upon them in a terrible rage.

Bug is like my characters, too. She doesn't know that some things are worth being scared of, and others really aren't interesting.

She confuses the two.

Nemo, unconscious in a dazzling kingdom, is almost as clueless as Bug and anything but heroic. Yet the heroes of most of my favorite books bear more resemblance to him than to Superman or Wonder Woman. To me the powerful, fulfilled, and well adjusted are of limited interest. Frankly, they're boring. Spider-Man was a little better; at least he was creepy and sneaky. Batman had his moments, too; he

161

knew how to dress, he was clearly in the closet, and he was possibly also a pedophile. But even these guys were always a little too proactive for my taste. The world of superheroes contains plenty of dark horses, but not many couch potatoes.

The reasons for that are mechanical: to have a story, you have to have events. Things have to happen. Passive characters can't carry it off, so men of action steal the day.

And you have to have story, right? Art without story is not enough for most people; they need linear, forward-moving structures of myth to imbue their own lives with meaning. Beauty is not enough because we can't easily glean meaning from it.

The job is just too hard.

To me, characters without tragedy lurking in their past or looming in their future—without flawed self-awareness or extravagant, secret faith—are predictable dullards. Once a character has enough self-love or corruption to be able to master the world, his soul is lost to me.

Curious but often confused, the people I like to read and write about most can live in a dream world but always finally fail to extend their dreams into waking life. If there is freedom in the world of dreams, there are also limits: even Nemo's dream world has all-too-finite borders. Dream is dream, everyday life is everyday life, and never the twain shall meet. *All good things must come to an end.* Nemo whirls through paradise only to end up in a small, plain room every morning. Where his dreams are elaborate and grandiose, *full of ideas,* his own room in the real world lacks any decoration at all. The wall, the bedspread, Nemo's pajamas, all the elements of the room are blank.

On the surface of it, Winsor McCay looks like the anti-Freud. *Little Nemo* seems to suggest that dreams, instead of doing complex important psychic work for the dreamer, are just fanciful vacations that we should enjoy while they last. Nemo's dreams are not keys to his own unconscious but just pleasure trips that leave him back where he began: in bed, with authority figures looming nearby, remote and vaguely disapproving. In *Nemo* it is gluttony, not secret desire, that brings vivid and overwhelming visions during sleep. (Winsor McCay was apparently obsessed with the link between gastric distress and dream images. His *Dreams of the Rarebit Fiend* also hinged on indigestion.)

Even so, the dreams are far more vibrant and spectacular than the daytime life from which they spring. Maybe that's all McCay wanted to say. Maybe, after his fashion, he agreed with Freud that the true, most vital self is not the conscious self at all. But maybe he felt that the true self was not the inward-turned core that Freud described— the self that is always about the self, that is eternally caught up in selfhood—but the part of the person that watches and loves the rest of the world.

What *are* characters to the writer who makes them up, anyway? Are they just pretend friends?

My own real friends tend to be articulate and well adjusted. They tend to have at least a semblance of control of their lives, cherish certain ambitions, move forward, and finally get at least part of what they want. True, the vast majority of them, being writers, artists, journalists, academics, environmentalists, and other denizens of subculture, are also clinically depressed; but that's what Wellbutrin is for. In a broad sense my friends are like me: privileged, observant, fat with their enjoyment of counterculture, and thin with worry about the dismal future. I admire them, but I don't usually write about them. I don't write about characters who achieve things and are high-functioning, live in pretty houses, eat and drink well, take reasonably effective action to have an impact on their society, and converse about politics or semiotics using polysyllabic words. Instead I write about underachievers, whose language embraces many possibilities but who never succeed in manipulating the world to their own benefit—though they may imagine they do for a fleeting moment.

I usually choose not to write about successful, middle-class people partly because existence doesn't strike me as fundamentally *about* these people and partly because—from my cheap seat on the margin of the cultural mainstream—I see the most interesting part of myself and others not in the trappings of normalcy but in the position of the underachiever, in the chronic outsider, the excluded and irrelevant. This is not self-deprecation, though—only the recognition that for me it is in desire, longing, and isolation that the soul tends to show its grace, in the understanding of separateness and the wish for communion.

The delusion of great size is a childish fantasy, and I love *Little Nemo* for the sweet and passive way it imagines a child's longing for a larger-than-life world, a life more beautiful than life, a life more real than real.

But later the delusion of size grows up and gets ugly, and becomes a delusion of power.

It strikes me that the main difference between self-reflective fiction and fiction that wants primarily to tell a story—at least in our culture—may be an assumption about what constitutes power.

Storyteller fiction often seems to work on the assumption that people run the world, and that people are in fact the center of the universe. Real power, this storyteller fiction seems to say, is power over other people.

And so storyteller fiction is chiefly about individuals' relationships to each other, the ins and outs of their romances and family dynamics and career paths and triumphs over obstacles. Further, it is written as though all ultimate truths lie in personal relationships. More than that, truth lies in the narrative *line* of these relationships, in the logical and orderly sequence of *what happens,* from beginning to middle to end. And all of *what happens* has to happen between people and other people. In general, with just a smattering of exceptions, what is most important does not happen between people and the rest of the beings in the world, people and their perceptions of the world itself, or even people and their own inner workings. Meaning resides in what humans do to each other, and just as there must be story, there must also be meaning. A world without meaning would be too cold to live in.

Not only that, the meaning must be highly visible. It should announce itself boldly.

Fiction that is full of self-consciousness, on the other hand—fiction of language, so-called experimental fiction, navel-gazing fiction, even, either prose or graphic—presumes a more subtle, submerged and ineffable universe in which humans, for all their foibles and strokes of genius, are powerless, in which meaning may exist but can never be grasped. It acknowledges with every phrase of its breath that people are only a small part of the world, and recognizes that somewhere in the air beyond our fingertips is a vastness before which we can do nothing.

But it is not silenced by this. It may tremble at the sight or revel in it, but before and after everything it shows how beauty brims all over, with or without significance.

TOM PIAZZA

The Convention Center in Jacksonville, Florida, is a small city in itself. Once a year, ComicCon, the big annual comics convention, becomes a city within a city. This year, I went there for the first time, to solve a mystery for myself.

I have always had a soft spot in my heart for the original Bizarro, the way one has a soft spot for the monster in *The Bride of Frankenstein*. The tragically imperfect Superman duplicate wants to do good but doesn't know how; he's scary-looking and people run away from him—sort of the way most comic-lovers are in high school. Ever since Lex Luthor's duplicator ray went awry and created him, in 1961 (an earlier version of Bizarro, a copy of Superboy, had been created and destroyed back in 1958), Bizarro has been a disturbing reminder of everything Superman is not. →

I never bought the idea of the "Bizarro World" feature that *Adventure Comics* inaugurated in 1961, with its multiple Bizarros and "Bizarro code" ("Us do opposite of all Earthly things! Us hate beauty! Us love ugliness!"). It seemed willed somehow—created only to cash in on the original Bizarro's popularity. The sinister, snarling, bellicose Bizarros on the cube-shaped Bizarro planet have their own version of normalcy, and they censure those who don't conform; they have become an establishment of their own, and they are no longer interesting. Certainly they have little in common with the original Bizarro, who wandered the earth mystified, befuddled, angry—but never mean or self-satisfied.

Of course, the original Bizarro's perversity and ingenuousness are no longer liabilities. The times have caught up with him and now those qualities make him cool. He has been invited to sing on record with U2 and Willie Nelson; Jim Jarmusch has hired him for several small roles; there was even a "Think Different" ad, which had to be withdrawn. Still, it hasn't been easy for him. Most people know the stories by now, from the tabloids. Since the breakup of his marriage to Bizarro Lois, he has been in semiretirement in Las Vegas, living off various lucrative licensing deals and occasional guest shots. He has, apparently, been mulling a move to Branson, Missouri; they are talking about opening a Bizarro Supertheater where the audience sits on the stage and Bizarro does his act from out in the seats. His trademark literalness and obtuseness still get him into trouble from time to time. The biggest recent flap was during his scheduled hour as a celebrity bartender at a Muscular Dystrophy evening, when Jennifer Aniston made the mistake of asking him for a Rusty Nail.

Big as the Convention Center is, finding Bizarro was not hard—or at least finding where Bizarro was supposed to be. When I got to the big tent area with paintings hanging upside down and chairs with no legs, a few dozen eager fans were milling around, hoping for a glimpse of their man. I asked where he was and his handlers shrugged. Lassitude; it was an incredibly hot day. Finally one told me that he thought Bizarro was over by Mr. Mxyzptlk. When I expressed some surprise about this, the official shook his head. "Mr. B loves the Little Guy. Don't ask me why. I guess it's an Old Days thing. You can find them in Area 5. . . ." and he showed me on a map. The map of the convention center was like a diagram of the inside of a computer. I began the long trek.

A television writer named David Mandel was the only other person, to my knowledge, to have interviewed Bizarro, for the introduction to the book *Tales of the Bizarro World* (DC Comics, 2000). Mandel had written the famous "Bizarro Jerry" episode of *Seinfeld,* but I had the nagging sense that he hadn't captured Bizarro at all in his interview, which felt shticky and superficial. The Bizarro of that interview drank heavily, was relentlessly sarcastic, and said things like "Cut the crap." It just wasn't in character. I even began to have eerie doubts that Mandel had interviewed the real Bizarro. Mandel himself asked "Bizarro" if Mr. Mxyzptlk, the Fifth Dimensional imp who would appear periodically to bedevil Superman, was making him act strangely. His subject denied there was any such being as Mr. Mxyzptlk. Despite Mandel's immediate acceptance of this, I wondered, myself, if the imp of the Fifth Dimension hadn't pulled a fast one on Mandel. In any case, I hoped I would have my chance to find out—both of the Old Stars were going to be at ComicCon, signing comics, posing for pictures.

In ComicCon terms, going from the Bizarro area, which was right in the middle of the DC "sector," to Area 5 was the equivalent of going from Times Square to Little Italy. Marvel was in another area completely. I made my way past the big *Classics Illustrated* IMAX theater, the Archie Comics Group Food Court, and the Gold Key tables, which were populated by some seriously freaky-looking people; there was a long hallway with tables and tents dedicated to *House of Mystery,* and *Mystery in Space* (Adam Strange was there, but he looked like an old man; I wouldn't have recognized him), and *Strange Adventures.* After

KLTPZYXM!

169

more twists and turns I finally rounded a corner and there was Mr. Mxyzptlk's table, the biggest thing in a section of crappy-looking stalls, a long, cavernous, grey cinder-block hall. Behind the table hung a gigantic black velvet hanging with the famous Hirschfeld caricature of Mr. M stenciled in gold, visibly frayed around the edges from being put up and taken down many times. People walked by, oblivious to the little man in the purple derby. Sure enough, Bizarro was there, sitting on a folding chair at the end of the table; as I arrived, he was busy signing a comic book (upside down) for a little kid. Mr. M sat alone, drumming his fingers on the table, visibly irritated by his colleague's presence, looking around nervously until he noticed me.

"Here—park it," Mr. M said, pulling out a folding chair with his small, gloved hand. "Sit down . . ." I noticed him looking me over, sizing me up. He shook his head, looking at Bizarro and the boy, and said, "He's not supposed to be doing that for free."

I settled on the chair and took out my cassette recorder. "You must be here to see . . . ?" and he cocked his head toward Bizarro. He looked disappointed, and I nodded contritely.

"So who's the article for?" he asked.

"It's actually for a book," I replied. I watched him surreptitiously as I got the recorder set and slipped in a tape. He was fidgety, glancing at me nervously.

"There's going to be another book about him? Great."

"It's not just about Bizarro," I said. "It's writers on all kinds of comics."

Mxyzptlk didn't seem to have heard. "What'll it be next?" he muttered, half to himself. "He'll probably get the fucking Kennedy Center Award."

Bizarro was finished with the boy, finally, and Mr. M introduced us. There he was, with that remarkable white crystalline skin that gave the phrase "chiseled features" a whole new meaning. Amazing. I put out my hand and told Bizarro how happy I was to meet him.

"Me sorry to meet you," he said, smiling.

"Right, right," Mr. Mxyzptlk said. "Hey—how many Vietnam vets does it take to screw in a lightbulb?"

"I don't know," I said. Already I was wishing that I could trick him into saying his name backward, the only thing that can send him back to the Fifth Dimension.

Belligerently, he said, " 'You don't know, man—you weren't there.' "

After a moment Bizarro started crying, and Mr. M rolled his eyes. "The same old shtick . . . I tell a joke, and he cries at the punch line."

I decided to just charge in and ask Bizarro a few questions, hoping that someone would come along to distract Mr. M. He was bugging me; the negativity was palpable. Maybe, I thought, he was unsatisfied with his placement at ComicCom. Or something.

But before I could ask a question, Bizarro spoke up.

"Me drink too much coffee. Have to go to kitchen."

"Don't go to the kitchen, you putz," Mxyzptlk said. "Go to the bathroom."

Bizarro stood up unceremoniously, said, "Me be back," and started down the hall. My stomach sank. The last thing I wanted was to be stuck there with Mxyzptlk. He was reminding me of someone, unpleasantly, and I realized right then who it was—Don Rickles. There was even a physical resemblance. Weird.

As Bizarro walked off, M shook his head. "I know you don't wanna talk to me. Who am I? I don't make the records with Willie Nelson. I don't have a good heart, I don't rescue blind girls. I make people think. . . . Like the time I changed the painting of Washington crossing the Delaware and put them all in ice skates . . . Or when I turned all the crooks in the jail into Supermen . . . So I'm a nuisance. . . . They want their good and evil . . . black and white . . ."

I asked him if he and Bizarro did a lot of these events together.

M snorted and said, "Together? He's up in the Big Money in his tent with the funny mirrors. He comes over because he's sentimental. 'Everything different,' he says. 'It am commercialized. . . .' "

"This had, actually, been my thought, too," I said.

"He's having an identity crisis," M went on. "Sheesh—I would, too, with thousands of duplicates of myself running around. Listen to this—he built a Fortress of Solitude in Las Vegas. Did you know this? Who builds a Fortress of Solitude in Las Vegas? He's not as stupid as he looks."

"What do you mean?" I said. "It sounds like typical Bizarro."

"He's doing a Greta Garbo number—it adds to the mystery." He looked pensive for a moment. "But you got a point. The putz has a listed number! He says he gets lonely! I'm over there and there's sales calls coming in every five seconds! Some Fortress of Solitude. Meanwhile I'm living in fucking Astoria."

"I thought you lived in the Fifth Dimension."

"Who can afford it anymore?" Mr. M shook his head, staring into the distance. "The guy's a fucking scream. When he makes a scotch on the rocks, they're real rocks. If he knew what he was doing he'd be a fucking millionaire."

"He *is* a millionaire," I said.

Shrugging this off, M said, "You know who he reminds me of?"

"Who?"

"Al Gore. Gore is the Bizarro version of Clinton."

"Well," I said, "in fifty years, probably nobody will remember Al Gore. But everybody will remember Bizarro."

I could see his expression change, so I quickly added, "They'll remember *all* the Superman characters. . . ."

Mr. M's face got red; he was suddenly seething with rage. "Superman," he spat. "The big hero. Superman's so great, so high-minded. Let me tell you something about Superman. If everything was so fucking aboveboard with him, where do all these spooks and dybbuks come from? Braniac? A guy with green skin, obsessed with destroying him? Lex Luthor—what's with all the bald guys? And then there's the obsessive double L shit . . . Lois Lane, Lana Lang, Lex Luthor . . . Total anxiety management. This compulsive alliteration . . . I have to be the

Silly Sprite. Or the Mysterious Mr. Mxyzptlk. The guy is obviously a mess. A total obsessive-compulsive. I mean, why doesn't Jimmy Olsen fall down and start dying every time he sees a green rock? Plus Superman's always talking to himself. You set yourself up as the big hero, and suddenly everything bad has to be outside you. But we know where it really comes from, don't we?"

"You said to Superman once, 'If it weren't for guys like me, super-guys like you would be out of a job.' "

"Not just out of a job," M said. "He couldn't *exist*. He'd be a contradiction in terms. In the Third Dimension, at least."

M chewed his lip a little. "What was his name? Siegel? Perfect. A Jew invents the biggest, strongest Dumb Goy in history. *Übermensch,* in German. The ultimate assimilation, right? But then the goy needs enemies, otherwise so what? Everything has to generate its opposite. That's the whole problem with the three-dimensional world."

We were silent for a moment, watching a young woman pass by. "Nice ass," Mxyzptlk said.

"I always wanted to get a job in the Marvel comics," he went on. "I always thought I'd be more at home there. But I'm too much of a caricature. They take one look at me, with the derby and the gloves, and it's like, 'Feh . . .' I'm not even a real devil. I'm Superman's idea of what a problem is. A square *goyishe* idea of a nuisance . . ." His eyes were red and he looked as if he was about to cry. "Look at this one," he said, gesturing with his chin in the direction of a young man with pink hair walking by. "With the fucking Bizarro t-shirt on. This year everything's Bizarro. Next year it'll be Perry White. Nazi bastard. I gotta walk around with the stupid fucking derby. I can't even get laid. Bizarro . . . they line up . . . please, I can't even talk about it with the angina. . . ."

"What do you mean?"

"The guy is hung like a horse. He fucked Lana Lang. He fucked everybody. Yeah. You're looking at me like I'm crazy. Everybody talks about how he was hitting on Lois, but Lana Lang was all over him.

Redheaded slut. She came on to me first, but I got so excited I said my name backward and then I had to wait for another episode and by that time she was with horse-dick. I'm such a putz."

Jimmy Olsen passed by with a couple of slick-looking guys in suits and waved at us, saying, "Hi, guys."

As they passed, Mr. M wrinkled up his features and simpered, " 'Hi, guys' . . . Fuck you."

His bitterness was unbelievable, and I was wishing Bizarro would come back from the bathroom, or the kitchen, or wherever he'd gone. I was getting really uncomfortable being with the imp, but I couldn't bring myself to leave him either. How many times do you get to have a conversation with a legend like that? Even a twisted, bitter legend. To pass a little more time, I asked M what he did when he wasn't doing comics conventions.

"I do the show thing mostly," he said. "We do the casinos—the Beau Rivage, in Biloxi, we played Tunica, Mississippi. . . . Some real shitholes . . . You go out and everybody's got the white shoes and the rat's-nest toupees. And they say I'm a freak. *'Mix-yez-pit-uh-lick . . . Whut kinda name is thay-ut?'* I'm on stage, thinking, 'I used to be able to slide in and out of dimensions at will, now I'm in Biloxi.' And the bands they put together for you . . . the trumpeter looks like Heinrich Himmler, the saxophone player looks like he's been dead for five years. . . . I used to know all of the stars, and I mean all of them. Mr. Lou Rawls, Mr. Warren Oates . . ."

I was listening, but something was still bothering me. The sound, the subject matter . . . I was thinking about the Mandel interview again, and I decided to bring it up. What was there to lose at that point? "Can I ask you something?" I said.

"Can I stop you?" he said, with an ingratiating smile.

"The interview with the television writer, in the Bizarro book . . . I've been wondering . . ."

Mxyzptlk was staring at me, shocked, apparently, and I didn't finish the question. I'd hit a nerve, and I had a long moment of dread—would he turn me into a circus animal? Or set me on fire?

"The Mandel interview?" he said. "Yeah, I did it," he went on, half defensively and half proudly. "That was me. I fucked him over. He deserved it. Why not put me on the fucking Seinfeld show? I can do comedy. That's my whole shtick. Instead I'm doing casinos. . . ."

I watched the little imp foaming at the mouth, railing about what a raw deal he'd gotten, and I realized I'd had enough. The shrillness, the self-pity . . . I didn't care anymore that he was a legend; I wanted to tell him off. I had come there to interview Bizarro, anyway, not him. I heard myself saying, "You know, Mr. Mxyzptlk, Bizarro gets to people. It's that simple. The way James Dean did." I could see that this hurt him; a look of pure childish pain crossed his face.

"He's a tortured soul," I went on, cranking up, "looking for his place in the universe. You're surprising, and you're lively, but you represent nothing more problematic than the spirit of anarchy. Plus you're full of self-pity, Mxyzptlk. Do you ever listen to yourself?" Even as I was saying this, I thought: I've done it now. He was looking at me with a combination of intense irritation and transparent hurt, a tinge of sadness as well, I thought.

"Not you, too," he said. " 'Place in the universe?' 'The spirit of anarchy?' Pardon me while I puke. When they started taking this shit seriously they were through. Who needs to go to comic books for Meaning? What kind of a moronic pinhead wants comic books to have meaning . . . ?" His face was bright red again. "One son of a bitch wrote that I represent an earlier stage of consciousness—the id. So now I'm old-fashioned, too. . . ."

There was no stopping him. From the corner of my eye I noticed Bizarro returning from down the hall, carrying two steaming Styrofoam cups. I was thinking, Thank God. Get me out of this. "Look at this," Mxyzptlk said. "It's two hundred degrees in this place and he's drinking coffee."

KLTPZYXM!

175

I saw Bizarro notice my expression—a quick moment of recognition, but unmistakable. After a moment, he said, "Mr. Mxyzptlk, me got fan letter but me can't read. . . ." and I saw an envelope in his hand, which he was holding out for the imp.

Almost apoplectic with irritation, M snatched it out of Bizarro's hand. "Moron . . . the one who can't even read gets fan letters, and me, with the sociology degree from Brandeis, nobody gives a shit I'm alive. . . ."

"You have a sociology degree from Brandeis?" I said.

"All right, it was honorary. But still . . . Okay, what is this," he said, pulling out the letter and unfolding it. " *'Dear Bizarro, You am my favorite Superman character.'* Jesus," Mxyzptlk said, "this guy writes like you talk." Frowning, he went on reading, " *'Me like when you Kltpzyxm. . . .'* "

A deafening crack and the smell of sulfur; I was blind, I was trying to open my eyes, I was in the middle of a cloud of smoke, clearing a little, and then I realized I was on the floor.

"What happened?" I said. Bizarro was looking down at me, offering his hand to help me up.

"Me trick him into saying name backward and now he go back to Fifth Dimension for ninety days. Me learn trick from Superman."

I was sitting in my chair, dusting myself off, and Bizarro was looking at me proudly, smiling.

"Wow," I said, with genuine admiration. "I always thought that was one of the hardest things Superman had to do."

"Me bizarre," Bizarro said, "but me not stupid. Want coffee?"

# CHRIS OFFUTT

One of my earliest memories is my father reading aloud the *Classics Illustrated* version of *The Legends of King Arthur*. I listened with rapt attention, following carefully as he moved his finger from panel to panel. He used different voices for the characters—Arthur, Merlin, Lancelot, Guinevere—and he read the prose narratives in a natural way that clearly set the scenes. →

Dad grew up in a log cabin in Kentucky, a product of the Depression and World War II. Eventually I learned that his father was a dairy farmer who despised comic books and forbade Dad from reading them. Dad didn't want to continue this transgenerational pattern of taboo, and began supplying me with comics before I could read.

Dad worked as a traveling salesman for Procter & Gamble food products in rural Kentucky. Many stores had a small comic book rack. To get credit for unsold comics, the proprietors merely had to tear the covers off and return them to the publishing company. They were supposed to destroy the actual comic, but some didn't. Each time Dad came home from sales trips, he set his briefcase on the table and went upstairs to change out of his worn traveling suit. He came back downstairs and very slowly opened the briefcase, while looking at me with a serious and dramatic expression. This was a ritualistic event: a warrior presenting a sword to his apprentice. Dad placed in my hands a dozen coverless comics. Most were Archies, but occasionally a surprise would emerge—the genres of war, western, crime-fighting, or horror. I read every word in them several times over.

Comic books were not available in my tiny community of Haldeman, a former mining town that had been owned and governed by the mineral company until the late forties. The subsequent decline was swift, then gradual. I grew up on dirt roads surrounded by woods, empty mines, and crumbling buildings. We had one store and its goods were limited to cigarettes, candy, pop, bread, milk, and a few canned goods. The only place to buy comics was Morehead, population 5,000—the biggest town within the Appalachian Mountains of eastern Kentucky. I went to town once a week, accompanying my mother when she bought groceries on Saturday. I spent the rest of the week walking the creek beside the blacktop road, gathering dirty pop bottles in a paper grocery bag. Often the bag split from the wet bottles and I hid my stash in the weeds until I could return with a fresh bag. On Saturday I took the bottles to town, converted them to cash, and bought comic books. The grocery store comics were in rough shape from being pawed over by children whose mothers were shopping. The drugstore comics were not as ragged but the covers were often stained because you were allowed to read them if you sat at the counter and drank an ice-cream soda. I tried subscribing but the comics arrived in a battered state. Finally I learned to visit the drugstore the day the new comics arrived so I could choose the most pristine copies.

This was during the late sixties. I didn't know anyone else who was interested in comic books, let alone collected them. I'm sure there were town kids who read comics, but they considered themselves superior to those of us who lived out in the country. I was thus spared the endless arguing over DC versus Marvel; who would win in a fight between Hulk and Thing, between Batman and Daredevil, between the Avengers and the Justice League of America; why no one ever shot Superman with a Kryptonite bullet; whether Mary-Jane or Gwen was a better catch—in short, the endless array of disputes that accomplish absolutely nothing except the hapless bonding of misfit boys.

Instead of a buddy, I had my father. Dad was a Spider-Man fan precisely because Peter Parker was neurotic. Dad took great pains to explain the difference between neurosis and psychosis, letting me know in a roundabout fashion that he was neurotic and that it was an acceptable malady. Iron Man struggled with alcoholism. Daredevil was blind. The Thing had an inferiority complex. The last remaining people from Superman's home planet were shrunk and lived in a jug. Captain America felt guilty over the death of Bucky. The Fantastic Four were a hyper-dysfunctional family. The X-Men were one classic set of institutional oddballs overseen by a paternal figure. And let's face it— Batman was an out-and-out sociopath protected by weather. That Peter Parker and my father were neurotic was no big deal.

As a kid, I read thousands of comic books—literally thousands. My bedroom shelves held piles of my favorite titles. Comics were stacked against the wall, beneath my plywood desk, in the closet, and under the bed. To prevent my younger siblings from damaging my best comics, I provided them with some ratty ones that I didn't care about—the castoff dregs of my collection. No one touched my main comics except my father and me.

There were no museums or art galleries in Appalachia. We received one TV channel, and the reception was fuzzy because the broadcast traveled through the hills from the foreign land of West Virginia. The only movie theater showed the same movie for up to a month. The result was my absolute reliance on comic books for visual art of any kind. Comics stood in for television and film.

In addition to reading the stories and letters in each issue, I studied all the advertisements. These were further evidence of a world that existed beyond the hills. Out yonder it was acceptable to stroll the streets wearing X-ray glasses, which allowed the wearer to actually see a lady's underwear beneath her clothes. You could get motorized go-kart kits, Judo lessons, a book safe, magic tricks, a seven-foot replica of Frankenstein's monster, genuine gold nuggets from Alaska, a hypno-coin, a spy camera. I pored over these ads, enthralled by possibility. The addresses were nearly all in New York or California, and I imagined the grand lives of kids who lived in those places. The detailed advertisements confirmed what I had already suspected—I lived in a place bereft of anything I liked. Comic books were my only window to life beyond the dark woods that surrounded my house.

At night and on the weekends my father wrote fantasy and science fiction, and began publishing in 1970. He and my mother attended science fiction conventions, known as cons, which included comic book dealers in the huckster rooms. At that time, before the era of highly specialized conventions, SF cons were a sort of countercultural, subcultural, proto-multicultural catchall. In other words, cons welcomed every underground freak in the country. Cons hosted comic book fans, *Star Trek* fanatics, B-movie buffs, vampire lovers, the fully costumed members of the Society for Creative Anachronism, dragonophiles, hobbiteers, and all manner of highly intelligent pariah, ne'er-do-well, scofflaw, misanthrope, and garden-variety nutjob. Cons were like a high school marching band or college theater department—a place where geeks could meet and feel safe. As a smart hillbilly kid who spent most of his time alone in the woods, I fit right in.

Many of the attendees were young hippies. Others were former beatniks. An astonishing number were quite overweight but completely comfortable with their bodies. The whole atmosphere was rife with a splendid liberty that included skinny-dipping in the hotel pools, pot-smoking everywhere, outrageously provocative clothing, and sexual rendezvous left and right. Many people went about armed with swords and space guns, wearing elaborate costumes carefully crafted from descriptions in their favorite books. Others spent the entire con hunched over a novel, reading in public as if doing something that was taboo.

My family never had an official vacation. Not once did we visit the ocean, a lake, or an amusement park. We never went camping, visited museums, attended ballgames, or stayed with relatives. Instead, all six of us drove to the cons that were close—Cincinnati, Nashville, and Champaign-Urbana. My brother and I shared an ancient leather suitcase with a canvas flap that divided the interior in half. My side contained comic books, with plenty of room to bring home my acquisitions. I wore the same clothes the entire time, which actually aligned me with the majority of con attendees who shared a similar habit. My parents had a room in one wing of the hotel. My three siblings and I shared a room on the opposite side of the building. At twelve, I was allowed to roam freely, independence granted through possession of my own room key.

Fans treated my parents like royalty. Mom wore miniskirts and no bra, unheard of in the hills of Kentucky but acceptable at cons. Dad dressed in bell-bottoms, wide belts, and open-necked shirts with long, pointed collars. His hair was longish. Mom's was pixie short. They were a compelling couple in this strange three-day world occurring at a distant hotel. I loved how they dressed, how they laughed a lot, and how everyone liked them.

Science fiction conventions introduced me to the world of serious comic collecting—the use of plastic bags for protection, the *Overstreet Guide,* and the prolonged tactics of barter. Because I was the son of a writer, I was always able to "rent" part of a table in the huckster room, which meant relieving the actual dealer during the slow times. I then bought comics cheap from the other dealers and doubled the price. Naturally I plowed my profits back into the comics I wanted.

At one of these early SF cons I encountered my first T.H.U.N.D.E.R. Agents comic book, and quickly gathered every issue. The art was fantastic, particularly that of Wally Wood, the tragic genius of comic book art. T.H.U.N.D.E.R. was an acronym for "The Higher United Nations Defense Enforcement Reserves," a secret government agency that battled the Warlord, an archvillain bent on global domination. He was aided by the Iron Maiden, a glamorous and brilliant woman clad in silver armor and a red cloak. The T.H.U.N.D.E.R. Agents were composed of a few super-agents—Dynamo, Menthor, and NoMan. Dynamo wore a belt that activated a change in his atomic structure, transforming him into the strongest man alive. Menthor wore a helmet that gave him the psychic powers of telepathy and telekinesis. There was also the T.H.U.N.D.E.R. Squad that ran black ops of infiltration and clandestine attacks. The squad included Kitten, the only female agent, who was described as being a "technical device expert." Although Kitten was blonde and gorgeous, I preferred the sexy wiles of the evil Iron Maiden, a desire that would unwittingly follow me far into adulthood, as I sought my own brand of femme fatale.

The super-agent NoMan was an android with pale blue skin, no facial expressions, and two black shadows for eyes. His secret power was a cloak of invisibility, activated by a dial in the clasp of his cape. This transformation was vividly depicted with ghostly striations that seemed to linger in the wake of his disappearance. He had a number of synthetic bodies, each with a receiver implanted in its head. NoMan could only occupy a single android at a time, but he could transfer his consciousness from one body to another at will, regardless of how far apart they were. When the body he currently inhabited was a few seconds away from being destroyed by a villain, he merely transferred his mind into another android. Some were stored back at T.H.U.N.D.E.R. Headquarters, but he soon learned the advantage of traveling with a spare blue body. NoMan immediately became my favorite comic book superhero.

My ambition as a boy was to be a comic book creator and I made several comic books, including the adventures of Catboy, Kid Knockout, the Buccaneer, and Fatman. I drew them on spiral-bound notebooks with wide-ruled pages, the same style of notebook I use today for writing. The T.H.U.N.D.E.R. Agents inspired me to write and draw the adventures of Buck Jagger, Agent of T.R.U.M.P.E.T. My father read *Trumpet* magazine, an above-average slick SF fanzine from Texas. One of my finest memories of childhood was coming downstairs in the morning and finding a piece of paper carefully placed on the table with the word T.R.U.M.P.E.T. in big letters. Printed vertically below each letter were the words that formed the acronym Dad had written for me: "The Raiders United to Master and Punish Errant Traitors."

Comic book crime-fighters are loners. Most young comic book fans are equally isolated. We were the smart kids who were lousy at sports—neighborhood outcasts who found in comic books an imaginary world that removed us from our dreary circumstances. Naturally, most boys identify with super-characters of great strength and invulnerability.

It has recently struck me as quite strange that I would identify so strongly with NoMan, a character who was essentially nonexistent, nothing more than an intangible consciousness. But the more I examined my interest in him, the more it made sense. NoMan was the most isolated of characters, which mirrored the degree of loneliness I felt growing up in a community of two hundred surrounded by the Daniel Boone National Forest in the Appalachian Mountains of eastern Kentucky. Life within the region was difficult. Unemployment was high, firearms were common, and alcohol was readily available. The threat of violence was always present in the hills. Car wrecks, shootings, and jail time were common among the men. The physical environment itself, for all its sheer beauty, is very tough to traverse. It's a slanty land, heavily wooded, with steep cliffs and narrow creeks. I was perpetually recovering from injuries sustained by the reckless abandon with which I played in the woods.

Having enormous strength wouldn't necessarily help me in the hills. Neither would speed or agility or telepathy or magic or powerful weapons. Instead I craved the ultimate safety of invisibility—which I found by wandering the woods alone. I was NoBoy. I wanted a spare body to withstand the various difficulties of a rough-and-tumble childhood. Having a spare body would allow me to return home rapidly when I was deep in the woods at dusk. NoMan's detachment protected him, and I was envious.

As a boy, I also envied the life of rocks, believing them to have the ideal existence. They could not be hurt. Nothing was expected of them. Their crucial flaw was the inability to move on their own. I believed that I helped them by throwing rocks on a daily basis. I also transported many rocks home, and often stored them in my bed, believing their presence would keep me safe. Every night I slept with rocks.

At the top of the steps where I presently live, conveniently located near my bedroom, stands a bookshelf containing more than sixty collections of bound comic books and graphic novels. The pile of books on my bedside table includes comics as well as poetry and fiction. It now seems natural that I would envy NoMan's safety and his mobility in the world. His flaw was an inability to know the love of a woman, but that didn't matter to me in childhood. Now, many years later, divorced and living alone, I sometimes wonder if I suffer the same cruel defect.

My house is full of rocks, some I've had since childhood, but I don't envy them anymore. Neither do I envy comic book characters or town kids or people living in California and New York. I no longer yearn for the safety of living as an invisible android. But I still read comic books and wander the woods, and sometimes I miss that crazy blue skin.

# GREIL MARCUS

Out of the pages comes the cry of patriotism: a strangled cry sounding out like a bugle call. That's the noise the two-issue comic book *U.S.—Uncle Sam* made in 1997. It's the language Americans have heard all their lives, in the schoolroom, on the nightly news, coming out of the mouths of leaders and used to sell everything from cars to wars to books—that language now wrapped around your neck like a rope. ➔

The premise of *Uncle Sam* was a paradox. The country may have betrayed every promise on which it was founded; that means the promises remain to be kept. That is not the way the story of the country is usually seen. At the time *Uncle Sam* appeared, it was John Grisham's legal thrillers that most directly addressed the question of the nation as ideal and fact, and they told the story very differently.

Beginning with *The Firm* in 1991, Grisham's strongest novels all pointed toward escape. What made a typical 1990s Grisham hero was his or her willingness to flee, to leave it all behind: job, family, country. At their most radical, as with *The Runaway Jury* (1996) and *The Partner* (1997), Grisham's books describe a national disease: a system of corruption that links public institutions, the law, corporations, and crime until none is distinguishable from the other, until the only choice a decent man or woman can make is to steal from thieves and disappear. The hero perpetrates a brilliant scam; reaps an unimaginable fortune; and abandons the United States for the gigantic fraud it has become. The hero takes up residence in a sunny place with nice beaches and loose, if any, banking regulations. The place may be just as corrupt as the United States, but it doesn't pretend to be anything other than what it is. Its air may be as polluted as ours, but not with hypocrisy. There are no national fairy tales of innocence and good intentions, no comforting bedtime stories like the Declaration of Independence or the Gettysburg Address.

What the Grisham hero really leaves behind is illusion. In his or her place of refuge, the hero is at home in whatever racket it is that calls itself a nation because, there at least, no one is fooled. Nothing— no ties of affection, nostalgia, or familiarity, no shared beliefs in liberty, equality, or the greatness of Chuck Berry's "Johnny B. Goode"—binds the Grisham hero to the land where he or she was born. In truth, except as a plot device, as a hall of mirrors for the hero to smash, in Grisham's books the United States hardly exists at all. And, leaving aside the corruptions immediately preceding the Grisham era, and erupting as Grisham's books followed one upon the other—the Nixon administration; the corporate state envisioned in Ronald Reagan's Grace Report; the coup Reagan staged against his own government with the Iran-Contra conspiracy, as was said at the time in essence "Selling off one half of his foreign policy," the insistence he would never negotiate with terrorists, "in order to finance the other half," the overthrow of the Sandinista government in Nicaragua—the presence of the country in Grisham's books as an absence creates a weird kind of thrill: see everything you ever believed in thrown away like a Big Mac box!

The same absence is the presence in *Uncle Sam*, written by Steve Darnall and illustrated and "coplotted" by Alex Ross. The thrill is different: the books are an argument not that the United States can be junked, but that it can't be. Everything you ever believed is going to go up in smoke ("The dream is under fire," runs one caption, "burning down from the inside"), but in *Uncle Sam* that smoke is the air you breathe. It doesn't occur to the authors that there is anywhere else to go—or, given the gigantic contradictions of the truths and lies that make up the U.S.A., that there is anywhere else worth going.

An old man lies crumpled on a big-city sidewalk. He has thin white hair, a long, white goatee, and is dressed in a black coat and red-and-white striped trousers. In the background, people pass on by: a man in a suit carrying a large documents case, two young men in jeans. There's a fat, feeding fly on the old man's smudged forehead. His left arm is stretched out toward you, almost off the edge of the page; his fingers are curled like a beggar's. He looks you right in the eye; his own eyes say he lies on the pavement not to ask for what you've got but to judge how you got it.

He's taken to a hospital ("Walks right into the hotel restaurant and begins assaulting the . . . uh . . . the Savings and Loan guy," an orderly says), then put back on the street. He starts walking—out of the city, and straight out of time. In the course of his travels, the man will find himself in slave ships and jails, modern political conventions and lynch mobs. He'll watch dumbfounded as for a moment a bearded politician turns into Abraham Lincoln. He will visit American killing fields: the battlefields of the Revolutionary War and Shays's Rebellion, the Confederacy's Andersonville concentration camp, the 1832 Illinois massacre of the Blackhawks by the U.S. Army, then a century later the deadly attack by police and hired thugs on striking auto workers in Dearborn, Michigan. All these sights and countless more—rendered in *Die Hard* scale, with big-screen, big-budget drama, heroic perspectives, and frames squeezed for the intensity of a tight close-up—leave the old man desperate and confused, except when his terror turns into comedy. He's half Charlie Chaplin's hideously disheveled tramp in the last shots of the 1931 *City Lights*, breaking down in shame under the gaze of a well-dressed young woman, half Joel McCrea's movie director in Preston Sturges's *Sullivan's Travels* ten years later, living as a railroad bum to research his social protest picture "O Brother, Where Art Thou?" then finding himself under arrest and shocked when the magic words "Don't you know who I am?" only get him a blow on the head.

When the reader first meets Uncle Sam, on the street, in the hospital, he has no idea who he is. All that comes out of his mouth is babble: presidential sound bites, recent political memory vanishing into Uncle Sam's political unconscious. "People have a right to know whether or not their president's a crook," he hears himself saying. "I am not a crook." "Message: I CARE!" "I don't care what the facts are!" "I've signed legislation that will outlaw Russia forever." But as the man begins to walk the streets—as his boots are stolen right off his feet, as he sits in an alley eating garbage from a Dumpster—the voices in his head come from every source. The shape the voices take is textbook schizophrenia; somehow, they remain part of the same shared, national language. The voices bring fragments of cultural speech onto a historical stage, where they seize the nation's political story and tell it as if it were new. "This is not my beautiful house," Uncle Sam says, quoting Talking Heads' "Once in a Lifetime," itself quoting the sermon of an African-American radio preacher. But then in an instant, Uncle Sam is riding in President John F. Kennedy's motorcade in Dallas as Jacqueline Kennedy turns her face to his. "This is not my beautiful wife," Uncle Sam says—and you realize you have gone through the looking-glass of your own house, which is the house Lincoln spoke of in Springfield, Illinois, in 1858: "A house divided against itself."

The books climax with a clash of the titans, the empowered, official, certified Uncle Sam and the derelict towering over the Capitol, two scary old men throwing punches at each other like two Godzillas, but the most powerful stop on Uncle Sam's journey comes when he finds himself in a junk store. He picks up a Dancing Sambo doll and winds the key. "Hey there, Mr. Bones!" he says. "What did they always say at the start of those minstrel shows?" "The crimes of the guilty land will never be purged except with blood," says a black lawn jockey in the corner. "Actually, I think it was 'Gentlemen, be seated,' " Uncle Sam says. "Actually," says the lawn jockey through his huge lips, "*John Brown* said that. Right before they hanged him." And then with a turn of the page you are staring into a panel so stark and luridly composed that you can't immediately see what it is. Uncle Sam and the black jockey are framed by the arms and bloodied face of a black man, hanging upside down. The jockey relates the man's story: He was a great accordion player. One night at a performance in Louisiana, a white woman passed him a handkerchief so that he might wipe his face. White men ambushed him after the show: "By the time they'd finished with him . . . he couldn't remember who he was."

By the end of *Uncle Sam*, after all of the old man's adventures, taking him again and again to the edge of madness, always with a sense of the absurd, of the impossible, the idea of a nation founded on ideals as shining as those of the U.S.A. seems more impossible than anything else. The great battle in the skies of Washington, D.C., is over; the tramp turns up muttering on the street again. A young couple asks if he's all right. "I'm okay. I'm fine," he says, looking at the ground. "We put a dollar in your hat," says the guy. The man is confused again; he wasn't wearing a hat. Then he sees a star-spangled white topper on the street, pulls out the dollar, puts on the hat. As he moves off, singing "Yankee Doodle," a new bounce in his step, he passes under a small, swinging sign with a pyramid topped by an eye. "Novus Ordo Seclorum," it reads: "New Order of the Ages." You might laugh; if you're lucky, you run your fingers over those words every day. Those are the words on the dollar bill. I laughed, but I felt privileged and happy, as if I'd just been told a secret. That the true history of the country should be found in a junk store, or that its motto should turn up as a come-on for—what? The sort of occultist shop where you get your fortune told? A welfare office?—seemed like the perfect shaggy dog joke. "Was that the country I heard?" "Naw, it was just a shaggy dog."

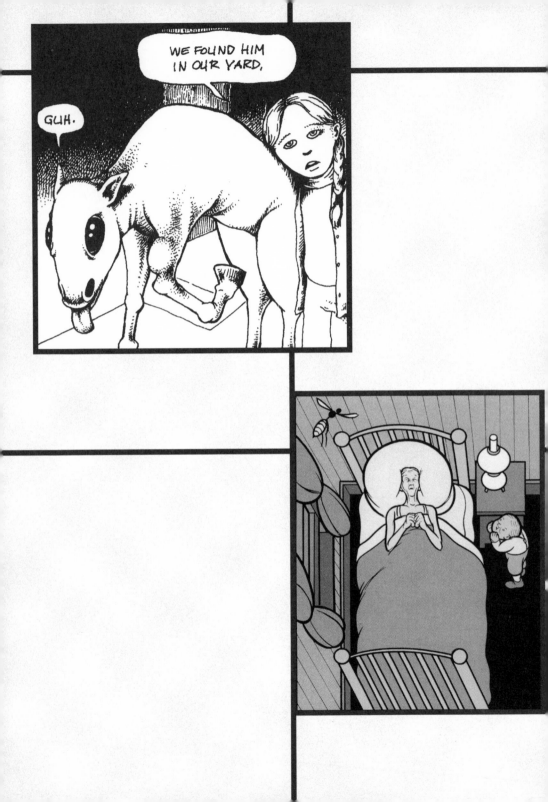

# THE EXQUISITE STRANGENESS AND ESTRANGEMENT OF RENÉE FRENCH AND CHRIS WARE

## MYLA GOLDBERG

In seventh grade, at Lizzy Pond's house, I saw my first comic books. She kept them under the bed, a location I had come to associate with other fathers' *Penthouse*s. I don't know whether Lizzy kept her comic books there because her mother forbade them or because the state of Lizzy's room made it the only reliable storage area, but their concealment lent a thrilling sordidness to the experience. Lizzy collected *Elfquest* and *X-Men*, the former an inarguably girly comic that included an elven romantic interlude in every issue, while the latter was one of the few superhero comics to include female superheroes. That →

afternoon I ignored Lizzy in favor of her comics, which I read with the abandon of a junk-food junkie inhaling a bag of potato chips. The experience, pleasant as it was, reinforced my preference for novels, which remained my preferred mode of escapism. For the next seven years I neither sought out comics nor did they cross my path. In the dearth of evidence to the contrary, I had no reason to expect any comic book could offer a reading experience commensurate to a novel's depth and intricacy. My snobbery lasted until college, at which point it was obliterated by my discovery of alternative comics.

For the first thirty years of its existence, the comic book was primarily a commercial art form, providing continuing narratives that ended in cliffhangers, inducing the purchase of next week's issue. Since the creation of a comic book required both acute visual and narrative talents, the comic book industry—like the film industry—was facilitated by a studio system. At least two and often as many as five people would, according to their individual strengths, divide the artistic demands of a comic to produce timely serials. This model was exploded in the 1960s when artists like Robert Crumb began to utilize the comic book as an instrument for individual expression, giving rise to the notion of the comic book auteur. If comic books, having essentially been invented in the 1930s, qualify as one of our culture's younger art forms, then the alternative comic book—which has been on the scene for less than three decades—is its incredibly precocious infant child.

The alternative comic book shares literature's lofty ambition to explore the human condition in original and resonant ways, with the added advantage that it includes the image in its arsenal. Unlike the passive experience of film, whose characters move and speak without any assistance from the mind of the viewer, the visual experience of the comic mandates outside participation, for it is still the imaginative, self-motivated act of reading that puts this world into motion and brings its characters to life. The result is an experience that inserts itself into the brain with both the intellectual force of text and the visceral force of the image, which at their best combine to create an intensity of experience mere text can't hope to match.

The catch, of course, is that this is extraordinarily difficult. It's tough enough to be a good writer or a good artist: either ambition generally involves a lifetime of hard labor, isolation, and self-doubt. Cartoonists tend to be superlative artists and mediocre storytellers, or excellent storytellers and average artists. This is their curse. And while most people are perfectly happy to appreciate a pretty picture or to lose themselves in a good story when these two intentions are discrete, their combination creates raised expectations. Merely enjoying one or the other will no longer do. The act of storytelling, no matter what its medium, contains the promise of escape, and for that escape to be complete there can't be any flimsy patches in the means of transport. Images have to meet or preferably surpass whatever a reader's imagination can supply, and narrative has to live up to the richness of the visual world that contains it. Most cartoonists are understandably unequal to such a task, consequently limiting their readership and their renown. For that reason, when cartoonists emerge who freakishly possess the ability to nest a complex narrative within a fully realized and compelling visual milieu, it is time to sound the trumpets. And so:

Renée French!!

Chris Ware!!

Maybe because I am a novelist I treasure the experience of reading a novel above all other pursuits, or maybe it's the other way around and I became a novelist because I could imagine no finer ambition than to attempt to provide for others the experience I hold in supreme regard. Whatever the ontology, I've never been shy about my bias: I rank the novel first among artistic endeavors. This preamble is to make absolutely clear my admiration and excitement when I say that reading Ware's work—more than the work of any other cartoonist I have encountered—is like reading a really good novel. The world he creates is utterly absorbing and multifaceted; it possesses an inner life that extends far beyond the page; and it is a powerful conduit not only for the thoughts and experiences of its creator, but for its readers.

Renée French's work amazes for precisely the opposite reason: it does things a novel cannot. As a novelist, this makes me both jealous and giddy. A novel is immersive, luring a reader into a world page by page to deliver its truths, which must first filter through the brain of the reader, where the cerebral alchemy of translating words into actual thoughts and feelings occurs. French's work is vascular in effect, conferring an intimacy that is immediate and intense and utterly unachievable through any other medium. Her images require no mental translation because they're already inside us, tucked into recesses beyond the reach of plain text. Reading Renée French can feel like uncovering a previously neglected sense organ—a second nose, perhaps, or a newborn stretch of exquisitely sensitive skin. Her work is an essential reminder that comparing the alternative comic book to other mediums is of limited value: its intrinsic power demands reckoning on its own terms.

An exquisite paradox about reading is that while it represents an inherent escape from the self and the larger world the self inhabits, it is simultaneously a quest for communion. One of the most coveted reading experiences is that rare feeling of connection when a story unexpectedly taps into a thought or experience previously assumed by the reader to be so wholly personal or deeply secret that he or she alone possessed it. To discover such a particular experience rendered on a page can feel religious in intensity. A perceived barrier between oneself and the rest of humanity is suddenly removed, and this removal is an embrace. To have this happen is to be reminded that none of us are strangers, and that for all the world's difficulty and obtuseness, we belong in it. The two most obvious areas ripe for this sort of communion—which not coincidentally are the two themes explored most often in stories of all kinds—are love and loss. But even rarer are those stories that touch on something kind of weird, something not universally affecting, something that inhabits a dimmer, less frequently visited corner of human experience.

This is what Renée French does. By definition, she doesn't do it for everyone. Not everyone enjoys the films of David Lynch, for example, but those who do are passionate about them. Like Lynch, French is explicit, she is brilliant, and she is unrelenting, making a tepid reaction to her work impossible.

Renée French is one of the most beautiful renderers of the completely disgusting that I've ever seen. With pointillist ink or soft, fuzzy pencil she labors over all that is strange and unsettling about bodies—their warts, their hairs, their loose or dangly parts. Her intent, however, is not to repulse her readers, but to call attention to the body's delicacy and mortality and to our fears surrounding these truths. She brings to her work a child's morbid fascination with disease, anomaly, and sexuality but with an adult's sensibility and perception, reminding us that the fact of having lived with our bodies for any length of time doesn't make them any less bizarre or wonderful, and that it is okay and even important to take a long, hard look at nostrils, skin, and moles. The guides to these truths tend to be children—children with freckles and large, Margaret Keane eyes—who inhabit a world ruled by unsavory urges and filled with misshapen animals and secretive adults. The uncertainty and pungency of this world is counterbalanced by its beauty. This is where the work's specific power as a comic book comes into play, because the style of the art that accompanies French's stories absolutely defies expectation.

In her story "The Ninth Gland," two girls come across a distressed horselike animal with a strange lump on its leg. As the animal seems to be in great pain—and because their curiosity is too great to leave the creature alone—they bring it to their friend Mr. Kittentank, a hospital custodian with a penchant for the anatomical, who presides over the hospital's basement. When Mr. Kittentank decides that surgery is called for, the girls are thrilled and watch raptly as Mr. Kittentank slices open the bulge in the animal's leg to reveal a strange fleshy sac containing an *Eraserhead* version of a baby horse. Were this story told in words alone, the images the mind would create to accompany it would doubtless be dark and menacing, but when French tells the story, the girls appear to have stepped out of a children's book and Mr. Kittentank has a kindly face.

French is an unapologetic sensualist. Her surfaces are rarely ever neutral, instead announcing their moistness, their smoothness, their softness, their hairiness, or their firmness in every panel. French is obsessed with texture and has developed a drawing technique to enable this obsession, her stippling and delicate pencil shadings providing a sensitivity to surface that a simple line would never permit. The results are beautiful and without imitators, likely because it's not only an incredibly difficult style to perfect, but insanely labor-intensive. The resultant forms are lovingly, carefully, and cleanly rendered so that even as the reader is faced with the alien internal anatomy of a bizarre creature the beauty of the image is inescapable. Through her unconventional anatomies French reminds us that the world is larger and stranger than most of us, in our daily lives, care to admit. Though the specifics of her stories often lie outside the realm of daily reality, they are grounded in environments otherwise wholly familiar. The banality of the living rooms, cellars, and kitchens her characters inhabit suggests that anyone can rediscover the stranger side of things if they dare to look close enough.

French's fearless specificity can be simultaneously unnerving and comforting, a disconcerting union I first encountered in a short piece called "Autocannibalism." Reading it, I felt I was being told something secret about myself that I'd never dared to confess because it was too private and embarrassing—something that French not only knew, but had the courage to reveal to the world at large. I will be the first to admit the intensity of my reaction was odd, but that is French's unique power: she can mine the small, strange urges that lie buried within us and polish their peculiar facets to a high shine. In "Autocannibalism,"

French painstakingly describes the process by which a man bites off a small piece of dead skin from his thumb and plays with it in his mouth. The images that accompany this description are repulsive and largely distinct from the action being described: in a living room, a boy torments a daddy longlegs while his obese father sits on an overstuffed chair with his legs spread wide enough for the reader to catch a glimpse of his genitals through his oversized right shorts leg. There is nothing about this scene to win our empathy or our favor; everything about it elicits our revulsion. And yet, by paying attention to such a minute, specific, and private act, French reminds her readers of the small, secretive rituals we perform on our own bodies, bringing us into a strange fellowship with each other and with this man that affirms the universality of even our most seemingly eccentric habits.

I suppose there are people out there who don't pick their noses or their scabs, who don't squeeze pimples or clogged pores, don't bite their nails or cuticles, or suck on their hair. These people will not enjoy Renée French. Even broader among people who won't like Renée French are those who might do those things occasionally—or even habitually—but who are so personally ashamed or disgusted by these private acts that French's work will read like an indictment. For those of us who remain, Renée French is that rare gift among artists—one whose work finds its way into the most guarded corners of our psyches and allows us to revel momentarily in all that is awkward, embarrassing, or sticky about being alive. The care French puts into her images and her clear-eyed, unflinching depictions of human curiosity, eccentricity, and emotion underscore her own wonder, fear, and fascination with the world and with the mysteries of human behavior. In her work the marriage of text and image is completely realized and both beautiful and frightening to behold.

Chris Ware's comics are just as powerful and disturbing as Renée French's, but they achieve their intensity through diametrically op-

203

posed means. Ware is an antisensualist: his line is precisely controlled, his figures flat. The world he evokes is coldly, poignantly beautiful, achieving its hold on the reader through its complete contrast with the welter of emotions and thoughts contained in the text. Since the mainstream press publication of *Jimmy Corrigan, The Smartest Kid on Earth,* Ware's name is known to some non–comics readers, but this small acclaim pales beside the celebrity status he has been accorded within the comics community, where his originality and brilliance are easier to parse because the language he speaks is more familiar.

A typical Chris Ware page teems with panels ranging in size from postage stamp to postcard. The pure density of information can be off-putting, especially to a reader unaccustomed to reading comics. The non–comics reader is, at best, prepared for an orderly page, one that contains perhaps six panels of equal size, divided into three neat rows that can be read from left to right. While this experience is qualitatively different from reading text, it bears enough of a resemblance to be comforting. Ware's pages rarely afford his reader such comfort, instead challenging our most basic assumptions about how to read. Panel groupings confine the eye to the left quadrant of the page before moving the gaze to the right, or force the eye to describe a counterclockwise path around a page's perimeter, the smaller peripheral panels amplifying or deepening a larger central image. Rather than assume in advance how a page is to be parsed, the reader is forced to pay attention to the page's overall composition for reading cues, a deepened level of collaboration that provides Ware another way to impact our reading experience.

Just as Italo Calvino, Julio Cortázar, and John Barth delight in challenging a reader's assumptions upon opening a book, Chris Ware pushes the limits of what a comic book is expected to deliver and how it is expected to be experienced. Using schematic diagrams, Ware places a single scene within the context of a dizzying chronological continuum that can include the various ancestries of his characters, as well as their futures. Playing on childhood associations, Ware interrupts his story with activity pages inviting the reader to construct meticulously devised paper amusements. These original designs range from stand-up figures to zoetropes and foreshadow or reflect the very adult events or settings in the continuing narrative. Encountering these devices was, for me, like reading Dos Passos's *USA Trilogy* for the first time: in both cases I received the electric feeling that I was witnessing an artist pushing the limits of his medium beyond established boundaries, an artistic sense of manifest destiny in which previously unexplored territory was being claimed before my very eyes.

Ware's narrative domain is the pain of isolation and loneliness, and the impossibility of true connection or understanding between friends, family, or lovers. The starkness of his imagery magnifies these assertions, often to a painful degree. By varying the size of his panels and grouping them in such challenging ways, Ware achieves rare control over the pace and focus of the reading experience. Readers of text enjoy a certain liberty within the confines of a story: their eyes can linger in one place or speed past others as they choose, effectively drawing out certain moments while minimizing others. A writer like Gertrude Stein wrested some of this power away from her readers by repeating words and phrases, forcing them to take notice of language, words, and moments they might otherwise disregard. Ware achieves a similar effect through his repetition of images. In *Jimmy Corrigan,* an entire page is given over to a young James Corrigan gazing at a wasp resting on the opposite side of a windowpane. A cluster of postage stamp–sized panels shows the wasp from the boy's point of view from inside his grandmother's house, while the next set of images depicts the identical scene, but this time from outside the window, permitting us to glimpse James's face as he stares at the insect and tentatively brings his finger to the pane to tap at the glass. By devoting an entire page to such a small moment, Ware effectively freezes time, forcing his readers to experience the terrible wait James endures as he stands

in the hallway, doing whatever he can to distract himself while antici-
pating with dread the doctor's call to him from inside his dying grandmother's bedroom.

Ware's images are classically "cartoony." Characters are evoked
with a minimum of lines and shapes. Eyes are simple circles, lacking
lids, pupils, or eyelashes; noses and mouths are curves. The simplicity
of these images is deceptive. These are the sorts of pictures we
enjoyed as children in the form of Sunday funnies and Saturday morning cartoons, images that were rarely threatening or challenging.
Because of this we let our guard down when we first see Ware's work;
we think we know what we are in for. With our defenses thus lowered,
we are confronted by a world of absent fathers and powerless children
grown into powerless adults, a world in which companionship is elu-
sive and love is either absent or suffocating. Betrayed by our expectations, we are effectively thrust into the world Ware depicts, where
people are betrayed as a matter of course, because betrayal is the
inescapable result of being alive. While the specificity of Renée
French's images is what cements her readers in place, Ware achieves
the same effect with his visual generality. Because Ware's world is
largely evoked in outline, the reader is invited to fill in the details, col-
laborating with Ware to flesh out the world he has presented in much
the same way a reader of text utilizes author-supplied details of a character's appearance to create within their imagination a unique creature of flesh and blood.

Like French, Ware is not for everyone. Ware explores discomfiting
psychological realities with the same unnerving specificity and relent-
lessness that French applies to corporeality. Some find his work too
relentlessly depressing to read. However, just as French has managed
to combine artistic maturity with a child's sense of fascination, Ware
puts his impressive intellectual and artistic acumen in the service of
raw emotions and thoughts that adulthood begs us to dilute. To
become successful adults we are expected to put aside our fear of not
fitting in; we are expected to be self-assured and confident. Ware's

work reminds us that the same insecurities that haunted us as children are still very much present in our adult lives. The scenes he creates validate and embrace the vulnerabilities we thought we had to ignore in order to be accepted into the world at large. Ware's work reveals personal, internal terrains whose topographies I had previously sensed but had never so accurately mapped. His unerring ability to define and explore the very psychological bogeymen most of us prefer to keep hidden bestows communion of an intensity that is uncanny and immensely satisfying.

In that Ware and French are not content to simply tell a story, but are continually searching for ways to expand what a story is, what it means, and how it engages its reader, they are very much products of the artistic foment that has defined alternative comics in recent decades. The birth of alternative comics marks the coming of age of artists like Jim Woodring, Jason Lutes, and Daniel Clowes, who, as devoted comics readers, have been seeking ways to expand the capabilities of the medium that influenced and nourished them as children. Though our culture embraces the limitless possibility of paired words and images in its insatiable appetite for film, comics are just beginning to be more widely recognized as a medium of equally expressive and intellectual potential. As a result, cartoonists are about as likely as poets to gain recognition or compensation for their efforts. They create comics only because they can't imagine not creating comics. Perhaps the fact that so few people have been paying attention has fostered the lack of artistic inhibition necessary for the provocative and resonant works of French, Ware, and their colleagues, but most artists are not Emily Dickinson: they want their work to be noticed. Now that the comic book has established itself as a medium of such enduring power, it's time for more people to start reading.

## STEVE DITKO'S HANDS

# ANDREW HULTKRANS

*It's all in the hands.* That's what I have to tell myself. How else can I explain my preference for the stiff, cartoonish, wildly inconsistent, occasionally downright bad art of Steve Ditko—cocreator, most famously, of Spider-Man and Dr. Strange for Marvel Comics—to that of his erstwhile coworker and inarguable superior Jack "King" Kirby, the Miles Davis of comics? It's perverse, outrageous—especially considering how repellent I find Ditko's cultish devotion to the pseudo-philosophy of Ayn Rand (hardly an outing, this: Ditko has spent nearly four-fifths of his fifty-year career promulgating Rand's blinkered views through superhero comics and self-published samizdat). I'd have an easier time →

proving that Syd Barrett was more important than Bob Dylan, or that the Pretty Things should have sold more records than the Rolling Stones. Help me out here. Bear with me. Be patient.

Kirby has all the advantages. He created, with writer/editor Stan Lee, every other classic Marvel character. His dynamic, muscular style influenced more comic artists than that of any other creator. His renderings of architecture and machinery introduced new levels of scale and detail to the medium. His uncanny feel for motion and impact made sound effects superfluous (even if they remained in the panels, turned up to 11). Kirby's output literally and figuratively dwarfs that of most artists to date: Steve Canyon jawlines as wide as the Grand Canyon; hawk-noses that could shatter brick; striated, steroidal arms supported by (god of) thunder thighs; blank, inhuman eyes staring from menacing metallic masks; thick, canvaslike clothing with skin-cutting creases; huge, crevice-scarred boulders; roiling, radioactive miasmas of toxic bubbles; massive, impossibly intricate machines and spacecraft; bazookalike handguns ("bazooka" sounds like a Kirby weapon looks) . . . *Sunset Boulevard*'s Norma Desmond could have been stumping for the Kirby Character Alumni Association when she snarled "I *am* big! It's the pictures that got small."

And yet, on the other hand . . . or hands, there is Ditko—puny Peter Parker to Kirby's Super Skrull, skinny Steve Buscemi to Kirby's Arnold Schwarzenegger, ninety-eight-pound weakling to bully on the beach. Stop kicking sand in my face and I'll tell you about him. If Kirby had been a film director, he would have specialized in Technicolor westerns, war movies, outerspace science fiction, and mythic sword-and-sandal epics. Like John Ford directing John Wayne in Monument Valley. On Mars. Under a flaming sky teeming with asteroids, space junk, hovering demigods, and the entire interplanetary fleet from *2001: A Space Odyssey*. If Ditko had been a director, he would have turned out nervy, attenuated film noir, moralistic sci-fi miniatures with ironic twists in the mode of *The Twilight Zone*, paranoid black-and-white horror reminiscent of *Night of the Living Dead,* and, stay with me here, the Salvador Dalí sequence in Hitchcock's *Spellbound*. Mostly, though, a 1960s Ditko comic resembles a Joseph Lewis or Phil Karlson noir—*The Big Combo*, say, or *Kansas City Confidential*, and let's throw in Rudolph Maté's *D.O.A.*—low-budget yet highly stylized, mingling stiff civilians in street locations with lemon-sucking grotesques in expressionist shadows. I hear you: Nietzschean undertones are *fine*, what in the name of Vishanti does this have to do with *hands*? Hold, as Thor might say. I'm almost there.

Not to sound arrogant, but I have beautiful hands. Hand-model hands, or so I've been told. My fingers are long and slender, and my knuckles are fluid and flexible enough to strike dramatic, widely separated, nearly hyperextended gestures. In other words, I'd make a good signer. Or magician. Or webslinger. When I first got into superhero comics, I must have been around seven or eight, tall for my age but a tad chubby, with the questionable coordination of a kid whose bones were developing faster than his reflexes. But I had lovely, expressive hands. With these hands I played piano, made detailed models of World War II armored vehicles and aircraft, and imitated the gestures I saw in Ditko comics. It was the closest I could get, you see. I had the hair of Thor, and the nickname of "Hulk," but the hands of Steve Ditko—twisty, hyperextended, commanding, yet delicate, graceful, almost feminine. I was the relative size of a Hulk or Thor, but I lacked the necessary strength, rage, and stilted vocabulary to personify these heroes in a satisfying way. I wasn't Incredible. I wasn't even Mighty. I could possibly be Amazing, though, perhaps even a Master of the Mystic Arts. And that, by the Hoary Hosts of Hoggoth, was what I became. I cathected to the panels. I was sutured into the narrative. Suddenly, I was a Ditko disciple. His comics were the only ones that invited me to reach inside their worlds—manually, astrally, emotionally; the only ones with which I could perform shadow-puppet plays from my side of the page-light divide.

But I'm getting ahead of myself. The first Marvel comics I read were those being published in the early seventies, whose value relationship to their Silver Age sixties predecessors was roughly parallel to that of early seventies music to late sixties music—Grand Funk Railroad to the Beatles, in other words, Bread to the Beach Boys. Looking at these comics today, it's clear that the industry was striving to be more adult, more "relevant," but that mattered little to a seven-year-old. If anything, it dampened my enjoyment. When your first media memory is your father sitting you down to watch Nixon's resignation speech on TV, you can be forgiven for wanting to keep your comics reality-free. But the real downer was the art, at least for a kid. An amplification of the increasingly detailed, almost icky physicality of sixties pencillers Gene Colan and Jim Steranko, the visual style of many seventies artists (Neal Adams and Jim Starlin, most obviously) would be named for me in senses literal and onomatopoetic by a word I learned a bit later from H. P. Lovecraft—*eldritch*. Anatomy was more perfectly proportioned and naturalistic, but the outlines of the characters, the cross-hatch shadows on their faces, even the air itself seemed to be made of cobwebs—an unconscious rendering, perhaps, of an optical fuzz I wouldn't experience until my first joint. Hair grew, hiplines fell. Sideburns were in full effect. Green Arrow and Green Lantern paused in the midst of *THWIP! THOK!* action scenes to debate drugs, poverty, and race relations. Horror comics returned after years of Code-enforced exile, and an atmosphere of downbeat, played-out mysticism permeated many superhero books. Starlin's inanely cosmic Captain Marvel, to name one, resembled an emissary from a black-light poster floating in a galaxy far, far away.

Such earnest politics and head-shop aesthetics transmitted the era's free-floating malaise to my tender brain, but I could only process the message as an abstraction: "There's something wrong." Filtered through the blame-the-messenger mentality of childhood, this quickly translated to: "There's something wrong with superhero comics." It wasn't long before the Silver Age art in archival hardcovers like *Origins of Marvel Comics, Son of Origins, Bring on the Bad Guys,* and especially in the gimmicky *Marvel Treasury Editions,* which reprinted strings of classic sixties stories—Kirby's widescreen Galactus saga from *Fantastic Four* #48–50, a lap of Ditko's genre-defining *Spider-Man* run—in massive tabloid format, rendered the contemporary stuff worthless. Having encountered my comic book Damascus, I embarked on a quest for twelve-cent Marvels—an arduous pursuit for an older-siblingless kid in the mid-seventies, comics stores and collector culture being not nearly as pervasive as they are today.

Lucky for me, then, that Marvel also seemingly lacked confidence in its current bullpen and began reprinting Silver Age series under generic monikers: *Marvel Tales* (Ditko-through-Romita Spider-Man), *Marvel Adventure* (Colan Daredevil), *Marvel Spectacular* (Kirby Thor), and the tellingly (accurately?) titled *Marvel's Greatest Comics* (Kirby Fantastic Four). (With hindsight, I attribute my terrible, impoverishing helplessness in the face of the remastered-with-bonus-tracks CD to my affection for these reprints.) I scooped up the reissues monthly and devoured them instantly, returning to contemporary material only in select cases—the new, overcrowded X-Men (which I ended up disliking fairly soon—art too eldritch, characters too absurdly international), the Defenders (a thrown-together anti-team with a rotating-door membership of every volatile or problematic hero in the Marvel pantheon), the Hulk (my childhood namesake and also a Defender, granting the fellow a previously hidden cooperative spirit that was less than, well, credible), and occasionally, Spider-Man and Fantastic Four (which, held up to their Silver Age forebears, didn't stand a chance).

Had I been old enough to understand the concept of nostalgia, I might have thought my retro snobbery pathetic, and, in a way, it was—still is. But that was the lot of children of the seventies (perhaps children ever since): too young to have been there for any seismic shifts in pop culture, too young, even, for the first tremors of hip-hop and punk. Today I realize that those reprints, along with a set of H. G. Wells novels, *The Twilight Zone*, the 1930s Universal horror movies aired on *Chiller*, and the Beatles' Red and Blue albums, were my first windows into cultural history, my first inkling that the newest wasn't

213

always the best, especially (if paradoxically) in pop. This was a lesson worth learning, and one I still carry with me as an adult, which is maybe more than you'd expect from drawings of spandex-clad mutants spouting ten-dollar insults and cheap wisecracks as they attempt to annihilate each other in the process of saving/controlling/destroying the world.

Or maybe not. The intervening years have seen the justifiable and largely successful efforts of creators and fans to make comics worthy of adults (Exhibit #8,166: this book) and even capital-A art, so it's been easy to forget how mortally *embarrassing* superhero comics were once a boy reached "a certain age" (usually twelve or thirteen—fourteen was pushing it, beyond lay the Forbidden Zone). Like Tamiya models and Testors glue, like that dalliance with *Dungeons & Dragons* or those disco 45s, or perhaps more than anything else, like Kiss, superhero comics seemed not merely incompatible with the fantastic new realms of girls, "serious" rock music, and intoxicants, but their dimensional opposite—antimatter to all that mattered in adolescence. Attempting to impress a cute fifteen-year-old girl with your *Spider-Man* collection was akin to asking her out in fluent Vulcan, fingers spread in a hard-won V. It just wasn't done.

So into a box they went, every last one of them, taped and tagged and destined for the deepest recesses of the closet. During my high-school years it would have been easier for my mother to find my pot or pornography than to unearth that hidden cache of comics with all their squirmy prepubescent freight. It still baffles me why I even allowed them to remain in the apartment. Throughout the eighties I stayed strictly comic-free, even if I silently cheered the occasional image of, or reference to, Silver Age heroes in the pop landscape, which, with the emergence and influence of that tireless engine of postmodernism, MTV, became increasingly frequent. Little did I know, so sophomorically concerned was I at the time with movies, mixtapes, and Literature, that an erudite, streetwise bunch of inkheads—Frank Miller, Alan Moore, Grant Morrison, and others—

were re-creating superhero comics by de-creating them, tracing their heroes' exit strategies instead of their origin stories, thereby making men-in-tights comics safe, or at least not scaldingly shameful, for adult males and, ulp, *females*. (True! My reintroduction to superhero comics came in the early nineties via a pass-along copy of Miller's *Batman: The Dark Knight Returns* from the approving, just-read-it-think-you'd-like-it hands of my girlfriend of the time, who, I swear, was not a gamer, a furrie, or an Otherkin.)

After Miller's truly dark trawl through the bubbling sludge of Bruce Wayne's middle-age psychopathology came Moore's sweeping, novelistic excoriation of vigilantism and the superhero's raison d'être, *Watchmen,* and I found myself furtively drifting into comics stores again (there were good ones in Berkeley, where I was living at the time), admiring the abundance of well-preserved, shrink-wrapped twelve-cent issues in neatly packed rows. This secret, sweaty reconnaissance went on until I had reached such a pitch of delirium that I flew back to New York to dig up that box of comics in my deeply unpleasant stepfather's country house (my mother having died a couple of years earlier), a mission that entailed confronting this man (already bad relations had degenerated), rejecting other of my mother's and my possessions that I probably would be quite happy to have if I ever woke up one morning to discover that I was a sensible adult, and pointing to the back of a closet (always the back, even when I wasn't in charge of them) and saying, "THAT! I want THAT! Nothing else, thank you, just THAT. Thanks! I'll be leaving now. . . ." and rushing out of the house and into the car with this large, wilted moving box on my shoulder and driving out of there feeling for all the world like I had just rescued a kidnapped version of myself from the arthritic claws of adulthood.

But back to Steve Ditko, or "Steverino," as cheeky Stan Lee often referred to him in what must have been a good-natured jibe, so impossible is it to reconcile the reclusive, sanctimonious, hard-line Objectivist, Fritz Lang-in-flannel figure of Ditko with this sobriquet, or indeed any grouping of sounds that would result in a word like

215

"Steverino." Ditko *qua* Platonic ideal is anti-erino, -oodles, -ado-cious . . . all silly suffixes. Which is one of the reasons why Steve and Stan, a silly suffix slanger on the order of Rob Schneider's copy-room guy on *Saturday Night Live,* were ultimately destined for divorce. Their prickly, or at least unlikely, working relationship was laid bare to fans at the peak of the pair's success in a three-page addendum to *Amazing Spider-Man Annual* #1 (1964), titled "How Stan Lee and Steve Ditko Create Spider-Man!" At the time, Lee fueled nascent Marvel fandom with his revolutionary blend of self-referentiality and ironic self-deprecation, but this was something else: an uncomfortably frank air-ing of his credit-grabbing, artist-effacing M.O. that couldn't have made original Spider-fans feel good about their favorite comic book. In the strip, written by Lee, drawn by Ditko, Lee awakes in the middle of the night with a story idea, phones Ditko, then after a late-night story con-ference, says "How *about* that, Stevey Boy?!! And just for kicks, we'll do *twelve* panels to each page!" To which a beleaguered Ditko replies, "Waddaya mean *we*?? *I* do the drawing while you practice signing your *name* all over!" Panels later, after Ditko pencils the new story and Lee mentions "a similar fight with Jack Kirby," the collaborators meet again:

> Lee: *Ptui!* It looks like you're learning to draw with your eyes *shut*!
> Ditko: *You* should talk after that corny *script* you wrote!
> Lee: Waddaya *mean* "corny"?? I copied it from one of the best classics I could find!
> Ditko: My friend *Sam* can write better than you—and he's a cocker spaniel!
> Lee: *Ah ha!! He's* probably the one who does your *inking* for you!
> Ditko: How come you don't use some of those gags in your scripts??
> Lee: What *for?* You'd only ruin them with your—ugh—art-work!

This sarcastic strip foreshadowed the Great Marvel Credit War of the late seventies, in which Jack Kirby's colleagues and fans waged an ultimately successful campaign to secure for the artist cocreator status on his Silver Age characters and plots and wrest his original artwork pages from the corporate clutches of Lee and Marvel. Although he was subject to the same chiseling work-for-hire contracts as Kirby, Ditko remained silent on this matter until recently. Unlike Kirby (or any other Marvel artist), however, Ditko received plotting credit as early as *Amazing Spider-Man* #25 (1965), an unprecedented concession that was most likely the result of Ditko's contemporaneous discovery of Ayn Rand's Objectivism, with its hatred of creative dilution and unearned rewards. But because Ditko never owned the copyright on the character or costume of Spider-Man, to date Marvel's most visible trademark, or had any legal rights to their creation, he hasn't reaped the considerable profits that Spidey has generated for the company since his 1962 debut. Nor has he actively sought them. It wasn't until the late nineties that the notoriously private, press-shy Ditko began to lobby for his rightful status as Spider-Man's cocreator, albeit in oblique, quasi-philosophical Objectivist tracts published in small quantities by Ditko fan and collaborator Robin Snyder. This effort eventually resulted in the twin triumphs of 2002, when Ditko was officially acknowledged by Marvel (in the pages of the contemporary *Amazing Spider-Man* comic) and by Sam Raimi's blockbuster film, which ran Ditko's name along with Lee's in the movie's credits. It isn't known whether this overdue recognition resulted in any monetary compensation for the artist, who, unlike Kirby, is still alive.

Like filmmaking, superhero comics are, with some exceptions, a collaborative medium, so it's impossible to know who was purely responsible for what unless you were among the involved parties. Even then, memory is imperfect and egos rarely impartial, particularly when the creation is a global smash on the level of Spider-Man. Nevertheless, after digesting the vociferous debates of obsessive fans, the writings of Lee and Ditko over the years, and what is known about Ditko's background, some educated guesses can be floated. Ditko was born in Johnstown, Pennsylvania, in 1927 to a family of Slavic descent. A shy, nerdy kid, he spent most of his childhood and adolescence in the company of his tightly knit family and between the panels of Will Eisner's *The Spirit* and Jerry Robinson's *Batman,* both of which became primary touchstones for his own artwork. According to Cat Yronwode, a Dr. Strange fanatic who researched Ditko over many years for a book project that never materialized, visual aspects of Peter Parker's life and surroundings could be directly tied to Ditko's high-school experience in Johnstown—architectural details of Parker's school building, for instance, and the model for his bullying nemesis Flash Thompson were both clearly present in Ditko's high-school yearbooks. Parker's profile as a bookish, bespectacled, socially ostracized, family-devoted teen also closely matched Ditko's own. The noirish urban moodiness and chiaroscuro lighting of Ditko's Spider-Man comics, as well as their cast of bizarre, grotesque villains (the Green Goblin, the Vulture, Dr. Octopus, the Lizard, Mysterio), owed a great debt to Eisner and Robinson. (When he first came to New York, Ditko studied under Robinson at the Cartoonist and Illustrators School, now known, with an expanded curriculum, as the School of Visual Arts.) Parker's boss and Spider-Man's most vocal critic, newspaper editor and consummate blowhard J. Jonah Jameson, seemed to be a repository for all of Ditko's proto-Objectivist bile as the conniving, hero-hating, tabloid smear artist, heralding Ditko's real-life contempt for the press. Finally, it has never been disputed, even by Lee, that Ditko was solely responsible for Spidey's iconic costume design, which, among its myriad qualities, was unusual at the time for its full-face mask—a crucial element that, along with the concept of the teenager-as-superhero, allowed for broad reader identification.

Lee should be credited, first and foremost, for making Marvel Comics possible—by rescuing Martin Goodman's Atlas Comics from financial ruin in 1957 and having the eye to hire Ditko and Kirby; this trio, beginning in 1961 with Lee/Kirby's *Fantastic Four* #1, would have the same impact on comics as the Beatles would on popular music. Lee's contributions to Spider-Man include the name, the concept (based on an undeveloped, pre-Marvel Kirby character) of an orphaned teenage boy with spider powers, the hero's wisecracking fighting style, Peter Parker's adolescent neuroses, his internal conflicts over his secret identity, his difficulties with girls, and all the soap-operatic aspects that humanized and propelled the narrative in a manner unique for the time and unquestionably Lee. And, of course, the self-reflexive, silly suffix-ridden dialogue.

Although Ditko's role as cocreator has been appallingly minimized over the years, it's safe to say that Spider-Man wouldn't have won such a wide readership without Lee's touch. It was Lee, after all, who initiated a paradigm shift in superhero comics by insisting that heroes not only have Achilles heels—Kryptonite, anyone?—but genuine physical handicaps, a full range of human feelings and failings, and perennial difficulties because of, not in spite of, their powers. As Ditko fell under the sway of Objectivism, his concept of a hero became more and more capital H: unswervingly righteous, generally infallible, unconcerned with Miranda rights or jury trials—Superman as a merciless right-wing extremist, essentially, or Dirty Harry with superpowers. Needless to say, this uncompromising vision was increasingly out of step with Lee's Marvel and its archetype of the imperfect, fallible, neurotic hero. Ultimately, Ditko walked out on Spider-Man (and Marvel) in 1966, reportedly due to conflicts with Goodman over the book's direction (more pretty girls) and Lee concerning the Green Goblin's identity (Lee: father of Parker's friend; Ditko: a nobody). Goodman and Lee would get their way, and increased sales, with the pleasantly smooth, romance-comic curviness of John Romita, Spidey's most popular artist. But enough about your friendly neighborhood cash cow, I'm really here to profess my love for what I always considered to be Ditko's peak achievement, Dr. Strange. And his hands. Steve Ditko's hands.

*"Unless I shatter this web of wonderment, all is lost! My mission will be forgotten—I will be doomed to a life of aimless imagery!"*
—*Strange Tales* #137

Make a heavy metal, devil-horns hand signal, thumb out straight, with your right hand. Hold at eye level with palm facing away from you, horns up. Then make the same gesture with your left hand. Hold at chest level with your wrist turned over, horns down. Presto! You're a figure from early Christian iconography—er, I mean, you're Dr. Strange! I wasted many childhood hours striking these and other Ditkoid gestures in front of a mirror—secret signs for a gang of one. I would imagine that the mirror was a portal to another dimension where the laws of time and space (as well as taste and palette) were bent beyond belief—the spindly shadow realm of Nightmare, say, or the demented Dalíscape of that irritating interdimensional hothead, the Dread Dormammu, or the relatively spartan Purple Dimension, indifferently overseen by Aggamon the All-Powerful. There, at the other side of Nowhere, vortex churning into vertigo, I would encounter Stygian voids, Spinybeasts, Cubes of Nothingness composed of Ribbons of Nihility, the gargantuan Gulgol, the inexorable, cyclopean Mindless Ones, and sundry weird domains existing in twilight areas on the edges of infinity.

I would mention here that Ditko's highly imaginative, protopsychedelic mystical dimensions are hard to describe, but as ever, Stan Lee already did—within the pages of *Strange Tales* itself. In issue #138, Dr. Strange casts an obscure spell that transforms his magic amulet into a porthole to the dimension of Eternity (an impossibly powerful character, not a concept). Jumping into the open amulet, Strange suddenly finds himself in—get ready—a Miró–Escher–Eero Saarinen collaboration on a virtual reality game for the Jetson family. That's the best I can do—really. Here's Lee's try: "Dr. Strange beholds . . . for the first time . . . the dazzling, description-defying dimension of . . . *Eternity!*" See? Dr. Strange, in keeping with his unflappable nature, merely notes, "I have finally reached my goal! But what inconceivable *wonder* awaits me now?" For anyone else, a cursory glimpse into the kaleidoscopic snarl of Eternity's stomping grounds would be inconceivable wonder enough. To the good doctor, it's just another day at the office. And this, perhaps, is what resonated with me most as a boy—Strange's poise in the face of extreme inconceivability. As an only child with an overactive imagination, I took solace and delight in the notion of interdimensional rabbit holes that could be accessed with the right incantations and hand gestures. But as a child of alcoholism, divorce, and a father whose brain would host a malignant tumor that, when removed, left him without spirit or intellect for my eleventh year, then returned to kill him for my twelfth, I drew strength and inspiration from Dr. Strange's acceptance and transcendence of the inconceivable. Still do.

Debuting in *Strange Tales* #110 (1963), Dr. Strange was an actual doctor, star surgeon Stephen Strange, before a car accident left him with damaged nerves and, in a nasty Ditko twist, shaky, ineffectual hands. Unable to operate, too arrogant to assist other doctors, Strange becomes an embittered waterfront drifter until he overhears some sailors discussing the legendary Ancient One, a mystic Methuselah with magical healing powers. Journeying to India, Strange reaches the Ancient One's remote mountainside sanctum and rudely orders the wizard to restore his nerves and dexterity. After telepathically scanning Strange's mind and perceiving the ruthless, egomaniacal, oddly Objectivist character within, the Ancient One deems him unworthy of aid—"I cannot help you, for your motives are still selfish!" Meanwhile, the first winter blizzard has fallen, forcing the angry, skeptical Strange to remain in the temple until the snow thaws. In the months that follow, Strange witnesses black magical attempts on the Ancient One's life by the guru's treacherous pupil, Baron Mordo, and eventually resolves to shield his elderly host from Mordo and all forces of darkness by becoming the Ancient One's disciple in the mystic arts.

As it unfolds over subsequent issues, the story of the Ancient One and Dr. Strange reveals itself as an ailing father/dutiful son narrative.

221

Though eminently wise and still powerful, the Ancient One constantly bemoans his age and infirmity, his inability to provide his "son" with adequate magical backup when he needs it most. In one brilliantly drawn sequence, Dr. Strange needs to retrieve a crucial spell from the unconscious mind of the Ancient One, in a deep coma after one of Mordo's countless attacks. When Strange begins to probe his Master's brain with his mystic third eye, the comatose Ancient One throws up a series of psychic defenses, each more powerful than the last, culminating in a "most dangerous" spell that causes Strange to hallucinate wildly, threatening to condemn him to *a life of aimless imagery*. Through deep concentration, Strange dispels the hallucinatory vortex and starts projecting mental images of himself (a parade of tiny astral heads) into his Master's mind—mini-Stranges bouncing off the forehead, hovering behind the neck, entering the ears, all pleading for access: "Hear me, Ancient One! It is thy disciple! Open your mind to me, Master!" This, too, moved me a great deal.

What's truly strange (sorry) about Dr. Strange is his utter incompatibility with Objectivism, the Randian creed Ditko embraced at some point during his *Strange Tales* run. Even more than Spider-Man, Dr. Strange was Ditko's baby. As in *Amazing Spider-Man*, Ditko began to receive plotting credit in 1965 with *Strange Tales* #135, but Lee, Ditko, and comic historians all acknowledge that Ditko was largely left to his own devices on Dr. Strange from the character's inception to Ditko's departure from Marvel in '66. There's no mystery to why an idiosyncratic stylist like Ditko would be attracted to the concept of a master magician operating in abstract, alternate dimensions, but it's curious that he'd want to continue with the character after becoming a staunch Objectivist, given that Strange embodied two of Rand's primary bêtes noires—mysticism and altruism.

Only three years after leaving Marvel, in his hectoring Objectivist strip "The Avenging World," Ditko presents Earth as a beat-up human figure—arm in sling, leg in cast, angry globe head wrapped in bandages—who barks, "The state I'm in was caused and there's a lot of people working hard, knowingly and unknowingly, to make sure my condition gets worse! I'll show you some types of people and the stupidity they practice that always leads to more misery!" Three of the culprits? The Mystic (a religious leader), the Enlightened (a psychedelic New Ager, surrounded by a miasma of "corrupt" concepts like "occult," "black magic," "mysticism," "visions," and "spirit world"), and the Humanitarian (an absurdly overwrought bleeding heart: "To HELP HUMANITY, the COMPETENT MUST BE FORCED TO SACRIFICE THEMSELVES to the INCOMPETENT NEEDY!" he bleats). Two conclusions can be drawn from "The Avenging World"—one, that Ditko's Objectivist agitprop, his most "personal" work, is about as entertaining as Maoist dinner theater, and two, that Dr. Strange, the mystical humanitarian who inspired his best, most creative work, is anathema to the living, post-Marvel Ditko. Both are dispiriting. I blame Rand. It's telling that the Ancient One's description of Stephen Strange's selfish personality in Dr. Strange's origin story reads like an Objectivist ideal: "You were proud, haughty, successful! But you cared little for your fellow men. Money, that was all that interested you, all you cared about. To you the problems of others meant less than nothing!" A = A? Yes. Ayn = Asshole.

It's a shame about Steve.


Some aspects of Ditko I've neglected:

1) The dominant emotion in Ditko's pre-'66 work is *anxiety*. It isn't known whether Ditko invented the quivering pen strokes best known as Spider-Man's "spider sense," which I think of as *tingle lines*, but he certainly perfected them. You could be forgiven for thinking these lines easy to duplicate, but try drawing them yourself. Yours will never look like Ditko's, while Ditko's are always unmistakably his. After his hands, these tingle lines are his visual signature.

2) Ditko is also fond of *floating heads*. In *Spider-Man*, the heads are often a Greek chorus of kibitzing New Yorkers, stirred up by J. Jonah

Jameson's editorials and sounding off on Spider-Man. In *Strange Tales*, they can be anonymous international sorcerers awakening to some mystic message, or that of an individual villain, usually Baron Mordo or the Dread Dormammu. Dormammu's head is perpetually *on fire*, so it lends itself to this effect. Ur-Ditko panels—those that combine hyperextended hands, floating heads, and tingle lines—include *Amazing Spider-Man* #21, p. 19, panel 2; *Strange Tales* #117, p. 6, panel 1; and, perhaps best of all, the splash page of *Strange Tales* #140.

3) While everything is stretched wide in Kirby, everything in Ditko is pulled thin. There's a bit of Edvard Münch in Ditko, just as there's a bit of Albert Speer in Kirby.

4) From 1958 to 1966, Ditko shared a studio with famed fetish artist Eric Stanton. The two men were close friends and frequently contributed to each other's work. Stanton has said that he suggested to Ditko that Spider-Man shoot webbing out of his wrists. Ditko, for his part, ghosted many erotic Stantoons featuring balloon-breasted women catfighting in constricting undergarments.

5) Ditko's 1950s and early sixties horror and science fiction strips for Charlton, Atlas, and pre-superhero Marvel are absolutely fantastic and criminally unanthologized. After *Dr. Strange* and *Spider-Man*, they are Ditko's greatest contributions to comic art and should be sought out by anyone who thinks his style is cartoonish, underdrawn, or lacking in fine detail. The stories boast covercopy like, "Were they really men? All that was known was that they had come 'FROM ALL OUR DARKROOMS,' " "In this great issue you will meet . . . 'THOSE WHO CHANGE'!" and "What was the dread secret of the . . . 'ROBOT IN HIDING'?" One title, "THE STATUES THAT CAME TO LIFE," could serve as an epigraph for the entire Ditko corpus.

6) One of the countless pleasures of reading *Strange Tales*, which, I should note, holds up much better than *Spider-Man*, is coming across thought balloons like this, from the flaming pate of the Dread Dormammu: "As I sit here, absorbing new power from within my magic triangle, I must *think*! How did the Mindless Ones escape?? Has some-

one dared to *betray* me??" I think we can all relate to that on some level. Alternately, there's this, from the mouth of Ditko's Objectivist crusader, Mr. A: "Only through black and white principles can man separate good from evil! The principles show man's basic choice of actions! Men can choose grey principles, to choose to be corrupt, but that choice leads to evil—and self-destruction!" The choice is yours. I'm sticking with the magic triangle, which, by the way, is a fetching sunburst orange, not grey.

7) Ditko's hometown of Johnstown, Pennsylvania, was the site of one of the worst disasters in American history, the Johnstown Flood of 1889. Death toll: 2,209. A century later, a massive flood in California destroyed years' worth of files that Cat Yronwode had compiled on Ditko, intending to write the definitive book on the artist. Ms. Yronwode is perhaps the world's biggest Dr. Strange fan. She has a website, "The Lesser Book of the Vishanti," that catalogs every spell Dr. Strange ever cast. Some samples (use with care):

Banish: Being from Whence It Came
Banish: "Living Wickedness" from Furniture
Banish: Subjective Vikings
Banish: Demonic Motorcyclist
Banish: Party-Goers
Banish: All-Purpose
Repulse: Humans, 5' Radius
Conjure: A Giant Hand from a Shadowy Dimension
Conjure: Illusion of Normality
Misc.: To Cease Dying

8) Over the years, I've found other uses for my hands, but I still strike a Ditko gesture now and then. In fact, I'm forming one right now. Good night. I'll see you in my dreams.

# ACKNOWLEDGMENTS

In addition to the seventeen remarkable talents who contributed essays, this collection was blessed with the intelligence and sharp instincts of Edward Kastenmeier; generosity and wisdom of Jonathan Lethem; patient guidance of Richard Parks; infectious enthusiasm of David Hyde; sound advice from Luc Sante and Jim Shepard; motivational words of Andy Greenwald; numerous conversations with fellow readers Alex Pappademas, Chris Ryan, Jason Altman, Mark Eckel, Emily Hoffman, Joel Ogden, Geoffrey Schmit, Justin Schofer, Mark Schwartzbard, and Jason Yung; encouragement of friends at the Criterion Collection; and relentless razzing from the staff of Roger's Time Machine on 14th Street. I'd also like to thank my family.

# ABOUT THE CONTRIBUTORS

Aimee Bender is the author of *The Girl in the Flammable Skirt* and *An Invisible Sign of My Own*. Her short fiction has been published in *Harper's, Granta, GQ, The Paris Review, McSweeney's,* and other publications. She lives in Los Angeles, right near Golden Apple comic books, a fine establishment.

Geoff Dyer's books include *But Beautiful* (winner of a Somerset Maugham Prize), *Paris Trance, Out of Sheer Rage* (a finalist for a National Book Critics Circle Award), and, most recently, *Yoga for People Who Can't Be Bothered to Do It.* He lives in London.

Steve Erickson is the author of seven novels, including *Our Ecstatic Days*, forthcoming from Simon & Schuster, as well as two books about American politics and culture. He writes about film for *Los Angeles* magazine and is also editor of the literary magazine *Black Clock,* published by CalArts, where he teaches writing.

Gary Giddins wrote the *Village Voice* jazz column, "Weather Bird," for thirty years. In 1998, he won the National Book Critics Circle Award for *Visions of Jazz*; his other books include *Bing Crosby: A Pocketful of Dreams, Faces in the Crowd, Satchmo, Riding on a Blue Note,* and the forthcoming *Weather Bird.* He has received a Guggenheim Fellowship, two Ralph J. Gleason Music Book Awards, five ASCAP-Deems Taylor Awards, and a Peabody Broadcasting Award, among other honors.

Glen David Gold is the author of *Carter Beats the Devil.* He recommends that everyone who collects comics (or anything) read Werner Muensterberger's *Collecting: An Unruly Passion.*

Myla Goldberg is the author of *Bee Season.* Her collection of essays about Prague will be published as part of Crown Books' *Journeys* series in fall 2004, and her new novel, *Wickett's Remedy,* will be published by Doubleday in 2005.

Andrew Hultkrans is the author of *Forever Changes,* one of the inaugural six volumes in Continuum's "33$\frac{1}{3}$" series of books on classic albums. From 1998 through 2002, he was editor in chief of *Bookforum* magazine. Over the years, his writings have appeared in *Artforum, Tin House, Cabinet, Salon,* and *Mondo 2000,* where he was managing editor and columnist for three years in the early nineties. He really does have beautiful hands.

Jonathan Lethem is the author of six novels, including *Motherless Brooklyn* and *The Fortress of Solitude*. He lives in Brooklyn.

Greil Marcus is the author of *Lipstick Traces* (1989), *The Dustbin of History* (1995), *The Old, Weird America* (1997), *Double Trouble* (2000), and *"The Manchurian Candidate"* (2002). He lives in Berkeley.

Brad Meltzer (www.bradmeltzer.com) is the author of *The Tenth Justice, Dead Even, The First Counsel, The Millionaires,* and *The Zero Game.* His books have a total of almost six million copies in print, have spent more than eight months on bestseller lists, and have been translated into more than a dozen languages. His critically acclaimed run on *Green Arrow* has been collected as *The Archer's Quest* by DC Comics, which was foolish enough to think it had to pay him to write comics.

Lydia Millet is the author of three novels: *Omnivores* (1996), *George Bush, Dark Prince of Love* (2000), and, most recently, *My Happy Life* (2002), which won the 2003 PEN-USA Award for Fiction.

Geoffrey O'Brien is the author of twelve books, including *The Phantom Empire, The Browser's Ecstasy, Castaways of the Image Planet,* and, most recently, *Sonata for Jukebox: Pop Music, Memory, and the Imagined Life.* He is editor in chief of the Library of America.

Chris Offutt is the author of *Kentucky Straight, Out of the Woods, No Heroes, The Same River Twice,* and *The Good Brother.* His work is widely translated and has received many honors, including a Lannan Award, a Whiting Award, and a Guggenheim Fellowship.

Tom Piazza is the author of the novel *My Cold War* and the short story collection *Blues and Trouble.* He is also well known for his writing on music. He lives in New Orleans.

Luc Sante contributed a comic strip (*Neanderthalman*) to his high school newspaper (1971–72), but life shunted him away from his original vocation. His books include *Low Life, Evidence,* and *The Factory of Facts.* He lives in Ulster County, New York.

Christopher Sorrentino is the author of one novel, *Sound on Sound*; his second is forthcoming from Farrar, Straus & Giroux. He lives in Brooklyn.

John Wray has a novel out called *The Right Hand of Sleep* (Knopf/Vintage) and plays in a band called Marmalade (*Beautiful Soup,* March Records). He has a box of *Dazzler* issues (#2–42, in Mylar covers) that he's looking to sell.